A DANCE TO REMEMBER

RIETTA BOKSHA

Copyright © 2021 by Rietta Boksha

All rights reserved.

No part of this book may be reproduced in any form or by any electronic or mechanical means, including information storage and retrieval systems, without written permission from the author, except for the use of brief quotations in a book review.

 Created with Vellum

ONE

Dance has always brought me happiness. Even when it seemed like the darkness was going to swallow me. If I could hear the music and become one with it, the darkness would not overtake the light.

It was 3 a.m., and I was dancing around my living room, trying to keep the dark cloud away. The dark cloud had been following me for a year now. Trying to take over what was left of my existence. Attempting to suck me down into a deep depression that I feared I would never escape. I loved dance from the moment I stepped into class as a kid. I knew I was in the right place and felt immediately at home. I never knew dance would save me from completely losing myself, but here I was. My neighbors probably thought I was possessed. Seeing odd shapes in the window from the one light that is on in the far side of the room, sweat dripping off the tips of my hair, but at that moment, I felt free, free from the nightmares. The nights are always the worst. I am sure that is what most people say who are battling depression. At least I was not sitting in the park down the street drinking. This had to be a healthier outlet. When I finally felt the darkness recede, I made my way back to bed hoping sleep came quickly. I didn't bother with a shower; I didn't want to give it too much time to potentially return.

I must have fallen asleep at some point. Sun was streaming through the curtains the next time I open my eyes. I made it through another night. Now was the time for shower and coffee. It was always a battle over which to do first. Today shower won, I could feel the salt layer left on my skin from my late-night dance routine. Standing in the mirror, I looked at myself. My blue eyes were brighter today, not as heavy with fatigue. My long brown hair was wavy from the sweat the night before and ready to be tamed. Once I was properly dressed and had my coffee, I went and sat out on my porch. It was my favorite place to sit. I could only partially see the mountains, but part is better than none. I have always loved the mountains, a large unforgiving force surrounded by beauty. Colorado was meant to be my home. I was only a few sips in when my neighbor Tara walked out with her pup, George.

"Hey, Drea, how are you doing this morning?" Tara asked.

"Better now I have my coffee," I said, holding my cup up to her.

"Good, I am glad to hear it." She paused like she had more to say but was searching for the right way to approach it. I could tell by her body language. She isn't the only one to act like this toward me.

"Just say whatever it is you are going to say and stop making it awkward, Tara," I finally said.

She smiled. "Well, I have a friend who works at the..." she paused again, searching for the right word. I signaled to keep it moving. "He works at this really cool facility for veterans and they are looking for someone to teach dance classes."

I felt my stomach drop. *It sounds like an amazing cause, but I just don't know if I can face that.*

Tara must have felt my panic as she continued. "It's just an idea, Drea, you don't have to, of course. It just made me think of you and how much you love to dance." She paused again. "Maybe your dancing has a bigger purpose."

I looked away from her, trying to take it all in. I wasn't even looking for a job. I took a sip of my coffee and without looking back replied in the most non-committal way, "Ya. Maybe."

"Just think about it, OK?" Tara urged.

I nodded at her. She smiled and headed down the block. I could feel my thoughts racing. Not really how I wanted to start my morning. I have enough racing thoughts at night. I needed to calm my mind before I really tried to make a decision. I went back into the house and turned on some music. This time I just lay on my bed and closed my eyes. Letting the vibrations from the music run through my body. My therapist asked me to try this in lieu of dancing. She loved my dancing but wanted me to have other ways to cope with my thoughts. While doing this, she also had me take deep breaths, counting each one and saying the word relax. I hate to admit it, but it works. There is something very calming about it. I guess this is what the Buddhists consider mediation. Just with music. And counting. I assumed her goal was to have me do it without music eventually.

"I think I want to do it," I said out loud to myself. "It could be good and... I can't just sit around here forever. I have to get back to work."

Wonder if I should ask my therapist? She would want me to get out, right? *I'll go talk to Tara later. Get more infor-*

mation. As I was contemplating getting up, a fluffy orange body lay directly on my face.

"Oh, hi there, Tigger," I mumbled from under the orange fur. "I wasn't sure if you were going to make an appearance today."

Tigger began purring, and I repositioned him on my chest. He wasn't happy but decided he would make do so that I could breathe. I was never much of a cat person. When my best friend, Victoria, gave him to me as another resource to battle my dark cloud, I wanted to forsake him. I hate to admit that he grew on me. He senses when I need comfort and leaves me be when I need space. So, the face-sitting wasn't a total dealbreaker. Just a slight annoyance. I am now a cat person, or maybe I should say a Tigger person.

When I did get up, Tigger made sure to let me know he was displeased and disappeared again. *I should eat.* I never thought I would have to remind myself to eat, but these days I do. So I went to the kitchen to make myself a sandwich. As I was assembling, I saw Tara walking back toward her house. I'm not sure what forces were in the works, but I ran out the door to catch her. Before I even made it to her I told her, "I'm in. Just tell me when and where, I will be there." She dropped the leash and hugged me. Apparently, I wasn't the only one who was ready to see me make some changes. I felt the load on my shoulders lighten.

Tara invited me over for dinner to give me more details. She had invited me for dinner frequently, but I always said no. I didn't want to intrude on her and her husband's life. No reason for them to be dragged down by my dark cloud. She never stopped asking, though. She was better at supporting me than some of my friends. *Wait, is she my friend?* Making friends has always been a struggle for me. Carrying around my dark cloud has only added to the issues. I have lost friends. Can't say I blame them, but doesn't make it sting any less. I have an amazing long-term friend who has always stood the test of time and you can probably guess who that is. If you are thinking the one who gave me the face-sitting orange cat, you are correct. Victoria. She has been my best friend since we were kids. Just like most young kids, I struggled to make friends. I was awkward and quiet, but Victoria didn't even hesitate to befriend me. We have been connected ever since. I don't want to say inseparable, but I couldn't imagine my life without her. So I like to say we are connected deep in our souls. I felt very anxious about going to Tara's house and actually meeting her husband. I had of course seen him in passing, but we had never had any real interactions. I think I scare him, and he wonders why his wife even bothers with me. When I knocked on the door, he answered.

"Oh, hey there Aundrea, come on in." It took me a minute to answer because I couldn't remember the last time someone used my full name. When it hit me, my stomach dropped and I had to quickly recoup.

"Hey, Liam, can you call me Drea please?" I asked, moving past him into the house.

The moment I entered, the house smelled amazing. The smell alone made the whole house have this cozy feel and I felt myself relax some. Tara came in and hugged me and motioned for me to sit on the couch.

"There is still about twenty minutes before everything is done. Can I get you something to drink?"

"Just a water would be great, thank you."

Tara quickly got me a glass of water and came back, placing herself next to Liam. I'm not sure if it was Tara's kindness all these months or the coziness of their house, but the words boiled up and came out without me even thinking.

"Thank you, guys, for having me over. I know it hasn't been easy living next to me, but I have appreciated it even if I haven't shown it..."

"We are so glad you finally agreed to!" Tara said.

"I just never wanted to bring my... dark cloud to rain on your parade."

This actually got a response out of Liam.

"Aun... Drea, we were honestly worried about you. I can't even imagine what you must be feeling, but you definitely would not be raining on our parade. Now, maybe if you came over every night that would be a different story."

I laughed, a real laugh for the first time. Tara's husband didn't think at all what I thought he did. Goes to show you, the scenario you make up in your mind is usually not right. Damn my therapist.

"Well, thank you for not giving up. I am really glad I came tonight. It smells wonderful in here; can I get the smell to go?"

This got a huge smile out of Tara. "I will work on that for you," she replied.

Over dinner I enjoyed hearing all about them. They tried to focus on me but hearing about what they do and how they met was a welcome distraction. It was the first time in a long time that I felt something. Maybe my dark cloud was finally going to start letting some sun come through.

The following day I went over to TLC for Troops. To say I was anxious about meeting everyone and talking about the program was a huge understatement. I didn't know if I was really ready or if it was even the first right step, but I had to find out. The guy who ran the program was named

Steve. Steve was a vet and after serving over twenty years with the Marines, he identified with serving and helping others. He designed TLC for Troops. It was a place where they could get rehab, hang out with other vets, receive therapy, and take classes free of charge. I don't know how he managed it, but it was an incredible place. After showing me around, he took me into his office to chat.

"Aundrea, I can't thank you enough for coming in. I have been wanting to incorporate dance into this program forever but could never find the right fit."

"Call me Drea, please, and you couldn't possibly know I was the right fit already," I replied, laughing.

He smiled back. "Trust me, I know good people when I see 'em, and you are good people."

"Well, thank you, I really appreciate that."

"When can you start?" he asked.

I hadn't even thought that far, but it is not like I had much else going on, right?

"Whenever you want," I replied.

"I wasn't sure if you needed some time. I heard that..."

I felt my blood pressure rise and I cut him off. "Look, Steve, I don't know what you heard or how much you think you know, but can we not? Please?"

My abrupt response set him back and he stared at me for several minutes before trying again.

"I'm sorry. You are right, it's not my place."

Suddenly there was a loud commotion coming from a room down the hall.

"Shit!" Steve blurted out before dashing from the room.

I sat perplexed for a moment before deciding I wanted to see what was happening. Aside from my cat, I haven't had much excitement lately. And my cat isn't even really exciting.

I stepped out into the hall and walked toward the noise. When I came to the door, I peeked around. Steve and another man were holding back one of the vets who, I assumed, stayed there. He was yelling and thrashing toward a guy who was on the floor with a bloody nose. I saw tissues on the table nearby and without even thinking reached for them and walked over to the guy on the floor. I squatted down beside him and held out the tissue box. He didn't notice I was there; he was still focused on the man yelling at him. If he was the one who gave him the bloody nose, and all evidence was pointing to it, I can't blame him for not wanting to look away. I gently touched his shoulder, and his eyes zinged in my direction.

"Here," I simply said, moving the box of tissues closer to him.

He looked at the tissues, than back at me. "Oh, thanks," he said and reached for a couple. I smiled at him and looked over at Steve and the other two men. Everyone appeared shocked. Like I was an angel that appeared out of the sky.

"Who are you?" asked the guy on the floor as he stuffed tissues up his nose and leaned his head back.

"Ya, who the fuck are you?" said the guy being held. He had stopped thrashing and was now completely focused on me. I felt the anxiety bubbling in my stomach as I realized how awkward the situation was that I had placed myself in.

"She's the new dance instructor," Steve replied. "Thanks for giving her a great first impression, guys! Hopefully she is still going to take the job."

"What the hell do we need a dance instructor for?" said the angry one.

"Shut up. Why do you have to ruin everything for everyone?" replied his punching bag.

"Drea, I am so sorry you had to witness this. I'm..."

Steve was cut off by bloody nose guy. "Hey, I'm Trevor and that asshole is Lucas," he said, holding out his hand. I laughed and shook his hand.

"I'm surprised you would even use his name after what he did to your poor nose."

Trevor smiled. "It's not the first time he has punched me, and I doubt it will be the last."

"You might want to get some new friends," I replied with a smile.

"Oh, don't come in here trying to act like you have any clue," said Lucas.

In that moment I felt a part of me come back to life. The part of me that wasn't going to take any shit from some asshole.

I stood up and walked over to Lucas, leaving only inches between our toes. "Want to know something, Lucas, I do have a clue. So back the fuck off."

A "dayyyyyyummm" made its way through the crowd of onlookers as I walked out of the room and back to my car. I was mad. Really mad, and I don't even really know why. I didn't know anyone involved, but it got under my skin. I was at my door getting ready to get in and drive off when I saw Steve running toward me. *Crap,* I thought. *He's pissed.* When he got to me, I couldn't believe what he said.

"I knew you were exactly what we needed, be here tomorrow at 10." And he hugged me.

TWO

10 a.m. felt like a lifetime from when I woke up. No matter how late I stay up, I am always awake at 4:46. Not 4:43, not 4:45, but 4:46. It's some sick joke my body has started. I pray every night that I will sleep even one minute longer. No such luck. I had already gone for a run, practiced a potential dance routine, showered, had breakfast, and packed a lunch by 7:30. I knew it was going to be a long day. Could I go bug Tara? Oh, wait, no, she was a normal person and had a job. Could I just show up early? I mean, it couldn't hurt, right? So I made the decision to drive over early. When I pulled up, Steve was getting things out of his trunk.

"You can't handle waiting either, huh?" he said as I got out of my car. *How did he know??*

"No, it's not really my strong suit," I replied.

"I knew I liked you. Come on with me."

We walked down to the end of the hallway, where there was a small room with a couch and a desk. He stood at the entryway and motioned for me to go in.

"This is your office, Drea."

"I get an office?!?!" I replied in shock. "What the heck do I need an office for? I am just a dance instructor."

"You are more than that, you just don't know it yet. Plus, you have to have a place to come eat your lunch and rest. I happen to know from a good source that couch is an amazing place for an afternoon siesta."

"I get an office and I am allowed to nap? Where has this job been all my life?" I said, giggling.

Steve shook his head. "So, 10:30, I am going to introduce you to everyone and let you do a little demonstration or whatever you want. Sound good?"

I nodded, and he proceeded to take my on a tour of the facility. TLC is much bigger than I had anticipated. It had everything you could think of, including a dance studio! It kind of reminded me of the fancy retirement facility my gran lived at. It has furnished rooms for the people who stay there permanently. A full-service kitchen that provides full breakfast, lunch, and dinner. Classes of all types. A beautiful outdoor area and game room. Steve spared no expense to give his brothers and sisters the best possible solace. To me it spoke to how much he cared. I mean, hell, he gave me my own office my first day. After the tour, I went back into my newly acquired office and thought of ways I could decorate it. Should I get a new laptop?? Wait? What would I use a laptop for? Mid internal debate, Steve came in and told me it was time. I was so glad I came in early. I would have been pacing a hole in the floor if I had stayed at home. When I walked into the dance studio and saw how many people were actually in there, I felt my anxiety start to rise. I did not expect this many right off the bat. Did Steve force people to come? Steve walked to the center of the room and began speaking loudly to get everyone's attention.

"Excuse me, everyone." He waited for everyone to quiet

down. "I am really excited to introduce you to Drea. She is going to be teaching us some dance moves and hopefully helping in some other respects around here. If you would please give her a warm welcome!" He started clapping and motioned for me to come join him. Beads of sweat were now convening in my hair line. As I stood next to Steve and looked around, I became frozen. All I could think was what was I doing here? It felt like hours had passed when Steve softly pressed his hand on my shoulder and whispered into my ear, "Drea, would you like us to stretch first while you get your thoughts together?" When I turned and looked at him, he had such a softness in his eyes. There was no reason for me to be worked up like this. I closed my eyes, took a breath, blew it out slowly, and forced myself to get it together.

"I want to take this outside. Is that OK, Steve?" I asked, looking back.

He shrugged and nodded.

"Great! Everyone follow me." When I got outside and the fresh air hit my nose, I felt all the anxiety fade away. There was a perfect open area that even had some shade if people got too hot. I went over toward it and motioned for all of them to follow me. It didn't take long for someone to make a snide comment.

"How exactly are we gonna have music out here?"

I looked for the person but couldn't find the source and before I could respond, Steve had the solution.

"From this," he said. "Now quit being a party pooper, Lucas." And Steve set down what looked like a small speaker.

I felt my eyes roll all the way back into my head. Of course it was Lucas. Who else would it be? Either way, I didn't care what it was as long as it had music.

"Can I connect my phone to this bad boy?" I asked Steve.

"Pretty sure that is its sole purpose. Hand it over."

I queued up the song and handed it over to Steve. I held up my hand to signal to Steve to wait for a moment so I could give instructions.

"All I want you to do today is to feel the music. You can dance however you want; it doesn't have to be technically sound, it doesn't have to be perfect, I just want you to dance. Whatever that might look like for you."

I got a bunch of military-sounding grunts, which I assumed meant yes, so I nodded to Steve to proceed. When the music started everyone stood still, trying to decide what they wanted to do.

"Don't think about it," I said. "Close your eyes and just let your body do the talking."

Most of the group followed suit. They closed their eyes and let the music take them to another dimension. I sat in the middle of them all and just watched in awe. It really was a spectacular sight. I took a picture with my mind so that I could remember that moment forever. It was the first time I had taken a mental picture in over a year. There were a couple of stragglers that didn't want anything to do with what we were doing. No surprise one of them was Lucas. He was laughing and whispering with the other non-participants instead. Normally this would bother me, but today I wasn't going to let it. What was happening around me was too wonderful. After the first few songs, I joined them. Taking their hands, swinging them around, having them jump over me or fall to the ground with me. Some were hesitant or confused and didn't want to, and some did it without even thinking. That was always my biggest challenge when I started dancing. To just do. To not worry about what someone else would say or think and just do what made me happy. It isn't as easy as you would think, but once you do it, it's totally freeing.

I felt really good about my first day and was heading toward my office when I heard a disgruntled voice behind me.

"You won't last here. They never do."

When I turned to look, Lucas stood at the end of the hall.

"I hate to disappoint you, but I am not going anywhere."

"Yeah, we will see about that. I give you a week max!" he shouted as I went into my office and closed the door.

THREE

The next week went by slowly. Steve only had me coming in once a week. He kept bringing up having me "contribute in other aspects" but still hadn't said what that might be. I wanted to know but at the same time didn't. I am really not good with people in any other avenue besides dance, so I didn't know how else I could be helpful. Especially if he knew. I was so excited to get there this week, I was in by 7:30. Steve didn't even say anything, just smiled and shook his head. I had brought some stuff to brighten up my office and keep me busy until I had to actually "work." I wouldn't call it work, because it was the one thing that I really loved to do. I think that is why I ended up diving into this job without hesitation. How could it be bad if it's something I love? Plus, it got me out of the house. It was getting to the point where the less time I spent in the house, the better.

I set a plant in the window behind my desk, and a picture of my brother, sister, and me on the desk along with my brand-new laptop. I hadn't bought myself anything since the day the dark cloud showed up at my door, so to me it was more than just a new laptop. I had also brought in pens, pencils, and a holder for them, some notebooks, my favorite candle, and some posters for the wall. When I got all set up I stood in the doorway to admire my work. Now THIS was an office.

"Hey, stop daydreaming and get to work. I can guarantee these guys won't do it without you."

I looked away from my new setup to Steve, a huge smile on his face.

"What's with the giant grin?" I asked him.

"You sound like my wife. Go do your thing and don't worry about my grin."

I laughed and jogged down the hall to the dance studio. I still wasn't ready for this room, so I took the group outside again where we could be wild and free. Lucas was quick with the smartass comments as per usual.

"What are we going to do when it gets cold outside?" he asked.

"Then we will dance in the snow. You scared to be cold?"

This got a laugh from the whole bunch except Lucas. His face hardened even more, which I didn't think was possible.

"I don't dance in snow and I don't dance, period. I'm out of here." And with that he left.

"I wish I knew what the fuck his problem was," said another one of the guys.

"Let's not worry about that right now. We are going to do the same as last week, just with different music. And remember, don't think, just do."

Lucky for me, everyone else was more than willing to participate. I wasn't going to let one bad apple spoil the bunch. It also made me realize how much I had missed working and interacting with others apart from my friends. I hadn't thought about work at all until Tara mentioned it, which is the total opposite of how I use to be. I had loved my job—hell, I had loved everything about my life. The dark cloud ruined everything. Everything but dance, and now here it was giving me a second chance. It's like the universe had been planning for this my whole life.

When I was done, I packed up and said my goodbyes to Steve. He said he loved what I did with my office and was really looking forward to me having an even bigger role here. He really wasn't going to let that go but at least he wasn't officially asking me yet. I did ask him if he forced people to participate in classes. To my surprise he said no. He said he encouraged them to try everything offered but didn't force them to do anything. Even therapy. Therapy is strongly recommended but not forced. I agreed with the sentiment. Even though I wasn't always a fan of therapy when I was at my darkest, looking back now, I needed it. I probed him with a couple questions about Lucas, but he didn't have much insight either. Steve had been trying to scale Lucas's walls for three years with no luck. He deserved a medal for his patience and resolve. Before leaving, I suggested that next time we start class with introductions. I had done a couple classes now without knowing everyone, and he agreed it was a great idea.

When I got home, I changed and headed over to Tara's. She had invited me over for dinner again. She wanted to hear all about my new job and what I was up to. Liam also had to work late, and she said she didn't know how to make food for one. She made it so I wouldn't say no. The moment I walked into her house I was engulfed with the smell of garlic. Garlic has to be one of my favorite smells. Guess that comes from living in an Italian household.

"Holy moly does it smell good in here," I said, setting my stuff down on the entry table. Tara poked her head out of the kitchen.

"Well thank you, honey," replied Tara. Guess I was playing the role of husband tonight. This made me giggle.

"You are welcome, baby," I said, getting a laugh from Tara.

When we sat down, I took in the fabulous spread Tara had prepared. No wonder she couldn't cook for one, she really couldn't cook for two either. This was meant for an army.

"I don't think we have enough food," I said, spooning some food onto my plate.

"I told you I have a problem," she replied, laughing.

"You sound like my mom. She can't cook in small portions either."

We started eating and I was enjoying every morsel when Tara couldn't hold it in anymore.

"Sooooo, how's the new job going?" she asked.

"It's... great, really."

This had Tara beaming, and she was containing herself from jumping out of her chair.

"Oh, I am just so glad, Drea! I was so worried about you there for a while. I was worried I was going to find you..." she trailed off, realizing she had taken it too far. "I was worried I was going to have to invite you for a sleepover. Yes, a sleepover, but grown women don't do that! Right?? That's crazy!" she continued, desperately trying to back pedal.

"Tara, it's OK. Relax. That was a legitimate fear for you to have. It was one of my fears too. Still is, but can we please not talk about it?"

She nodded her head, her eyes glued to her plate. I decided to try and break the awkwardness.

"There is this guy though, he is really rude to me."

"He must like you," Tara replied, slowly returning to normal.

"Guys still flirt that way? I thought that ended in fifth grade, but there is no way. Pretty sure he hates me, hates everyone for that matter."

"I Wonder why?" Tara asked.

"Yeah, me too."

FOUR

I walked out of Tara's house straight into a storm. The wind was so strong I couldn't even get off her porch and I clung to the pillar. The dark cloud was hanging low and dumping rain, soaking me to the bone, and I struggled to get air into my lungs. As the wind swirled around me I could feel my grip giving out and I decided it was time to let go.

I snapped awake in my bed. An orange, fluffy body was on my face. I pushed Tigger off and sat straight up as I gasped for air in my pitch-black room. I was soaked in sweat and the sheets were wrapped around my legs. As my heart rate slowed and my breath came back, I lay back down. Tigger was still near; I heard him purring. He eventually deemed it safe to come closer. He lay next to my head, pressing his butt against me. He continued to purr until it faded as he drifted back to sleep. Lucky cat. I lay there for what felt like hours before finally falling back asleep. When I woke the next time, there was light filtering in and Tigger had long since vacated. I rolled over to check the time: 9:52.

"SHIT!" I yelled, untangling myself from the sheets and running for the shower. I am not sure if I was more shocked that I slept past 4:46 or that I woke up with just barely enough time to get ready. *Wait, should I even bother with the shower? I am going to dance anyway and maybe if I leave now, I can still make it.* I decided to scrap the shower. Stripping off my pajamas, I sprayed fresh deodorant under my arms and grabbed my toothbrush. As I was brushing, I grabbed clothes and using one hand to brush and one hand to dress managed to get myself somewhat put together. I made it to the car in three minutes. I don't think I had ever moved that fast in my whole life. When I parked in the lot it was 10:02, just barely late. When I came barreling in the door, the whole group was chatting on the floor, including Steve. They all looked my direction and then quickly returned to their discussion. Apparently being late isn't a big deal here. I walked over to the group and sat down next to Steve. Just as I was about to say something, my favorite voice made itself known.

"Nice hair, have you heard of a hairbrush?" asked Lucas.

Damnit, I forgot to brush my hair before I left. Lucky for me, I did grab my purse. I took out a mirror, a hair tie, and my brush. My sister taught me to always have a hair tie. I gently brushed my hair into a decent-looking mane and then tied it up into a messy bun on top of my head. Before I returned everything to my purse, Steve leaned over.

"I thought it looked fine. Kinda fun, like Einstein," he whispered.

I burst out laughing and slapped Steve on the shoulder. "You shush, I don't need it from you too."

Steve laughed too and everyone was looking at us wanting to know what was going on. I cleared my throat and addressed the group.

"Well, now that my hair is up to par for your high standards, why don't we start the intros. Steve, since this is your place, why don't you start?"

Steve smiled. "Well, my name is Steve. I spent twenty-six years in the Marine Corps. First as a young dumb grunt and finishing as a CWO4. It wasn't always easy, but I love my brothers and sisters. I was tired of seeing them not having everything they needed and deserved, so I started TLC for Troops. I have been married to my amazing and tolerating wife Courtney for thirty-one years and we have two kids. Bret, who is just about to turn eighteen, lord help me, and Kara, who is fifteen.

"I love how you had to add tolerating as a characteristic for your wife." I smiled at him.

"Hey, it's true."

"OK, who's next?" I asked.

"Why don't you go, Rob?" Steve said, looking at the guy next to him.

He smiled and began. "As Steve said, I am Rob. I'm twenty-four, from Waco, Texas. I was a Marine for six years before getting injured in Afghanistan. I was inside a Humvee when we ran over an IED. I hit my head on the fifty-caliber machinegun and suffered a severe concussion and TBI. I'm still working on regaining my memory after the blast. I am not married and as Lucas constantly reminds me have no girlfriend, but I am hoping to change that someday."

"Hey Steve, you didn't say your age," someone said from the other side of the circle.

"You don't need to know my age," he replied.

This got a laugh from everyone. The introductions continued around the circle. Everyone had served in different branches, men and women, but they all had a deep love for their country and had suffered some kind of injury. Some more serious than others. I listened to each, intently making as many mental notes as I could. As much as I wanted to take actual notes, I didn't want them to feel uncomfortable. When we got to Lucas, we all stared and waited. He didn't even notice we were all looking at him. When he looked up and saw, he seemed slightly startled but quickly recouped with a snarky response.

"I hope y'all aren't expecting me to say anything, because it isn't going to happen."

We all gave him a collective annoyed sigh as Steve tried to reel him in.

"C'mon, Lucas, we are all in this together."

"We want to hear your story," I added.

"You do, princess?" he said, looking at me with hate in his eyes. "You really think you could handle my story? Something that isn't just rainbows and butterflies?"

Why did he hate me so much?

"I just listened to everyone else talk and their stories weren't all rainbows and butterflies."

He rolled his eyes, gave me the middle finger, and left.

"Ignore him, Drea. He is like that with everyone, it's not just you."

I looked to see who made the comment and found myself looking at Trevor.

"Alright, punching bag, you are the last one, let's hear it," I said, forcing a smile

"I'm Trevor. Twenty-seven from Chicago, Illinois. I was in the Marines as well until I lost my left leg to an IED." He lifted up his pant leg to reveal a prosthetic. "I am very lucky to be alive and even luckier to have an amazing wife. Her name is Paige." He smiled just saying her name. "We have been married eight years and have one son named Paxton."

I found myself smiling back at him. "I would love to meet Paige and Paxton."

Trevor returned my smile. "What about you, Drea? What's your story?"

My eye started twitching violently and I was not sure if I was suppressing tears or anger. Crap. I didn't think about the fact that they would want to know about me too. Could I do it?

"My name is Aundrea, but I prefer Drea. I'm thirty-one, from Highlands Ranch, Colorado.

I'm...

I....

Can't."

I got up and left the room. The twitching was trying to turn to tears. I made it to my office. Closed the door and pressed my back against the door. Taking in quick breaths to stop the tears, I slid to the floor. *Drea, you are going to have to talk about this eventually. You can't pretend like it didn't happen, remember what your therapist said.* As I was collecting myself, I heard a soft knock on the door. I opened it expecting to see Steve but instead saw Trevor.

"Hey look, I'm sorry I didn't..."

I cut him off. "Trevor, it's OK. It's only fair you guys ask me about myself too. I just didn't prepare myself for it."

"What's got you so... crushed?"

Wow, crushed. Now that was the right word for how I felt.

"Well you certainly picked the right word," I replied. "Honestly, I haven't talked about it yet and... can't."

As I was driving home after fumbling my way through class, my mind was cluttered, thinking about my dream, Trevor, Lucas, and the attempted icebreakers. Thinking about Lucas seemed like such a waste—he had never spoken a nice word to me—but he had the ability to get under my skin. He made me see red and feel deep anger, and I am not even an angry person. I had to figure this out. I had to figure him out, even though the hatred between us continued to grow.

Every time I showed up to teach, Lucas made a point to sit in the corner with his buddies Rob and Sam and stare. If he wasn't staring, they were laughing and, I can only guess, making jokes. It made me angry, but I was not going to let him see that. I just kept working and if I got really mad, I would close my eyes and get lost in the music. Just like I do at home. It did have me wondering, though. Why even bother to sit there? Just to make me uncomfortable? Or was there an ulterior motive. My goal was to one day get him to dance. I had started teaching actual choreography at this point. Some loved it and some hated it. You would have thought they all would have loved it being former military. Being told what to do was normal, but this wasn't as easy. Plus, not everyone had the memory for it. Thankfully, I had taken that into consideration and was making fairly easy routines. Trevor had the memory for it and learned fairly quickly. He wasn't a bad dancer either. I watched him improve each day. That is, until he told me I was making him uncomfortable and that he didn't think his wife would appreciate the way I was watching him. I laughed and got up and moved to the other side of the room where it wouldn't make him so uncomfortable. The move did however put me closer to Lucas and his snide friends.

"Hey! Fat ass. Move," said Lucas.

I was going to make a comment back but decided to just shake my ass and give him the finger. This made the whole group laugh. I knew I wasn't a "fat ass." I've been active my entire life. I didn't have a six pack, but my stomach was defined, along with the rest of me. As for my ass, that is a mix of genetics, dance, and squats. I worked hard for it and had never had any complaints before. So fuck him.

"Can you really even dance?" asked Rob. I didn't acknowledge him either.

"She can't dance, I have never seen her do anything other than basic steps," Lucas replied to his friend.

I was starting to become uber frustrated but instead of engaging with them, I moved over to the other side of the room. There was no point in bringing myself to his level anymore. It didn't solve anything, and all it did was make me angrier.

Not worth it, Drea, I whispered to myself. After they had practiced the routine to my satisfaction, I released them to get some water and do whatever they wanted. It was a nice way to end things as it gave them creative freedom. Trevor was getting some water, and I decided to talk to him about his progress.

"Hey," I said, coming up next to him

"Hey, creeper," he replied, setting down his water.

"Hey! I was just impressed how far you have come already, especially with a prosthetic. Did you used to dance before?"

"Not officially, but I enjoyed doing it. Luckily, prosthetics have come a long way and it just took some getting used to."

"Really, Trevor, you are doing awesome. Your wife is one lucky gal," I replied, winking at him.

"Really? You are winking at me. I am going to have to tell my wife on you."

"Trying to make me look bad. I see how it is."

The following morning, I had an appointment with my therapist. As I said before, in my darkest days when the dark cloud hung just inches above my head I used to hate going, dread it actually, but for about the past month I hadn't had to force myself out the door. I used to show up late all the time and now I was always early. I guess that's progress, right? I was sitting in the waiting room reading when the door opened and the patient before me walked out followed closely by Dr. Cox. They nodded to each other and she watched her walk away. After several moments she looked over at me and smiled.

"Look who's early again."

"Always making progress, Doc." I replied.

"Well, come on in."

She held the door open, letting me enter the room first, and came in behind me, closing the door. Her room was actually very comfortable. Whoever decorated it made it not feel like a therapist's office. I have been in some rooms that the moment I walked in I had to leave. I took a seat on my favorite chair, took off my sandals, crossed my legs, and placed the pillow in my lap. She sat across from me.

"So, how are you doing today?" she asked.

"I have been feeling pretty good lately," I replied, smiling.

"I have noticed a positive change in your attitude."

This made me smile even more. I was always known as the person who walked into the room and everyone gravitated to. I thought I had lost it, so it was a wonderful feeling to know it was coming back.

"What do you think is contributing to this change?" she asked

"I think my new job. Getting out of the house, interacting with people, helping them feel better too. I look forward to it all week."

"That's wonderful, Aundrea." She was the only one I

allowed to call me by my full name. Mainly because she insisted on it.

"Yeah, it really is, isn't it."

"So, tell me about these people you work with, what are they like?"

"Well, they are all veterans from different branches of the military, both males and females, and they all have amazing stories."

"What do you mean by amazing?" she asked, probing for a deeper response.

"They have all been through hell and back.... And they are still here to talk about it. Still pushing forward, being positive, using each other as support."

"Sounds just like you."

I felt my throat close slightly. "No, I'm not like them."

"How are you not? You have been through your own hell. You are still here, still pushing..."

"I'm not positive though. Not all the time. Not like I use to be."

"You really think they are positive all the time too? Or anyone is for that matter?"

She was right. I was being too hard on myself. Why does she always have to be right?

"Yeah, I guess you are right. As usual," I replied.

She chuckled. "It's not about being right, Aundrea, it's realizing you aren't alone in the fight. You have more in common with them than you even know. Have you told them about..."

I cut her off before she could finish. "No, Dr. Cox."

"Aundrea, you are going to have to talk about it sooner or later."

"Then it's going to be later. I am not ready yet."

"Are you really not ready, or are you just telling yourself you aren't ready?"

On the drive home I was torn. I was feeling more comfortable each day at TLC, but at the same time I didn't know if they would ever truly accept me as one of them. I'm not really, or maybe I was letting Lucas get to me more than I cared to admit. It's hard to ignore when someone is constantly trying to bring you down a peg.

FIVE

That night I lay in bed thinking more about what Dr. Cox said. Was she right again? Was I not ready to talk about it, or was I just telling myself I wasn't ready? Or did I just not want to because it just makes it even more real? I felt like I would know when it was time. There would be a moment that without thinking I would just tell my story. God bless the poor soul who would have to hear it. I imagined I would be a hot mess, or maybe it would be easier than I thought. All I knew was right now I couldn't keep lying here thinking about it. I already didn't get enough sleep thanks to the dark cloud without keeping myself awake. At least tomorrow I was going back to work again. Even though I wouldn't really consider it work, it was fun.

WHEN I GOT TO TLC, STEVE WAS WAITING FOR ME outside his office. I could tell he was waiting even though he was trying to casually lean against the door frame flipping through a folder. I made sure to walk by really slow to give him the opportunity to keep up his charade. Sure enough he called me into his office so we could "chat." I had a feeling where this was going. He had only brought it up a few hundred times already. Steve wanted me to be a mentor/counselor. I thought it sounded completely out of my league, but he insisted it wasn't. He said it was basically what I was doing already but not limited to just dancing and the studio. I was to be there if they needed someone to talk to, confide in, or just hang out with. I asked him what made him think I would be good person to confide in and he became uncomfortably quiet. This meant only one thing. He knew. I guess I should have figured considering Tara got me the hookup here. Knowing Tara, she went about it in the most eloquent way possible. Steve said he still hoped I would talk to them about it someday and I just nodded along. I didn't want to argue with him, he was just trying to be kind, but I was feeling a mix of betrayal and anger. Betrayal that she would tell him without even letting me know she did and anger that he knew this entire time and let me think that he didn't. I found myself wiggling in my chair wanting to escape. When he was finally done talking, I smiled, nodded, and left Steve's office for my own. I sat at my desk for what felt like an eternity until my phone reminded me it was time to teach. At least I had the next thirty to forty-five minutes to get lost in the music. I had to give it a serious thought later. Right now I was too upset to think about it clearly.

I HAD A GREAT CLASS WITH EVERYONE. IT WAS THE BEST in a long time because Lucas wasn't even there to make comments. We had a totally uninterrupted practice and then free movement. It still amazed me how much everyone loved free movement. Most people overthink it. Trying to plan their moves ahead of time to make it look good when the point is to just feel. Let the music make the movement for you. Maybe after all the years of being told what to do it was nice to do whatever they wanted. Either way it made me happy that they enjoyed it.

On my way home I got myself a big juicy burger, some fries, and a milkshake. I sat and watched trashy TV and ate. It was glorious. The perfect ending to my day. Once I was happy and full, I went out onto my back porch and lay in the hammock. As the hammock softly swung back and forth, I decided to call Victoria. She was mad I didn't invite her over for burgers and trash TV but thrilled to hear about Steve's offer. I guess I was the only one who didn't see my potential. I still didn't get how someone who has a therapist could mentor someone else. As usual she told me to stop overthinking and just do it. The worst thing that could happen was that I would try it for a while and decide it was not for me. I didn't know why I hadn't thought of that, and she told me it was because I was only thinking of the ways I wasn't qualified instead of the ways I was. Before hanging up, she told me to have a beer and sleep on it. That was an idea I could get behind. I grabbed a beer and returned to my hammock. I spent the rest of the night watching the stars and enjoying my beer. Remembering.

SIX

When I woke up, I was still in my hammock. I slept all night in the hammock?? Where did the blanket come from?? *Was someone going to kill me and then decided, "Nah, she isn't worth it, let's just leave her be"? Really, Drea? That didn't make any sense.*

I was on the porch mulling it all over with my coffee when Tara walked by with George.

"Morning, Drea," she called, waving from the sidewalk

"Morning, Tara," I said, half smiling at her.

"What's wrong, everything OK?"

I felt bad for making her concerned. "Oh, yeah. I am fine, just confused is all."

"What are you confused about?"

"Well, I fell asleep last night on my hammock and magically woke up covered in a blanket. I don't know if a potential murderer took pity or what?"

Tara busted out laughing. She was laughing so hard she was hunched over and looked like she was going to collapse on the sidewalk.

"Hey! It's not funny. I could have been killed!" I said, trying not to laugh.

Somehow through the laughter she managed to get out three words. "It... was... meeeee."

"I'm an idiot," I replied and started laughing.

When she had finally regained her composure, she came and sat down on the porch with me. George without any commands found a spot in the sun and lay down.

"I haven't laughed that hard in a long time," I said.

"Me neither!" she replied. "I thought I was going to pee my pants at one point! You didn't really think a murderer covered you with a blanket, did you?"

"I mean, it's possible, right?" I laughed. "I couldn't come up with any other logical explanation."

"Really? That was your logical guess? You never thought your overly concerned and protective neighbor would cover you? I woke up in the middle of the night debating if I should cover you with a second one."

"OK, OK, I got it, it was a ridiculous thought."

"Ya think?!?"

And we started laughing all over again.

Later that afternoon, I was back in my hammock. Apparently, I did some of my best thinking here, minus the whole serial killer scenario, and I really wanted to take the time to think about Steve's offer. When I thought of it as more of a mentor role, I could wrap my head around it. Being a counselor seemed totally outlandish. Are there therapists out there who have therapists? Or was that something they just showed on *The Sopranos*? I had to admit Steve hadn't steered me wrong so far and maybe he really saw something in me that I didn't have the ability to see in myself right now, just like Victoria said. I took my phone out of my pocket and called Steve. He answered on the very last ring.

"Well, hello there, to what do I owe this great pleasure?"

"I was just lying in my hammock thinking about you..."

He cut me off. "Hey, how many times do I have to tell you I have a wife?" He was trying really hard not to laugh.

"Very funny, Steve."

"I'm sorry, I couldn't help it." He cleared his throat. "Go ahead, I am listening now."

"I was thinking about your offer, and I think I'm going to do it. There is just one condition."

"Anything," Steve replied.

"If I decide it isn't for me, I want the ability to go back to just doing dance. I don't want to have to quit completely."

"I'll take it. At this point I am just glad you are willing to try. I honestly think you will be very helpful to some of our vets, and it may even prove to be helpful for yourself."

I paused before asking the next question. "Can I ask why?"

"Drea, I don't know if you have noticed but you have the ability to really connect with people. You can sense what is needed in a situation and react. Like that first day I met you and you got involved in that tussle between Lucas and Trevor. You didn't even hesitate, just went to the aid of Trevor."

I sighed. "Damnit, Steve." I could feel him smiling from the other side of the phone. "Are you smiling right now?"

"See, point proven. Come in tomorrow?"

"I'll be there." And I disconnected.

I think that's the nicest thing anyone has said to me in a long time. We will see how this goes, and at least I have the ability to back out, I thought. Later that evening I went and had dinner with Tara and Liam. I was actually really excited to share my news with them and see what they thought. Of course they both agreed that it was a wonderful thing and were so glad I was embracing it. I have to say after everything that had happened, I had found support in the most unlikely of places. Now it was my turn to have faith in myself. It seemed everyone else did, and I needed to not only believe them but believe in myself. That way I could really offer TLC and all its vets the very best of me, which is what they deserved. I became determined to prove Steve right.

With coffee in hand, I drove out to TLC the following morning. I decided I wanted to be there early and let the crew know my door was open and I was there to serve them. Hopefully I wouldn't need to say much more than that and we would all be on the same page. When I arrived, Steve wasn't even there yet and everyone was in the dining room having breakfast. It smelled delicious, which reminded me I hadn't had breakfast myself. I was too caught up in making coffee. I texted Steve to ask him if it was alright for me to have breakfast there. When I finished typing and went to walk forward, I almost immediately ran into Trevor. Apparently, he had been standing there waiting to see if I would notice him.

"Good thing I'm not crazy. I could have slit your throat and ran without you even noticing."

"I don't know if I should laugh or be terrified," I replied.

"Hungry? I was just about to grab some breakfast."

"Actually, I am, I was just texting Steve to see if it was OK for me to eat here."

"Oh yeah, the staff eats with us all the time. C'mon, I will show you."

I followed Trevor into the dining room. It was a great space. Lots of windows with tables all around. I couldn't decide if it was warm from the food or the sun shining in. He led me over to the buffet area, where there was a wonderful spread of food and a lady standing at the end making waffles and omelets. Trevor walked right over to her and stopped.

"Linda, this is Drea, she is one of our new teachers. Can you cook her up something nice?" he said, winking at her.

She smiled and looked over at me. "Nice to meet ya, Drea, what is your pleasure?"

"Hi Linda, it's nice to meet you. I would love a waffle. I can't remember the last time I had one."

"You got it!" she replied and went to work.

A short time later she had a perfectly crispy waffle on a plate for me. She pointed over to a table and I nodded and walked to where she pointed. On the table was every kind of topping you could think of. Strawberries, blueberries, bananas, chocolate chips, whipped cream, powdered sugar, and so much more. I decided on some strawberries, bananas, a few chocolate chips, and whipped cream. To top it all off, I added some warm syrup and found my way over to Trevor. Trevor had an assortment of food in front of him. Omelet and a waffle, some fruit, eggs, and bacon.

"Someone is hungry," I said, sitting next to him.

"Don't judge me."

I held my hands up and replied, "No judgement here."

We had just started eating when several others from the group came to sit with us. Everyone was chatting about their evenings and what they all wanted to do for the day. I was enjoying listening when it came to me that this would be the perfect time to let them know I was here for them in more ways than just dance class. I clinked Trevor's orange juice glass with my fork, and everyone looked over.

"I'm sorry to interrupt, but I wanted to let everyone know something. That OK?"

"Yeah, Drea, what's up?" Trevor asked.

"I am going to be here every day now, and my office door will always be open. So, if you need anything, I'm here."

"Whoa, wait are you the new mentor Steve has been telling us about?"

Damnit Steve, always working things up to being bigger than they needed to be.

"Uhh, yeah, I guess that's me. I don't like to think of it as anything official, though. Just think of me as a resource... no... I don't like that either. Just think of me as a friend who you can come to at any time."

"We are supposed to go to you for advice?"

I knew that agitating voice. It had been a while since I had heard it, but there was no mistaking it.

"No one said you had to, but if you ask me, you are the one who needs it," I replied.

"I don't need anything from you. You aren't a vet. You have no combat experience. Hell, I bet you haven't had a single bad thing happen to you in your whole life."

I closed my eyes, pushed back the urge to choke him, and cleared my throat.

"Pretty sure we have covered this before, but again, you don't know anything about me."

"I know you don't have a fucking clue. If something bad had happened to you, you wouldn't still wear your heart on your sleeve."

"Wow, Lucas, have you taken into consideration you might be the one who doesn't have a clue?"

It was getting harder to control my composure, so I got

up and left. I knew if I stayed, I was going to say something I regret. Even if he deserved it.

I was sitting outside on a bench when Trevor came and sat down beside me. We sat in silence for a while before Trevor decided to make conversation. I was perfectly content sitting in silence.

"I have tried to get through to him," he said. "He has his walls built so high I can't climb them. It's why he lashes out at you; he does at anyone who might find their way in."

"There must be something really bad in there," I replied.

"There is something he doesn't want anyone to know."

"The more I interact with him, the less I care."

"I know it's hard. We have all tried to be friends with him, include him in our outings, but he is stubborn as a mule."

I laughed and smiled to myself.

"What?" Trevor asked.

"My dad used to say that about me all the time."

"Used to?"

"Yeah, I'm not as stubborn now. I try not to be anyway."

"So, your dad is still around?"

"Oh yeah! I'm sorry, that was confusing. Yeah, my mom and dad live about twenty minutes from here. I haven't seen them in a while. I'm not ready."

"Why aren't you ready?"

"Maybe one day I will tell you. Today just isn't that day."

Trevor shrugged and shuffled in his seat. I didn't mean to make him uncomfortable. I had to let him know.

"I really do appreciate you asking, and I have a feeling you may be the first person I tell. I just can't talk about it yet."

This made Trevor smile. "Really? Me?" he said in a goofy high-pitched voice. "Just know that I think you are giving Lucas control that he doesn't really have."

I chuckled at him. "Yes, you, you are the first person that I have actually felt a connection with. And before you give me the whole 'I'm married' line, I don't mean a connection like that. Just a new, fresh friendship connection, and you are right. I am giving Lucas the power to affect me."

"Well, even though you ruined my joke, I feel the same way but I need the 'I'm right' part in writing."

This random job that Tara offered me had turned into so much more than I ever expected. I was not only working and finding a purpose again but making new friends. You know the quote "hard times will always reveal true friends"? It's true. I know it's true because it happened to me. During the hardest time of my entire life, people I would have never expected, walked away. I never thought I would be willing to open up again, to find new friends, because I was so terrified to be hurt again. Yet here I was with Trevor, feeling like I really could make new friends. Better friends. Guess it goes to show you that you find what you need when and where you least expect it. I decided to confide in Trevor. Just a little.

"Lucas really gets under my skin."

"Yeah, he has that uncanny ability," Trevor replied.

"No one has been able to get under my skin like he does. I don't know what it is about him."

"Me neither. Pretty sure I have perfected my right hook because of him."

"Wait, you have punched him?! When you guys got into that tussle when I first arrived, you didn't."

"No... I have never punched him. Unlike him, punching people isn't on my daily agenda. Even though I definitely owe him a few. We have some punching bags hanging in the gym. That is what I punch and pretend it's his smug face."

"Wait, you guys have a gym here?!" I didn't remember seeing the gym on the initial tour, but there was so much to take in I must have just forgotten about it.

"Out of all that, that is what you hear?"

I smiled at him.

"Yes, we have a gym. Want me to show you?"

"Yes! Please!" I don't know why I was so excited about them having a gym, but I had to see it.

I followed him down a few corridors until it ended at two large double doors. He pushed through the doors and we came into an awesome gym. There were mirrors on every wall, several complete sets of dumbbells, a squat rack, cardio equipment, and, just as Trevor promised, two Thai bags. To our surprise someone was working out on the one on the far side of the room. The sun was shining in and we couldn't make out more than just an outline.

"Who is that?" I asked Trevor.

"Not sure, but based on that right cross I have a good feeling."

"Lucas?"

He nodded.

An urge to protect me came over Trevor and he wrapped an arm around me and started moving me quickly toward the door.

"I don't think Paige would appreciate that, Trevor," called a voice from the far side of the room.

Trevor motioned for me to stay put and then turned toward the voice, pressing his back against mine. I stood motionless, waiting for whatever Trevor was thinking was going to unfold.

"Wow, you actually remembered something about

someone else. But don't you worry, Paige knows all about Drea."

"Yeah, I'm sure she does." And I could hear the quick three-punch combo he laid into the bag.

Trevor went to continue guiding me through the door when I come out from behind him and walked several steps in Lucas's direction. I couldn't keep letting him get to me.

"You ever going to stop the tough guy act?" I asked him.

He stopped and took several steps toward me. I heard Trevor behind me sound like he was hyperventilating.

"Act? This isn't an act, sweetheart."

"Yeah, it is, and it's getting old," I said, taking a few more steps toward him.

He walked until there were only a few steps between us.

"You have no idea who you are messing with," he replied as he puffed up his shoulders.

I walked past him and made my way over to the bag. I lay in a quick four-punch combo followed by a side kick. I turn back and close the distance again, so we were toe to toe.

"Neither do you, and regardless of what you think you know, we are trying to help you."

I could feel his breath on my shoulders. He was at least six inches taller than me. His body was tense, in attack mode. I could sense Trevor's discomfort from across the room. It finally came to me that Trevor really feared that Lucas would hit me. Lucas may be a lot of things, but I didn't think he would lay a hand on me. I decided to take the bull by the horns.

I looked up and asked, "Do you want to hit me, Lucas?"

His facial expression quickly changed. The question

seemed to have almost brought him pain, and he released his fists.

"You seriously think I would hit you?" he asked.

"No, I don't, but I think Trevor does," I replied, glancing over at Trevor. Trevor shrugged and put his hands up.

"Why don't you?" Lucas asked.

"I don't think you are that type of person, Lucas. I don't think this whole persona you give off is you at all."

"I agree," said Trevor.

Lucas was totally taken aback and didn't know how to respond. He had put up this front for so long, I think he lost who he really was.

"We want to get to know the real Lucas," I said.

The brief moment of his walls being down was over, and the hard look returned to his face.

"Well, you are both wrong." And he went back to hitting the bag.

Trevor and I started walking slowly down the corridor back to the front of the building. When we made it to my office, I sat in my chair and Trevor was leaning against the doorway, smiling.

"What on earth are you smiling about?" I asked.

"You almost had him."

SEVEN

Trevor had left me wondering if I really almost had a breakthrough with Lucas. I guess that was the first time we hadn't had a totally snippy exchange. Holy shit, was Steve right? That I really had the ability to help people? Of course, after the revelation, I couldn't wait to tell Dr. Cox. Which then made me second guess if I could really help. I hated always having this internal battle. That was when it hit me. Maybe me going through this, had a greater good: to help others to get through their issues. Six months ago, that would have made me really mad. Now, in this moment, it made me kind of happy. I guess therapy was working. I would have to tell Dr. Cox that too. I gave her a lot of resistance, especially in the earlier months. It would probably be nice for her to hear that I was actually noticing some changes. That first visit with her was brutal. I ruined her favorite pillow. Literally ripped it to smithereens. Come to think of it, I never replaced it. *OK, that's it, I am leaving this office to go get her a new pillow.* I grabbed my stuff, waved at Steve telling him I would be back tomorrow, and sprinted to my car. I was going to ride this excitement train as long as I could.

I drove over to the mall to begin my search. I figured the mall was my best bet, lots of options without having to drive around to multiple stores. I started off looking for a pillow that was an exact replacement. I soon realized that this would probably be impossible without knowing where she got it or even the brand. So I decided to just look for something that would match her setup. I had been there enough to know what everything looked like. She had a lot of blue and green. Pictures of waves and trees, basically trying to bring nature indoors the best she could. Thinking about it now it made sense. Where do people go to find calmness? Where do they go to relax? They go to the beach, or on a hike. As I wandered the aisles, I came upon a display. On this beautiful cream-colored couch were two pillows. They looked like they had been painted. One was a beautiful ocean with a sky. It was a mixture of blues and teals and made me feel like I was looking at the ocean. The other one looked like a forest. Tall green trees reaching up high to eternity. I know this sounds like they wouldn't go together, but for some reason they did. They were the perfect match. I searched the aisles for the set but couldn't find them. Apparently, I wasn't the only one who liked them. I snatched the ones off the couch and went to the checkout. I'm not going to say how much they were, but I will say I had never spent that much on pillows. I seriously debated putting them back, but now I had a nice gift to surprise Dr. Cox with tomorrow.

The next day I was so excited to give her the pillows I could hardly contain myself. Dr. Cox said she thought I was going to explode with happiness. I had packaged up the pillows in a beautiful bag filled to the brim with tissue paper. I stashed it behind her couch to give it to her at the end, but I didn't even make it two minutes before I told her I had a surprise. When I gave it to her and when she finally made it through the ridiculous amount of tissue paper, she was blown away. She loved them, saying how beautiful they were and that I had gone way overboard. I of course told her it was long overdue, which it was, and apologized to her for how I had acted previously. She in her ultimate grace forgave me and proudly put the new pillows on display. I forgot how much making other people happy also made me happy. My heart was singing over these dang expensive pillows, how silly, but you gotta enjoy the little things. She told me this was exactly what we had been working toward. I was able to feel general happiness without the guilt.

We eventually dove into our actual therapy session. I told her all about Lucas, and what had been happening. How I felt like I was making a difference over at TLC and every day I felt better. How Steve had ask me to be a mentor. She did agree that I would be a wonderful mentor and said it sounded like I was already making progress. She always reminded me that no matter how small the progress seemed, it was still progress. I also told her about Trevor and how I felt like I could confide in him and he might be the first person I finally opened up to outside of my circle. She was so pleased with everything she didn't give me any "homework" and told me to continue on the path I was on. It was nice to have a break and to know I was breaking down barriers on my own without it having to be assigned.

I decided after therapy to go take advantage of the beautiful gym at TLC. My dad used to pretend spar with my brother and me. It got me interested, and he signed me up for classes. As an angsty teen looking for ways to get out my emotions, I fell in love with it. There is something very therapeutic about punching a bag, so I was getting a double dose of therapy today. I swung by the house and grabbed my bag filled with all my goodies before heading over. The gym was quiet since it was later in the evening. Exactly how I like it. I wrapped my hands, put my headphones on, and went to work. It had been a while since I did bag work, but my body certainly didn't forget. I started adding in kicks and elbows by my third round and was feeling so good I did ab work in between rounds. Figured I might as well tire myself out. Helped to keep the nightmares at bay if I was knocked out from exhaustion. Just as I started my sixth round, there was a tap on my shoulder. Turning around, I come face to face with Lucas.

"Holy shit, you scared me," I said, taking my headphones out and putting my hands behind my head to get air to my lungs.

"What are you doing in here?" he asked sarcastically.

"Umm, doing bag work. Pretty sure that is what this room is for."

"This is my time in here."

God, he couldn't even give this a rest when I was doing my own thing. *Who said he had to tap me on the shoulder? There is another bag.*

"What's stopping you?" I went to put my headphones back in and continue, but he didn't let up.

"Get out."

"Lucas, you have to be kidding. There is another bag over there. Just pretend I'm not here."

He rolled his eyes as if I was being the annoying one.

"You are really bothersome, you know that?" he said. At this point I was too irritated to argue.

"Fine. I'll go, but I'll be back tomorrow, and you are going to have to deal with it." And before he could even respond, I grabbed my bag and left. *Why does he have to be such an ass? The room is plenty big for the both of us.* I wasn't going to let this bother me anymore, though. I had a good therapy session and I got five rounds in. It was a good day. It did, however, give me an idea for tomorrow.

EIGHT

The next morning when I showed up for work, I could feel the tension the moment I walked in the door. I don't know what had happened that morning or even last night, but something was brewing. I kept my coffee close and hoped that some dance would ease whatever was building. When I walked into the open gym, everyone was in there, including Steve. Even Lucas and his little posse were hanging in the back. The little hairs on the back of my neck stood up and a bubble of anxiety starting swimming in my stomach. I took a sip of coffee, set it on the stage, and addressed the group as calmly as possible.

"Well, good morning, everyone. Nice to see you all here."

Steve responded immediately, "We need you today, Drea."

"Me?" I gulped hard to keep the anxiety bubble in my stomach.

"Yes you, we need you to bring us together."

"HA!" said Lucas from his corner.

I closed my eyes and took a deep breath. *You can do this,*

Drea. Remember what Dr. Cox said, you are stronger than you even realize.

"Awww, did we break you already?" asked Lucas.

My eyes snapped open and the words came out of my mouth like vomit.

"Come here, Lucas."

The smile disappeared from his face and it returned to the cold, hard, emotionless face I was used to him showing. I imagined this was his war face, but I would never know for sure.

"Yeah right, you think I am...."

"Come. Up. Here," I said, cutting him off with as firm a voice as I could manage

"Dude, just go up there and get it over with. Show her what's up," said one of his buddies.

Lucas rolled his eyes, pushed up from his chair, and walked over to me. He left two strides between us and continued to stare me down. I have to admit there was something about him that was intimidating, but I wasn't going to show its effect.

"Steve, would you turn on the song that is queued up, please?"

"You got it!"

As the music began to fill the room, I immediately felt myself relax. Even with all their eyes on me, this was my arena now. I started to dance around Lucas. My eyes not leaving him. He seemed confused at first and then slightly amused.

"Is this supposed to intimidate me, Aundrea?"

He always used my full first name just to be extra annoying.

"Nope, but you better start doing something or I'm just going to keep showing you up."

Then it happened. Lucas grabbed me by my waist, spun me around, and pulled me into him. We were eye to eye for the first time since we met. His eyes were a brilliant turquoise blue I had never noticed before. Under those eyes and the firmness of his chiseled face, I could feel a softness coming through. He must have noticed my feelers and swung me down into a dip. As he pulled me up slowly, he used his right hand to raise my leg up his side. *Holy shit. He knows how to dance.* I instinctively wrapped an arm around his neck and pulled myself back in close to him. Our noses were now touching. It was his turn to get uncomfortable. He lowered my leg and musically made some distance between us. As he moved me around the floor we became in sync. It was like we had danced together before. There was this intense draw between us that was also being pushed apart by the hatred. We were two magnets with the opposing ends facing each other. I pushed back from him and just glared at him. He wasn't speaking, but his eyes were. They were saying, "Now what?"

"All this time you knew how?" I asked him.

"I guess you are just that good of a teacher," he said, smirking.

"Bullshit."

"Oooo language, young lady."

I suddenly became very aware of everyone else in the room. All eyes were on the two of us and Lucas was winning. I don't know why I was always so focused on who was winning, but all I knew was I couldn't "lose" to Lucas.

"If I am such a good teacher, show us."

"I only dance with a partner."

"I don't believe that for a second. You have always flown solo, unless with your posse and you are clearly the leader."

This made Lucas smile. "You do pay attention. I will give you that."

Lucas walked over to the far side of the room and grabbed a chair. He brought the chair over and placed it in the center of the group. He turned to me and motioned for me to sit in it. Pretty sure my heart skipped a few beats before I finally made the decision to sit in the chair. He went over to my phone and started scrolling. The only thing he could be looking at was my music playlist.

"I'll give you one other thing, you have some good music on here."

He set the phone down and music started coming through the speakers. As he walked my direction, I realized what song he'd put on and the hairs on the back of my neck stood up. Everyone around us pushed back, making the circle bigger. This couldn't be happening. The song he had chosen was "Beg for It" by Chris Brown. I gulped hard as he completely closed the distance.

He pulled a ball cap out of his back pocket and slipped it on. He slid one hand down his stomach as he started to move his feet just like Usher would. Then he did a spin toward me and fell forward, clasping the back of the chair on either side of me. He pushed his chest into me and paused. I would be lying if I said he didn't smell good. From here he rolled his body in a sexual grinding motion and I felt the heat move from my face to my Netherlands. I tried to think about the last time I felt that kind of heat but was quickly pulled back into Lucas's trance. He removed a hand and put his right leg up on the chair and the grinding continued and was getting too close for comfort. I went to touch Lucas's leg when I noticed it was a prosthetic. Just as I was about to make contact, he put his leg down, spun around, and sat on my lap just enough so that I could feel every movement. He then leaned back on me and, pressing harder into my lap, sent hot breath into my ear. I shuddered under him instinctively and it sent me into full panic mode. Just as he went to stand and turn, I slid off the chair and ran for the door.

NINE

I was sitting against the wall right outside the dance studio when Trevor walked out right on cue to look for me. He eased himself to the ground next to me and put an arm around my shoulder.

"You OK?" he asked, concerned.

"Yeah, I'm OK."

"You sure? I have yet to see you back down from Lucas."

This made me remember Lucas's leg.

"Lucas..." I trailed off, still trying to process what I saw.

"Lucas what? Sexed you up? Yeah, kind of, but it seemed like you enjoyed it." He smirked.

"Wait, what? It did!? Damnit, game face, Drea, game face!"

Trevor laughed. "Hey, let's be honest, I'm pretty sure any women would have liked that. I'm impressed you were able to walk away. I just want to know why you walked away."

"No, wait. Lucas has a prosthetic."

"Are you sure you weren't just drunk on pheromones?"

"Trevor, shut up, I'm serious."

"Well, it would explain why he never wears shorts."

"I tried to..." again I trailed off, leaving Trevor in suspense.

"You really need to finish your sentences. I can't handle this."

"I'm sorry, I'm just still taking it all in. I tried to touch it, but he wouldn't let me."

"If he hasn't even told anyone, it doesn't surprise me he wouldn't let you touch it. Can we get back on track here, though? I don't give a shit about Lucas. Why did you leave? I know there is something else to it. Like I said, you have never backed down before."

I felt the story coming to the tip of my tongue, but I still couldn't get the words to come out, the dark cloud was hanging low. I tried. I really did. But whenever I went to speak, no words came. Trevor sighed in frustration.

"I want to tell you. I just... can't."

Trevor let out another sigh.

"I know it's frustrating, I do. But thank you for being here."

"It's what Marines do," he replied.

That evening I lay in bed replaying the whole situation in my mind. What started off as something so innocent quickly became something I was not prepared to handle. As I fell asleep, I found myself in more unfamiliar territory.

The dream was as vivid as the afternoon dance-off.

Lucas is next to me in bed. In my bed. He is shirtless and laughing. We are laughing. He throws the sheets over our heads and as I giggle and try to get away, he kisses the soft spot behind my ear. How did he know that was my spot? As I melt into his body, he kisses down my neck. The sheets move around us and I lose sight of us temporarily. When we reap-

pear, we are facing each other. Nose to nose. Legs intertwined. In what seems like slow motion, with his eyes never leaving mine, he kisses me. Soft at first, but then harder. Sexier. Forcing his tongue into my mouth and twisting it with mine. As he reaches to undo my bottoms, I wake up.

I was under the sheets and covered with sweat. I quickly threw the sheets off of me and gulped the cool fresh air. I sat up, turned on my light, and looked around the room. I was alone, with the exception of Tigger, who was purring at the base of my bed with his eyes still closed. He was not digging the lights being on. I pinched my leg just to make sure and when I felt the sting I laid back onto my pillows and started counting the bubbles on my ceiling. My bedroom still had that old popcorn ceiling. As I felt my heartrate slow, I tried to figure out what was happening. I mean it was just a dance. It's not like that has never happened to me before. I used to perform with partners all the time. It had been a long time though, and a long time since I had… well, you know. I sat up, grabbed Tigger, and curled up with him. He protested briefly before deciding cuddling with me wasn't the worst, and we passed out.

When I woke up again the next morning, Tigger was nowhere to be seen and every blanket and sheet was on the floor. I don't remember having a nightmare, but typically the bed being disheveled was a sign I had. I took it as a win that I didn't remember and went to turn on the coffee. As the coffee brewed, I peeled off my sweaty clothes and got into a hot shower. I stood under the water with my eyes closed, letting it run down my face. I felt all the tears and pain from yesterday and last night wash away. I turned and let the water work its magic on my tight neck and shoulders and when I finally exited all pink and warm, I felt rejuvenated. It's funny how sometimes a shower can feel like a chore and certain days its everything you need. After I was dressed and ready, I poured myself a coffee and went out to my favorite spot. I had brought my phone with to call Victoria as I was way overdue to call her. Before calling I saw I had several messages from Steve. The messages seemed to get more concerned the longer I went without answering. I sent him a quick text saying *I was fine and would be in shortly,* before calling Victoria. I wasn't sure she would answer as she was working, but by the second ring she picked up.

"Hey stranger, I was just starting to wonder if I should worry about you."

"Hey, I'm sorry I haven't called. I've actually been... busy." It felt weird to say that.

"I am really glad. You needed something to keep you busy. So, how is the job? I am guessing you are liking it?"

"Vic, I love it."

Don't ask me how, but I could hear Victoria smiling on the other end of the phone.

"Stop smiling over there," I said.

"How can you always tell??" she asked, perplexed.

"It must be a best friend thing," I said, laughing.

"Drea, I am so so happy for you. You deserve this and so much more."

"Thank you for always being in my corner. I don't know if I would have made it through the last year without you."

"Yeah, you are so damn lucky to have me." She couldn't even finish the sentence without laughing.

"Yeah, you are right. I am."

"So, fill me in. Give me the down and dirty."

"I am just really enjoying spending time with these vets and helping them find joy in their lives too. Well, except one who is a giant pain in my ass, but something weird did happen yesterday. He kind of gave me a lap dance. I think."

Victoria was silent for several beats before finally responding. "How do you kind of give someone a lap dance? I don't think there is much room for a gray area in that situation."

"OK, well... He did or was until I ran away."

"You... ran... away? Why on earth would you run away? Was he fat and you were worried he was going to crush you?"

I almost sprayed coffee out my nose at that comment. "NO!" I said, choking the coffee back down my throat. "It's just that he and I... we... are kind of enemies."

"What is with you and kind of? You have never had an enemy a day in your life either, so I am going with no."

"No really. I don't know why, but we hate each other."

"He hates you, but he gave you a lap dance? Is this crazy backwards world or are you leaving out vital pieces of information?"

"Prior to that, the only interactions we have ever had were very rude and snippy. Like two teenagers trying to prove who is a bigger badass."

"So, how exactly did we get to the lap dance?"

"Frankly, I don't know. I had been trying to get him to dance ever since I started there and finally yesterday, he did. I challenged him and he accepted."

"Is he hot?"

"No!!" I blurted out without even thinking.

"Your mouth says no, but the way you say it says yes."

"What?! How can you get that from a no?!?"

"Because of how quickly you said it and with such forced hatred."

Was Victoria right? Did I really not hate him?? This

was an odd new thought. Well, I guess it wasn't new considering my dream last night...

"I did dream..." I stopped to think

"You dreamed what? About this guy? OK, what is his name?"

"Lucas."

"Guys named Lucas are usually pretty hot in my experience."

"This conversation is over."

"Noooo, it's just getting good!!"

"I'll call you back later after I process this information you have just brought to my attention."

"You sound like one of those robots when you call the claims department at the insurance company."

"Goodbye, Vic," I said and hung up the phone.

Victoria noticing this over the phone had me in a panic. I couldn't go back into work. Everyone would be able to tell. Or would they? No one knows me like Victoria. *Ahhh! This is worse than I ever thought.* That must have been why Steve had sent me a bunch of messages. He had sent more even after my response letting him know I would see him when I got there. Now I didn't even want to go. I had to, though, or I would be letting Lucas win. Pretty sure after yesterday he was already way ahead. I couldn't give him any more.

"Shit," I said out loud to myself. "I better get myself together and go face the music."

TEN

As I walked through the hallway toward my office, I wished I had put some whiskey into my Hydro Flask instead of water. I tried to hurry past Steve's office before he saw me, but no such luck. He bolted toward the door and escorted me in, closed the door, and had me sit down. We sat looking at each other for a while. It was starting to get awkward when he finally found the words to say.

"Drea, I'm sorry..."

"Steve, wait, you don't need to apologize."

"I feel like I do..."

"For what?! You didn't do anything. Hell, Lucas really didn't either. It just got... weird."

"All I know is you walked out and hadn't been back since."

"It's only been a day, not even really. Now if I didn't show up for a few days I could see being concerned."

"OK, touché, I just worry. I don't want you... I don't want anyone to be uncomfortable."

"Steve, really, it's fine."

"Is it, though? Someone you... have an extreme dislike

for gave you a..." he trailed off, trying to find the appropriate word.

"Lap dance? You can say it, Steve. We are adults here."

"It just sounds so wrong to say lap dance."

"You are ex-military and struggle with the word lap dance?"

We both laughed. "That is actually two words," he said.

I resisted the urge to give Steve the finger.

"I have never seen Lucas act like that, ever!" Steve continued.

"I'm not sure if that is good or bad," I replied.

"I am going to go with good. Anything has to be better than snarky asshole Lucas, right?"

"Guess we will find out eventually."

"You going to talk to him about it?"

"Noooooope."

"Don't you..."

And as Steve was giving me some sort of explanation on why I should talk to Lucas, I walked out and went to my office.

By the end of the day, I was ready to punch some bags. I had missed yesterday due to the whole lap dance situation, but I wasn't going to miss another one. Even if Lucas was there. I was sure he would give me a bunch of shit about yesterday, but I wasn't going to stop my plans because of him.

Sure enough, when I got to the gym Lucas was already in the room working the bag. He had great form and had spent a lot of time perfecting his craft. He reminded me of a guy I went to high school with. Anything athletic tried, he excelled at. Didn't matter what it was: football, baseball, swimming, he could do it all. I had a feeling Lucas was like that. I walked in, dropped my bag, and started wrapping my hands before Lucas noticed I had walked in. He gave me a scornful smile but kept working. Guess that meant I was allowed to use the room today, not that I was going to leave anyway. I popped in my ear buds and got to work. In between rounds, I did my ab work. Plank holds and crunch and punch. In the middle of my plank work, Lucas decided to set up next to me. I took out one of my ear buds and addressed him.

"Is everything a competition to you?" I asked.

"No but it's fun to beat you."

Here we go, I thought.

"Glad you are enjoying yourself," I replied snidely. I went to work on the bag again and remembered my idea. I took my Thai pads out of my bag. Strapping them to my arms, I turned to Lucas. "You want to beat me again? Let's go."

"Oh, honey, please. You can't handle this."

"Are you going to hit the pads or be a pussy?"

This provoked him, just as I thought it would, and he came toward me. I took my stance and held up the Thai pads. As he began to strike, he was trying to do it as hard as possible in attempts to knock me on my ass. What he didn't realize was that I had done this many times and knew how to hold my stance. The more times he hit the pads and I barely moved, the more aggravated he got, and his form began to fall apart. He was wasting his energy trying to prove himself. He gave the pads one final punch before finally stopping.

"My turn." And I unstrapped the pads and gave them to him. I didn't think he would actually take them, but he did. The other day he didn't want me in here with him, and now we were holding pads for each other. Even if he was pretending to knock my head off. I worked the pads like I normally would, throwing up a mix of punch and kick combos. Lucas knew how to hold the pads—no surprise. When I'd had my fill, I dropped to my planks. This time he didn't join me. I decided to try and lighten the mood.

"You aren't going to suffer with me this time?"

He gave me a quick no and undid his hand wraps. I guess he was feeling defeated, which wasn't my purpose. I thought if anything it would make him feel better to pretend like he was knocking my block off since he always acted like he wanted to. As I tried to think of something to say, he left. That night as I was picking at my food trying not to think about Lucas, I was thinking about Lucas. Why was he so defensive? Why did he have to be so confrontational with everyone? There was something he was hiding. I had now seen brief glimpses of the person under the surface. I wanted to know more about that guy and why he was hiding.

The following morning, Trevor was waiting for me in my office. Evidently, I wasn't the only one trying to figure out what was under the surface.

"Good morning, Trevor. What brings you into my office?"

"I am here for a better explanation of the other day. Take a walk?"

I sighed and set all my stuff down. We walked out the back doors to the garden area. Steve had hired someone to make the back of the building beautiful. It was like a Buddhist garden. Lots of beautiful flowers, greenery, ponds, and fountains. I had only seen it when I first came to tour TLC. I made a mental note to come out here daily, and maybe even have a weekly meeting with the crew. Trevor led me over to a bench by one of the ponds. As we sat, I listened to the slow trickle of the fountain on the far corner.

I knew Trevor wanted me to say something, but I didn't even know where to begin. *Guess I could start by telling him that...*

"Trevor, I don't know what you want me to say."

"I want to know what's going on. I know it's not really Lucas. He is just somehow playing a factor."

I thought for a moment, not sure how to go about it. I needed to talk about it, and Trevor had been nothing but supportive.

"I was married, Trevor... His name was Ryan."

I stopped for a moment so I didn't start crying. Just saying his name made my heart ache.

"He died in Afghanistan. KIA... and I haven't even thought about another man since. So, when Lucas started doing... that... I felt things come to life in me that I wasn't ready for. Someone I don't even know, or really like for that matter, made me feel stuff..."

Trevor was wringing his hands and looked like he was holding back tears. Not really a reaction I was expecting from a tough Marine.

"Drea... I... I'm sorry."

I placed my hand on top of Trevor's to get him to stop fidgeting. "I haven't talked about him in a year. It hurts every time I do. Just like the first time I got the news."

"Now I don't know what to say..." he replied, trailing off.

"You don't have to say anything." I squeezed his hands. "I was dead before I came here. Dead with a dark cloud following me. My therapist tried everything to pull me out, but all it was doing was getting me by."

"Well, you are helping us too. Even if you don't think so. My wife even made a comment about how I seemed happier."

I couldn't help the smile that came to my face.

"Thank you for that," Trevor continued. "I just hope he is proud..."

"Ryan."

"I have no doubt," Trevor continued.

When I got back to my office, I sat there for a minute thinking about Ryan. What he would think about this whole situation with Lucas. Would he be disappointed? Disappointed that someone I didn't even like was bringing out sexual feelings in me? I doubted he would expect me to be celibate for the rest of my life and it's not like I was ever going to actually sleep with Lucas. He probably would be more upset that I walked around with my pain by myself for so long. He was my husband and he died. Not talking about it wasn't going to make that any less real, but it could help me cope. I promised Ryan right there that I would no longer be scared to talk about him or let others use my full name. Since he had passed, whenever someone spoke my full name I could hear his voice saying it. It shattered me every time. Now, I would find peace in the memories I did have.

ELEVEN

Every day after that, it was like a giant weight had been lifted. I no longer felt anything when I saw Lucas. Not fear. Not hatred. Not sex appeal. Just nothing. He had just become a fly on the wall, and he hated it. He did everything to get my attention. Snarky comments. Getting his buddies to follow me around. Whatever he could think of that day. He didn't dance, though. I am not sure if he thought I would run off again or if he was worried his prosthetic leg would be exposed. Trevor still didn't believe me about it. Said I hallucinated in my drooling sex state. I refuse to acknowledge that anything about Lucas was sexy.

I did start a new thing. Instead of boxing every night, I started rotating it with dancing in the studio. I didn't want to force my presence on Lucas all the time. He deserved his own time just as much as I did. Even though I really wanted to figure out what his problem was. That evening when I went to box, I kept to myself. Ear buds in, staying on the far side of the bag, giving him all the space he could want. He seems especially out of sorts, but I didn't want to press. He never responded well to being pushed. When I finished, I sat down to unwrap my hands and stretch. Between dancing and boxing, my body was sore. I wanted to be able to get out of bed tomorrow.

"You are scared of me and ignoring me now?" Lucas asked, leaning against the bag.

"No, Lucas. I am giving you your space. You clearly don't want me around."

He laughed at this response. I'm not sure what is funny about it, but whatever.

"It must be nice to be so sheltered," he replied.

Sheltered. He thinks I am sheltered. I took this moment to be vulnerable.

"My husband was killed in Afghanistan, Lucas. If you want to call that sheltered, sure, I am sheltered."

Lucas was looking at me, trying to figure out if I was telling the truth or not. I was trying not to cry, but I had promised myself the other night I would talk about him. So I was doing this for myself more than for Lucas. I doubted he would care anyway.

"Seriously?"

"Oh yeah, cuz that is something I would lie about," I said. I was trying to be catty but chewing on my lip to keep the tears back. I wanted to be vulnerable but not totally exposed.

"When?"

"A year ago."

He stood silent as I packed up my bag. People often didn't know what to say. At his funeral most people just went for the hug, which offers comfort without having to say anything. With that, I slung my bag over my shoulder and walked out, leaving Lucas to stew.

Of course I had to call Victoria and give her the update. She was impressed that I not only confided in Trevor but that I tried to use my pain to get through to Lucas. I highly doubt it did anything, but Victoria told me not to throw in the towel so quickly. After all this time of giving me shit about not having a clue, he probably felt stupid. He wasn't going to want to fess up to that right away. That I agreed with her on. He didn't strike me as a person to admit anything, but I have been wrong before. The lap dance situation proved that. Losing Ryan still didn't make me one of them. It just gave me a little street cred. At least, that's how I looked at it.

The following morning, I went out to the bench by the pond. I like the change of scenery from my porch. The way the sun comes up and reflects off the water is so peaceful. I can close my eyes, feel the warmth of the sun and how quiet it is. Just me and some ducks. That was, until someone sat next to me. Expecting it to be Trevor when I opened my eyes and looked over, I was stunned to see Lucas. Having no idea what he wanted or what to say, I just kept drinking my coffee. I still didn't want to let him get to me.

"Why didn't you say anything sooner?"

I was surprised by his question. It wasn't like he would care anyway.

"It's not like it makes a difference. Plus, it's not really something I go around telling everyone."

"Anyone else know?"

"Trevor. After I walked away from our... dance, he knew something was up."

"That is why you left?"

"That is the short answer."

"What's the long answer?"

What is with all the questions? Why is he so fascinated by me all the sudden?

"Not sure I am ready to spill my guts to you, Lucas, just because you gave me a lap dance."

Lucas smiled and ran his fingers through his hair. This was the first time I'd seen him do it. I read it as a sign of discomfort. We sat taking in the quiet for a while. I was surprised by how relaxed I felt. Usually when Lucas was around, I felt like I had to be on the ready. Even when I stopped interacting with him, I still kept my guard up. He started to shake his knee. There was something he was holding back.

"You OK?" I asked.

"Don't worry about me. I'm fine." And he got up and left. I wanted to say something to him, but I didn't know what. That was the first nice conversation we had ever had. No verbal punches thrown. Maybe telling him did make a difference? I guess only time would tell. It would be nice to not be constantly bickering with him. As much as Lucas aggravated me, I was there to help. Maybe that was what brought me there. To get through to him. To pull him out from under his dark cloud.

While I debated my next steps with Lucas, I decided to tackle another issue. The bad coffee. Figured it was something simple I could do and would make everyone happy. No one likes bad coffee. First step was to check out the current situation. The first problem was they were using Folgers. Yuck. With how much money and effort Steve put into TLC, I was surprised. This would not do. They were also making it insanely strong. I like strong coffee, but how they were doing it would make hair grow on your back. I went to the store and picked up better-quality coffee in whole beans, a grinder, some cinnamon, and a French press. The French press I would leave out by the hot water in case anyone wanted to make it that way. The next important part was to throw out the bad coffee. The people in the kitchen looked at me like I was insane. I'm not usually one for waste, but this was an exception. Taking out a new filter, I got it slightly damp and put some cinnamon on it before adding the fresh coffee I'd just ground up. The moment it started brewing, all the noses in the kitchen were curious. I asked them who usually made the coffee. The answer explained everything: Steve. His poor wife. Once it was done brewing, I poured a cup and walked to Steve's office. He was busy working on his computer when I set down the coffee in front of him. He looked at me confused before taking a sip.

"Holy moly, that's good coffee. Where did you get it?"

"The kitchen."

"No, you didn't. Do I taste cinnamon?"

"Yes, I did and yes, you sure do. I got rid of your crappy coffee and did it the right way."

"Well, this is just... delicious."

"I can come and do it every morning if you want or I can write down how to do it for you. It's really simple."

"You do not need to be here that early. Write it down for me, please."

I wrote down the directions and set them on his desk while Steve continued to work. When I walked out, he called after me.

"Thank you for doing that. Little things matter."

I smiled and waved. Glad to see I am not the only one who appreciates the little things. It turned out Steve wasn't the only one either. As word got around that I had doctored up the coffee, I got little thank you's all day. Just as I thought; no one likes bad coffee. Except maybe Lucas, or he at least pretended to like bad coffee. He would find a reason to complain about the new coffee once he knew it was my doing.

    That night was dance studio night. The music was vibrating through my skin. I could see it as I moved. I closed my eyes and I could feel it. Feel every sensation and every beat. I took myself into a leg hold pirouette and when I landed, hair still spinning, there he was. Lucas. Watching me. Normally I would stop, but I didn't. I kept spinning, twisting, turning, and shaking as Lucas inched his way closer to me. The next time I spun around I was face to face with him. Before I could continue, his hands were on my waist, pulling me into him. My inner womanhood was somewhere between screaming no and screaming hell yes. The warmth of his hands was very inviting. Placing a hand between my shoulder blades, he super-dipped me. Just like Johnny did to Baby in *Dirty Dancing*. As my eyes met his, I felt the hair on the back of my neck stand up. Ignoring the inner screaming, I danced with him, letting him lead at first until the hell yes womanhood took over. Turning my back to him I bent forward, and as I came back up, I pressed my booty into him and ran my finger through my sweaty hair. Taking a gasp for air, scared of how he would react, one hand ended up on my hip and the other moving my hair to expose my neck. There went the hair on my neck again. As we grinded to the beat he very gently just grazed my neck with his lips. All the blood went straight from my face to my nethers. As I attempted to break away, he turned me so I was facing to him. Our eyes were piercing each other as we panted for breath.

    "Don't go."

    Two simple words and my heart stopped.

    "Why?" I asked, managing not to add a snippy comment on the end.

He stared into my eyes and I could feel the pain behind them. Without thinking, I pulled him into me closely and started dancing slowly, closing whatever distance was left. His hand went to the back of my neck, his thumb slowly tracing the indent. I feel my breathing catch in my throat.

"I need you."

So much for my breath. I am pretty sure I stopped breathing. This man, who had done nothing but fight with me, said he needed me.

"I..."

He placed one finger on my lips.

"You don't need to say anything."

I wanted to say something, I just had no idea what, so at the moment I just kept dancing with him. My iPhone somehow was sensing the mood as the music stayed slow. It of course wasn't just slow either; it was sexy. Lucas lifted my leg with one hand and slow super-dipped me with the other. I felt sexy. Powerful. As I came back to standing, he went to drop my leg but I held it up, straightening it slowly and than spinning underneath his arm. As I came back into his frame I ran my nose along his collarbone. It was his turn for his hair to stand up.

"Don't," he mumbled through gritted teeth

I found myself smirking and moved my nose from his collarbone to his ear, letting my hot breath mingle.

"Don't," he repeated.

"Don't what?" I replied.

"You know what."

"So only you can tease?" I asked as I grazed my teeth over his earlobe.

Taking both my wrists in one hand, he pushed me back away from his ear so I could see his face.

"I can't be responsible for my actions."

A small portion of blood returned from my nethers to blush my face.

"What actions?" I asked, biting my lip.

He looked away, clenching his teeth.

"You gotta stop."

"Why? Is your anger finally going to turn physical?"

He turned back and his eyes were now angry. I kept the snippy comments at bay for as long as I could. One was going to slip eventually.

"You think that's what I want? Like I'm a narcissist? No, this is what I want."

And he kissed me.

TWELVE

His lips were soft and inviting. I tried to resist, but he was pulling me in like a magnet. Before I knew it, my hands were in his hair, pulling him deeper into me. He let out a groan as his tongue requested my lips to part. Letting his tongue intertwine with mine, the heat between us rose and we couldn't control it anymore. We kissed. Deep. Passionate. Hard. A mix of the hatred we thought we had with whatever it was becoming. He somehow managed to pull out of the kiss, bite my lower lip, and pick me up. Wrapping my arms around his neck, I nuzzled into his, biting and kissing every inch of it.

"Unless you want me to strip you right here in the hallway, knock it off."

I debated briefly if I cared, but he was quick and we were in a room with the door closed before any decisions could be made. He set me down and just looked at me. I could feel the heat between us even though the distance between us was the greatest it had been in a while. Just as I started to feel uncomfortable, he spoke.

"You are a fucking goddess."

I ran and jumped into his arms, my tongue quickly finding his. My hands were back in his hair and his in mine. That moment seemed to stand still until he set me down and pulled my shirt over my head. I became very aware of my sweatiness and thought of the smell and tried to cover up.

"Oh no, I don't think so."

And my sports bra was gone. Game on. I reached for the bottom of his T-shirt and he didn't make any move to stop me. As I slid it over his head, the reality of his body came to light. I might have even gasped. He was all muscle. Like a statue. It turned me on and made me feel very not up to par. He must have read my thoughts because he pulled me over to the bed, sat down, and put me in his lap. His hands running up and down my naked back, he kissed and pulled on my lips. A groan escaped my own mouth and I couldn't think of anything but wanting him. Pushing him back onto the bed I climbed off his lap. Unzipping his pants, I slowly started pulling them as I kissed, nibbled, and blew on every inch of skin. Several groans were escaping his gritted teeth as he ran his hands through my hair. Once I reached the top of his knees, I pulled them all the way off. My hallucination proved correct. He has a prosthetic on his right leg starting right where his knee would start. The rest of him was just as muscular as his chest. I sensed his discomfort rising and I continue my assault just as he did for me. Reaching up, I touched the top part of the prosthetic. I notice there was a button on the side and assumed this had something to do with releasing it. I placed a finger on the button and look up at Lucas. His eyes were deep with concern, but he gave me a single nod and reached his hand down and placed his thumb on mine. Together we pressed down and held. I heard a subtle kind of swish noise and he released my finger. Looking back at him, he nodded again and I assumed that was my sign to take it off. Gently with both hands I pulled, and it came off with no struggle. I set it down gently on the side of the bed and came back to him. He was trying to undo the blankets and get under. It was my turn to speak.

"No," I said simply.

He paused, and I could see him debating. I went back to his right leg and began kissing just above whatever the bandages were that were under the prosthetic. Each one of my hands was on one of his legs, making their way up to his boxer line. My kisses were getting closer to the same location. Just as I got close, he took both of my wrists in his hand again and rolled me onto my back on the bed. His breath was deep, almost panting. He moved my hair off of my eyes and tucked it behind my ear as he kissed me. It sent electricity through my entire body. My hips pressed up toward him begging for him to end the torture. With one thumb he slid down my leggings, and I am guessing he was pleasantly surprised by the grin he gave me. I had no underwear on under my leggings. He kissed and bit my hips as he pulled off his boxers. My heart was racing. He dropped his boxers and reached into the nightstand. I closed my eyes and heard crumpling as I was trying to contain myself. When I felt his body next to mine again, his fingers begin tracing the outline of my hips. As he got closer to his destination, I couldn't bring myself to open my eyes. For a brief moment I thought of Ryan, and this whole thing felt wrong. That was until one finger was slipped inside of me and my breath slipped away. I rolled my head to the right and let out a soft groan. As he added a second finger and began to swirl my g spot, I bit my lip and pressed my hips into his hand. He gently pulls out his fingers and I was instantly longing for him. I opened my eyes and saw him lying in awe beside me. Now he really looked like a statue. Not moving, didn't appear to be breathing. I reach for his face and pulled him into me, kissing him deeply. Curling my fingers around his neck and into the base of his hair. He climbed on top of me and pulled away. He was about to speak but before he could, I placed one finger on his lips and with my other hand guided him into me. He let out a deep groan as every inch filled me. I wrapped my legs around him and pulled him in deeper. I found myself wanting him as close as possible. In response, he deepened the kiss and began to go in and out slowly. We groaned into each other's mouths as our hands explored each other's bodies. He was no longer stopping me or concerned about his right leg. His strong, muscular body was so warm and inviting. I couldn't get him close enough. As he tried to pick up speed, I forced him to roll by biting his lip with my full weight, rolling to the same side. He had no choice but to follow me. As I took my position on top, I sank low and slow, pressing my hips into his. His back arched slightly and he groaned through gritted teeth. I rode him slow, taking every inch in and out. His hands went from rubbing my back to my breasts and ass. As I felt him getting closer, he sat up and pulled me down on top of him. His hands were running the length of my back and he was looking into my eyes as he kissed me. He quickened the pace, pulling me into him so that every inch of us was touching. This was where we stayed until we both climaxed.

I let my head fall to his shoulder, my body completely relaxed for the first time in over a year. He was caressing me from the base of my spine up to the nape of my neck. Our bodies still intertwined, frozen in the moment together. I closed my eyes and inhaled his scent. It was refreshing but manly, even after all the sweat. I moved my hand from his side to shoulder and ran my fingernails from the base of his hair to around his ear, and I found myself kissing his shoulder. *How the hell did we get here?*

He leaned his shoulder forward, forcing me to sit up and make eye contact. I brought my hand around from his to his face and moved the longer hair away from his eyes, dragging my fingers down his cheek. As I went to pass his mouth, he took my hand and kissed the palm. I took this moment to voice my thoughts.

"What the hell just happened?"

He smirked and released my palm.

"To be honest, I have been fighting this for a long time," he said as he lay back on the bed and covered himself with the blankets.

"Fighting what?" I asked, lying down beside him

"You."

"Yeah, you have been fighting me, but not in this way, not..." I trailed off, thinking of the right words. "You hated me."

"No, I didn't, Drea. I wanted to hate you."

"Why?" I asked, seeing if this sudden open heart was going to let me in.

"Because you were happy. Together. Beautiful," he said. "You have it all and I lost it all and it made me angry. Angry at you even though it isn't your fault."

I laughed. "I definitely do not have it all together." I sighed.

"I know now."

Wait, he all of a sudden decided I was "worthy" because I told him my husband was KIA?? That is fucked up! I pinched my eyes closed and clenched my teeth to stop the vomit from forming in the back of my throat.

"What? The death of my husband made me sexy?"
"What? No, Drea, that's not it..."
"I am a fucking idiot."

How did I not figure this out before letting this happen? He found out I had scars too and wasn't this perfect princess he imagined, and he thought, "Hey, I'll sleep with the messed-up girl and we can be messed up together." I felt disgusted. I had to get out of there. Ripping back the sheets I jumped up, threw on my T-shirt and pants, and grabbed everything else. Lucas was trying to get himself together behind me, but I was too quick for him. I went back to the studio, tossed my stuff in my gym bag, and headed for the door.

The tears were starting to flow. I was not sure if they were angry or sad tears. Maybe a mixture of both, but I couldn't stop them and didn't even bother to try. I passed several people in the hallway, but I didn't acknowledge anyone or even register who they were. Either way, I wasn't going to stop moving until I got outside and in my car. As I started to back out, I could see Lucas in the distance running toward me. I couldn't help but wonder why he was chasing after me, but I wasn't stopping. His smooth moves may have gotten me once, but that wouldn't happen again. Ever.

Sticking my phone to the dash, I asked Siri to call Tara. She answered on the second ring.

"Hey, neighbor! What can I do you for?"
"Are you home?" I managed to garble between tears.
"Aundrea, what's wrong? What happened?"
"Are you home?" I repeated again, louder.
"Yes."
"Please be there when I can get home," I practically begged.

"You got it." And she hung up.

By the time I was in my driveway I had stopped crying. I put on some meditation music after hanging up with Tara and did my breathing exercises. One of the best things I learned from therapy was the breathing exercises. When I was first dealing with the loss of Ryan, I couldn't go a day without having a panic attack. Once I learned to breathe, the days got longer. Who knew just remembering to breathe would be the key? I got out of the car and walked up to the house where Tara was sitting on my porch. I can imagine what my face looked like based on her reaction. She swiftly got up and hugged me. I had to keep breathing, or I would have started crying all over again. This neighbor. This friend. Who knew this woman who didn't really know me before Ryan passed would become such an incredible blessing?

"Thank you," I said, releasing her.

"That is why you invited me over? To thank me? Ya know, a text works." She smiled. I loved that she was trying to lighten the mood.

I smiled back. "No, I didn't just ask you over to thank you, but it did need to be said. You have given more than I could ever imagine."

"It's been my pleasure, Drea."

Realizing she said my full name on the phone, I said, "I'm sorry if I sent you into a panic. You never say my full name."

"I have to admit I was pretty freaked but when you said to meet you, I at least knew you were safe."

This got my brain on a different track. "Did you worry I would commit suicide?"

Tara shifted uncomfortably in her chair before answering. "Yes. Not because you aren't strong, but because if it was me, I know I would consider it."

Her honesty surprised me and warmed my heart. She continued.

"I am guessing that isn't why you called, though. What the heck happened? I was worried you were going to pass out, you sounded like you were hardly breathing."

So I told Tara the whole thing. Spilled my guts, as they say. Every shitty interaction with Lucas. How I told Lucas my deepest, darkest secret in a crazy attempt to get through to him and how somehow our dance-off turned into a bedroom dance. By the time I was done we had gone through two beers. Tara decided about halfway through we were going to need some.

"All I can say is wow. That is like a movie."

Taking a sip of my beer, I said, "I know, and I am not sure who I am more mad at, myself or Lucas."

"Don't be mad at anyone," she replied.

She's kidding right?!

"How can I not be, Tara?"

"Why should you be? For what? You followed your gut, so did Lucas. I mean hell, you said he was running after you. Why would he run after you if he just wanted to sleep with the "messed-up girl," as you put it? Which I don't agree with that assessment, by the way. I think he just felt like he related to you and it made him open up. Honestly, I thought he liked you a while ago and was just holding it back. After he heard you have been through hell too, he couldn't hold back anymore. You are reading into this all wrong."

Swallowing another sip of beer, I nodded.

"I take your nod as you reluctantly agree."

I smiled. "Yes, that's the perfect way to put it."

A black truck glided to the curb and stopped in between Tara's house and mine. We both waited to see who was here. I figured it was someone for Tara or her husband until Lucas stepped out. He walks around the front of the truck and halfway up the sidewalk before stopping. Tara sipped her beer, looked over at me, and whispered, "Please tell me that's Lucas." Holding the smile back, I didn't respond. My eyes were locked on Lucas. Tara decided to be herself and break the ice.

"WHAT'S THAT, HONEY?? IT'S DINNER TIME?? I'LL BE RIGHT HOME!"

"Well, looks like I gotta go, see ya tomorrow," she said, winking at me, and she dashed home.

I couldn't help but laugh as I felt the panic rising in my belly now that I was alone with Lucas. Neither of us had moved, like we had involuntarily ended up in a staring match. I took a sip of liquid courage and asked the first question.

"How did you find me?" I asked, replacing the beer on the table.

"I was in the military, c'mon now," he said, trying not to smirk.

Stalking is not something I smile about, and he could tell I was not satisfied with this answer.

"Steve gave me your address."

Wow. Way to protect me, Steve.

"Well, you wasted your time," I said, collecting the beer bottles and walking to the door.

"Please. Can I come in?"

"No." And I closed and locked the door.

Half an hour later, my cell rang. Finding it lost under my blankets in the couch, I answered.

"He's still out there."

"Tara?"

I could hear her eyeroll through the phone.

"What, you didn't look at your caller ID? Yes, it's me and he is still out there."

"On my porch??!" I ask, panicked.

"No, he is sitting in his truck. Let the poor guy in."

"Poor guy?? The poor guy who fucked me just because he felt bad after months of torturing me???"

"Drea, if that was true, he wouldn't be sitting outside right now."

Damnit. She was right. This was her subtle way of telling me I was exaggerating. I hung up without a goodbye and walked to the door. Taking a few deep breaths, I opened the door and walked to his truck. I couldn't see in the truck with the tint on the windows, and I didn't want to just open the door, so I rapped softly on the window. After a few second delay, the window rolled down and there sat Lucas.

"Come inside, you are making my neighbors uncomfortable." And I walked back to the house without waiting. I left the door open and walked back to the couch. Tigger had used the opportunity to take over my spot in the warm blankets. I picked him up and carried him off to the bedroom. When I returned, Lucas was standing in the middle of the living room, running his hands through his hair. I sat and wrapped the blankets around me, returning to my movie.

"Didn't peg you as a cat person," he said, eyes on me, mine still on the movie.

"He was a gift. You going to sit or what?"

He stalked over to the chair by my reading lamp and sat. I'm guessing he didn't want to chance sitting too close to me. He made the right choice. As much as I knew Tara was right, I still didn't want to admit it fully.

"What is so important, Lucas?" I asked.

"You just left, didn't even give me a chance to explain."

"Explain what? That my deep, dark scars made me suddenly worthy of you. I'm not sure what is worse. That it turned you on, or that I let it happen."

"That's not what happened."

"Then what? This is all just a part of your asshole plans. Now you can go tell your buddies you fucked me."

"That wasn't fucking," he said, and our eyes met. "I've been an ass because I didn't want to feel what I felt. I was attracted to you from day one, but I knew someone as perfect as you wouldn't want anything to do with me. So I did everything I could to make you hate me. Once I found out you had wounds, that you were human, just like me, I couldn't fight my feelings anymore."

"You know that's kinda fucked up, right?" I asked.

"Yeah. I know. But I can't change it. I can change, but I can't handle you being mad at me."

His eyes are dark and serious but somehow sexy. He can't take me being mad at him? Maybe he really did have feelings for me. There was still a part of me not wanting to trust any of this.

"I have every right to be mad," I replied, eyes still closed.

"Maybe you do, but you don't want to be."

He got up and closed the distance between us. Kneeling down at my feet, he took both of my hands into his and looked up at me. As he kissed each knuckle, in between each kiss he said, "Please. Let. Me. Make. It. Up. To. You."

The blood had officially left the upper half of my body, and I started to squirm. In one swift movement, he took the blanket off my lap and picked me up. He looked around, not knowing where he was, and without thinking I pointed to the bedroom. He beelined to it and sat me softly on the bed. I was in my PJs, and whatever he had planned, there were only two small articles of clothing stopping him. Pushing me back on the bed, he slid his knee in between my legs, forcing them to separate. I lay back and tried to focus on slowing my breathing. He worked to do the opposite by placing his first kiss on my inner thigh. Tracing his way up my thigh, he stopped at the hem of my PJ shorts. With his teeth he pulled them down, just starting to expose the top of my clitoris. He moved his kisses up to the newly exposed skin and across but when he reached my sex, he just blew a soft puff of air. I arched my back and groaned in reply. Going over to my opposite thigh, he began the same assault, this time pulling my shorts far enough down so he had full access. Kissing across my hip bones again this time, his mouth stopped on my clitoris and began swirling and sucking. I could barely contain myself. He added one finger, slowly swirling my hot spot as his tongue continued to caress me. Everything was building inside me, and all I wanted was him. Sliding a second finger inside, he orchestrates the perfect balance between tongue and fingers until I crashed into climax.

As I was trying to catch my breath, he continued kissing up my stomach, removed my shorts the rest of the way, and moved over to his jeans. Unbuttoning them and sliding them down, he revealed an amazing erection. Being caught up in the moment before, I'd never noticed how spectacular he was. How could this guy think he couldn't be good enough for me? My fingers quickly found the hem of his shirt and slid it over his head as he disposed of his jeans. He took a moment to sit and remove his prosthetic, and I took the time to remove my PJ shirt. When he turned back toward me, he smirked with pleasant surprise.

"I'm glad to see you aren't hiding yourself this time," he said and started kissing my hips again.

"I could say the same to you," I groaned as I ran my hands through his hair.

Crawling up to me, his lips found mine and we were lost in a sea of passionate kisses. His warm lips pressing deeply into mine showed me how desperately he wanted me. Leaving one hand in his hair, my other hand grabbed his back, pulling him on top of me. My hand fit perfectly in the crevasse of his back. I wanted to feel his skin on mine. His strength drowning me. I went to reach to put him inside me and he pulled back. Reaching over to his jeans, he grabbed a condom, unwrapped it, and rolled it over himself. As he crawled back to me, I held him at arm's length.

"You were planning for this, huh?" I asked, giving him my best seductive look.

"A guy can hope, can't he?" He brushed my arm aside and pushed himself inside me.

THIRTEEN

The sun was warming my skin, the hammock rocking me back and forth keeping me somewhere between sleep and materiality.

Somehow, without disturbing the hammock's gentle rock, his body is next to me, his nose in the crook of my neck taking in my scent.

"Your scent is what got me through my first tour in Afghanistan," he says softly, knowing I am not completely awake.

"You could smell me without actually smelling me?" I manage to ask.

. . .

"Yeah. It's hard to explain, but it's like you would just appear in the wind. Right when I wasn't sure how I was going to make it."

"But you didn't make it."

Wait? Did I just say that? I am trying so hard to open my eyes, to see his face, but they will not open. I try to move my hand to touch him but I can't. It's like I am in my body but have no control.

"I did make it, just not the last time.
 But my last thought.
 The last thing I saw.
 The last thing I smelled.
 Was you..."

And my eyes snapped open. Lucas was next to me, sound asleep. Tigger was in the crook of his arm. The morning light was peeking in through the curtains. *Holy crap. I slept all night.* No nightmares. I was not sure what to think of that dream, though. I had dreamed about Ryan many times, but we had never had a new conversation. I usually was revisiting old memories and remembering old conversations. Living in some of my favorite times with him. Was his last thought really of me? Could he smell me without smelling me? The guys who had been with him when he died had always offered to talk to me about that day. I never took them up on it. I couldn't. Or at least I thought I couldn't. Now I had some questions, but would questions based on a random dream seem crazy to them? As I steered my mind away from my current dream, I took the moment to try and remember the last time I slept with no nightmares and enjoy the view. I had never seen Lucas look so peaceful. I mean, he even let Tigger stay. That, or he hadn't noticed yet. I thought back on all our jabbing back and forth, and the more I thought about it, the more I could tell it was forced. A forced hatred. I still wouldn't have known why or that it would lead to this, but it was all for show. I wondered if his friends knew and just played along?

Lucas rolled toward me and opened one eye. "You know it's rude to stare, right?"

I smiled. "I thought you were sleeping."

"I was until I could feel your stare."

"You could feel it, huh?"

"I can feel a lot of things when it comes to you," he said, pulling me into him and kissing my forehead.

I kissed his chest and took in the scent. *Shit.* Here I was back in the smell thought. I don't know what it is about how he smells, but I couldn't get enough of it. I found myself kissing along his collarbone out to shoulder and back up.

"If you want more, I need sustenance." He smirked, kissing my forehead again.

Smiling up at him I said, "That I can manage," and stole a kiss before grabbing a shirt and heading to the kitchen.

I set my iPhone into the music dock and let it begin to shuffle through. Dancing and shimmying, I pulled some eggs and bacon out of the fridge and got busy. Lucas came and sat at the breakfast bar and watched me work.

"Now this I could get used to."

"What, a woman barefoot in the kitchen cooking for you?"

"I was more focused on you dancing in the kitchen..."

As we sat to eat, I figured it was time we actually talked. Maybe I could even ask about the smell thing.

. . .

"Why did you come here?"

"I couldn't leave it how it was. You made me feel like a cheap hooker running out on me like that." He laughed.

"Well, it was deserved."

"Was it really? What did I say that was that bad?"

This was the second time I realized my counterpart had a point. All he was trying to say was he realized he wasn't alone in having scars.

"Do you want to know about Ryan?" I asked.

He nodded. I was not sure if he really wanted to or if he was just appeasing me, but I decided to go with it.

"He was a Marine too. The Osprey helicopter he was riding in was hit by an RPG. His entire squad didn't make it home." My fork started to shake in my hand. Closing my eyes, I took a few deep breaths before continuing. "I tried to stay close with the other wives, but I couldn't. It was too much for me to handle at the time. The guys even offered to talk to me."

"I'm really sorry."

"Thank you," I said, doing my best to smile at him. It was weird to talk about him with someone I'd just slept with, but it also felt good to talk about it. "Do I get to hear your leg story?" I asked, turning the subject back to him.

Lucas took a deep breath and it seemed for a moment he was having an out of body experience.

"If it makes you feel any better, you are only the second person I have actually told my story to. My close friends all found out through the grapevine. I couldn't talk about it either."

"Well, you shared your story, and the way you just..." he trailed off again.

"You mean other women have freaked out on you?" I asked, pushing my plate aside.

. . .

"Freaked out is an understatement. That, or they want me to do weird things with my stump."

"You are fucking kidding?" I asked, trying not to laugh. He couldn't help but smile as he put his plate on top of mine.

"No! I'm not. There are some fucking weirdos out there." He took a few breaths before continuing. "But Afghan seems to take a lot of things. It's where I lost my leg too. I got caught in some heavy machine-gun fire. I'm honestly lucky to be alive and not just missing my leg."

"Well, I'm glad you are." Saying the sentence felt so right but so wrong at the same time. It felt like a betrayal to Ryan, but I couldn't deny whatever this was with Lucas.

"Thanks... I gotta ask," he continued, "why didn't my leg freak you out?"

"Why would it? It's not like its infected and smells."

He laughed. "Touché. I'm just not use to such a... loving reaction."

. . .

Reaching across the table, I took his hand in mine. It may be messed up, but it was nice to know I wasn't the only one battling more than one demon.

"I'm sorry I was such an ass to you. Ever since I lost my leg, and each time I get a bad reaction to it, I just built a bigger and bigger wall." He looked up to my eyes. "But that is no excuse."

"Hey, I was an ass too," I replied.

"Only in defense. I just couldn't bear the thought of getting close to you for you to just end up being repulsed by me."

This shocked me. *Has he looked in a mirror?*

"Repulsed? You can't be serious. The moment I saw your abs I wanted to hide under the covers. You are way out of my league."

This brought out a full laugh from Lucas. It was deep and sexy and I knew from this moment I wanted to hear it as often as I could.

. . .

"You can't be serious? I told you I was attracted to you the moment I met you. I could tell you were a goddess."

There was that word again. Goddess. I have been called a lot of nice things in my life, but goddess had never been one of them. Ryan called me his queen. I loved it. It made me feel sexy, strong, powerful and independent all at once. Goddess would take some getting used to. Lucas must have sensed an argument coming.

"Don't even try to tell me you aren't a goddess, or I'll have to spank you."

"Is that a threat or a promise?" I smirked at him.

"A promise," he said. Then he threw me over his shoulder and smacked my ass swiftly and sharply, once on each cheek.

He set me back down and was grinning ear to ear. He was very pleased with himself. I was somewhere between turned on and shocked. Deciding to clean up the kitchen, I got up and turned on the water. Lucas came over. He grazed his lips down my ear and whispered, "You cooked. I clean. Go sit."

. . .

I sat across from him and watched him work. I decided while he was semi-distracted by another task I would ask the question. Or at least ask him if I could ask the question.

"Hey, umm.. can I ask you something kind of weird?"

He smiled up at me as he rinsed a plate. "Weird questions are my specialty."

"Can you smell someone without actually smelling them?"

"I think I know what you are getting at, but can you give me a little more to go on?"

"Like, have you ever been able to smell someone's scent without actually being in their presence? Like their perfume or... lotion."

"Absolutely."

"Really?"

. . .

"Yeah. Why do you ask."

I got kind of uncomfortable at the thought of bringing up Ryan, but I didn't have to tell him I had this dream last night or even that it was a dream at all. Hell, I could just say someone said it.

"A friend of mine said something about being able to smell his girlfriend's lotion while he was at work. That it would come to him at just the right moment."

"It was Ryan, wasn't it?"

Shit. How the hell did he know that? Am I that transparent? He must have been able to see my wheels turning.

"You had me until you said it came to him at the right moment. When you said that, I knew it was Ryan."

"How?"

"It has happened to me before. I don't know if it's the universe trying to remind you of the things that are important to you in a moment of peril or what, but... yeah...

the wind will blow and it suddenly smells like your girlfriend's shampoo or favorite perfume."

We spent the rest of the afternoon talking. He told me all about his family. He had a brother. He was older. His brother was a former Marine as well. He was the reason Lucas joined and now he worked construction. His mom and dad had been married for forty-one years and lived up in the mountains in a little town called Pine. I swapped some family stories as well and tried to get down to why he had never been married before, with no luck. I basically learned that everything I thought I knew about Lucas, was wrong.

I lay in bed that night replaying it all. The dance. Us together. The dream. It made everything seem like it was a dream and I would soon be ripped from this reality to another. Instead, I awoke sitting straight up in bed. The book I had been reading lands on the floor with a thud. My hairline and chest are covered in beads of sweat. I don't remember what I was dreaming, but whatever it was, it was not pleasant. It was still dark in the room, so it must have been early. I looked over to the opposite side of the bed. It was empty, not even Tigger. I found myself wishing Lucas was there. Having a night's sleep with no nightmares was a welcome change. Hell, even the cat liked it. That has to be a sign, right?

I gave myself a mental head slap. *Really, Drea?? You think just because he let the cat sleep in the crook of his arm, and you didn't have nightmares, that he is it.* Lucas being it was a scary thought in and of itself. I never thought I would marry again. I never wanted to. It felt like such a betrayal. Dr. Cox had told me a number of times that Ryan would want me to be happy. He would want me to keep living and that would include getting remarried. I just can't imagine he would want to see me with someone else. Ugh, I had sex. With someone else. It's only been a year. This time I actually slapped my forehead and tried to wipe away the sweat. The panic was starting to swell. I was feeling overwhelmed by feelings of regret, loss and ecstasy. *Good thing I have an appointment with Dr. Cox today. She can help me sort through these crazy emotions.* I tried to go back to sleep but I couldn't get my mind to shut off. I just lay in the darkness watching all the scenes from the past twenty-four hours replay in my mind over and over again.

On my way to my appointment, I rehearsed all the ways I wanted to tell Dr. Cox what was going on, trying to make it sound it as sane as possible. Until I realized how insane practicing to sound sane was. When she called me into her office, I walked right by, sat down, and got comfortable. This was going to be interesting. She sat down across from me, crossed her legs, and smiled. *Why is she smiling like that?*

"What have you been building up in your head since last night?" she asked. *Damn, she knows me so well.*

"I don't even know where to begin."

. . .

"The beginning is usually the best place."

So I gave her the run down. Similar to what I did for Tara but with a lot less detail. She listened patiently and nodded, occasionally letting a smile slip.

"I had a feeling this was going to happen," she replied when I'm finished. Had a feeling? How did she know, and I didn't?

"How?" I asked.

"By the way you described your interactions with Lucas and the way you fought your emotions."

"You mean you knew all along that I had a thing for him?"

"No. I knew he had a thing for you."

"Why didn't you say anything?" I asked.

. . .

"You needed to find it out on your own. You wouldn't have believed me anyway."

She was right. I wouldn't have believed her, just like I didn't believe Tara.

"What do I do now?"

"You aren't going to like my answer, but you need to just go with it. Get out of your head, Drea, and just let things happen."

"But it's so... weird."

"I know it seems weird now, but you have to open yourself up to these new possibilities. You can't mourn Ryan like this forever."

"I can't forget him either," I replied.

"I'm not asking you to forget him. He will always be a part of you, but that doesn't mean you can't make a new life either."

. . .

Damnit. She was right. As always. At least I was getting what I pay for.

"Drea, you have something amazing unfolding for you. See what it turns into."

"What if I get hurt?" I asked.

"You always take that chance when entering new relationships of any kind, but wouldn't you rather find out than wonder what if?"

FOURTEEN

As I drove over to TLC, I still felt conflicted. Conflicted but with a dash of hope. I knew Dr. Cox was right, I just needed to figure out how to embrace it. I was not good at embracing things. I used to be. I use to get a thrill out of trying new things, but ever since Ryan I became too afraid to lose anything else. As I entered the building, memories of what happened here last night with Lucas flood my vision. I felt a flame starting to form as I remembered dancing with Lucas in the studio. *Crap. Stop it, Drea. You can't be getting turned on now.* I fixed my hair and went into my office. I decided to do a writing practice to help me work out my thoughts and feelings. This is another technique Dr. Cox taught me to help me sort through things. It also helped me to see it all out on paper, or should I say computer screen. I am a visual person

When I showed up to class, everyone was there. Everyone including Lucas and his crew. *Shit. I wonder if he told them.* I decided to teach them a routine to the song that kinda fits how I am feeling: "Burn" by Usher. I broke down the first minute or so, and then we practiced slow. Once I felt confident that everyone had the idea, we added the music and took it on. Walking around the room, I helped the ones having a harder time catching on. When I reach Lucas it was no surprise, he had it down, so I kept walking. Before I was even two steps past him, he called after me.

"Want to have a dance together, teach? Think this routine would look better with a couple," he said.

Did he say just couple?

"You couldn't handle it, Lucas," I replied, increasing the distance between us.

"How about everyone else? You guys wanna see Drea and me dance together?"

Of course everyone said yeah and started clapping. How did he always manage to get his way?

"Alright, alright, if that is what the people want."

Everyone found a spot against a wall in the room. Some were chanting my name, some Lucas's. I thought we were doing this together, but I wasn't surprised there was a split. Trevor went over to the iPod to restart the song as Lucas and I met in the center. He was smirking, way too happy with himself. I took a breath and shook off the fear and gave him my best smile back. *I can do this*, I said in my head.

The music started and before he could move me, I was circling around him. I figured it was my time to shine after the whole running out incident. As I completed the circle and came back in front of him, I brought myself into a leg-hold pirouette. Still holding my pirouette, my eyes focused on his, I rose on to my toes before spinning down and just like that he caught me and dipped me back. I felt all the air rush out of my lungs as he dipped me and quickly refill as he brought me in close to him. *How did he time that just right? Maybe we really do have something here.* I turned so my back was to him and we began grinding to the beat. I raised my arms above my head and he in turn ran his fingers down my inner arms to my waist. I could tell he was resisting the urge to touch my ass. At this point the room was empty. I couldn't hear and see anyone anymore but Lucas. We get lost in this incredibly sexy dance. In all my years of dance, I don't think I had ever connected with a partner like this. I couldn't add Ryan in the comparison because the only dancing we ever did together was at weddings and other formal events. It wasn't bad, it just wasn't... this. As the song came to an end, we finished nose to nose, breathless and aroused, both trying to resist the urge to rip each other's clothes off. That is, until we heard everyone clap and cheer and suddenly it was not just the two of us in the room anymore. Snapping myself back to reality, I pulled away from him, smiled and took a bow.

As I was getting my things together to take off for the night, Trevor came over to me.

"Great class tonight. That was fun."

"Hey, I am glad you liked it," I replied, taking a sip of water.

"When did you and Lucas start sleeping together?"

Water came shooting out my nose and I started coughing as I choked on the water left in my throat. "What??"

"C'mon, it was obvious, and you shooting water out your nose just solidifies it."

Wiping off my face, I looked up at him. "Was it really that obvious?"

"I was waiting for you two to rip each other's clothes off."

"Maybe we are just really good performers."

"I will give you that, but there was some extra... heat?"

"Heat?"

"I'm sorry, I couldn't think of a better word." He smiled. "So, you going to tell me what the fuck is going on or leave it to my imagination? I want to warn you my imagination can get really carried away."

Not wanting to let his imagination make up some *Fifty Shades of Grey* scenario, I told him what happened last night. I didn't give too much detail. It didn't seem necessary or appropriate. It wasn't like talking to Tara or Victoria. Trevor, true to form, had a hundred questions. Questions that I didn't want to nor was prepared to answer, so I just left it as, "It happened, I'm not sure why it happened but it was good." Later that night as I lay in bed, I found myself wondering if I could really do this. Could I date again? I never thought I would have to think about this again, but I am sure most people when they get married don't plan to ever again either. Yet here I was. Single and finding myself incredibly attracted to a man I thought I hated just a week ago. I thought about his deep blue eyes and dark hair and felt my cheeks flush. *No. No. I can't get myself worked up now, I don't think straight when I'm turned on. Maybe we can just keep this casual. I mean I'm not going to marry the guy; I don't ever want to marry again, and I highly doubt Lucas is the marrying type. So yes, casual is good. Right?*

In efforts to keep whatever this was casual, I started to avoid too much contact with Lucas. I focused on everyone else in dance class, helping them learn the steps and how to move fluidly with the music. As a result, his snippy comments would make appearances. Apparently, he wasn't liking the distance I was creating. Trevor must have noticed something was off because before the week was over, he found me on my lunch break out by the pond. He even approached me with very exaggerated caution.

"Am I allowed to grace her highness with my presence?" he asked.

"Her highness? Where is my crown?" I asked, smiling.

"Maybe you should ask Lucas?"

"You did not come out here to talk to me more about Lucas."

"Actually, I did. Is that weird? It's weird, isn't it."

"It's really weird considering just a few weeks ago all we did was make snide comments at one another."

"And then you slept with him and wouldn't answer all my questions."

"I didn't answer all your questions because I don't have answers for all of your questions. I haven't even thought about everything." I was starting to question Trevor being my confidant. At this point he was being too nosey. He didn't really expect me to give him details about my sex life. Even if it was with Lucas.

"There is one question I would really like you to answer... HAVE YOU LOST YOUR MIND?!"

Why was he yelling?!? Oh, right. He's an asshole. Damnit, what do I say? How to I even begin to explain this to Trevor?

"Woman, you better start talking," he prodded me.

"He's not who he pretends to be."

"Damnit, Drea, how do you know that? He probably just wanted to be able to tell his buddies he fucked you."

"It's funny, I made that same comment. To Lucas. When he showed up at my house after I ran out on him."

"Wait, he showed up at your house?"

Shit, now there was going to be more questions.

"Trevor..."

"I just don't want to see you get hurt."

"Trust me, I don't want to either, and I don't even know

what 'this' is, which is why I have been ignoring it, but I would be lying if I said I wasn't enjoying it."

"Well…. Enjoy it then and just be careful, OK?"

I nodded, picking at the last bits of my sandwich.

It was Trevor's turn to get quiet. I knew he was thinking of more questions. Always with the questions. Of course, it didn't take long for him to deliver.

"So… his leg… didn't bother you?"

"You know what's funny? He asked me the same question. No, it didn't. Why would it?"

"It freaked my wife out at first."

This gave me pause.

"It probably freaked her out because she knew you before you lost your leg and it was more of a shock, pain thing. She was feeling your pain. Does this make sense? I mean she wasn't judging you."

"I know she wasn't, but it still was something for her to get used to. I'm impressed you could just dive in."

"It doesn't make him any less of a man. He can't help what happened to him."

"You are getting deep on me, Drea."

"That's what he said," I said, trying not to laugh

"Annnnd you ruined it."

After my conversation with Trevor, I was feeling more relaxed and decided I owed Lucas an apology. The problem was I couldn't find him anywhere. Just when I was about to give up, I realize the one place I didn't look. The dance studio. Sure enough, there he was. I opened the door as quietly as possible and sat against the wall right inside the door so as not to disturb him. As I watched him move, my appreciation for him deepened, or maybe I was just turned on. I wasn't sure. Either way, I liked it. As the song ended and he went to change it, he caught a glimpse of me and paused. Running his fingers through his hair, he looked over to me. Even though I could not see his eyes, I could tell he was upset.

"How long have you been sitting there?" he asked.

"At least one song worth," I replied.

He didn't say anything. Just turned away and started to pack up his stuff. Crap. He was really mad. I got up and walked over to him. Gently grabbing his arm, I turned him to face me. Now that I could see his eyes, I could feel the pain. Guess I had become the asshole.

"Lucas listen..." he cuts me off

"Drea, I don't need an explanation. You realized I was a mistake. You aren't the first person to think that."

And he grabbed his stuff and walked out. I wanted to run after him but figured this wasn't the time. In all my worry and stress about what "this" was, I never took into consideration Lucas's feelings. I got so caught up in saving myself that I hurt someone else, and I think that stung more than him being mad. I put myself above him. We may have had our differences, but we also shared some very raw moments. I had to fix this and if not for me, for Lucas.

I went home and sat outside on my porch with a beer and a notepad. I was never much of a writer, but I knew writing down what I was feeling would be better than going in empty-handed. I have a tendency to get sidetracked. This was too important for me to get sidetracked. The weird thing was as I thought about Lucas, I thought about Ryan too. What I used to say to him when we would get into fights. No, this isn't working. I ripped off the page, crumpled it up, took a sip of beer and started again. *Focus, Drea. You can do this.*

At some point I had migrated to the bedroom. I am not sure how long I worked, but when I woke up the next morning, I was surrounded by crumpled papers and Tigger's tail. As I attempted to blow his tail away with a giant exhale, I hoped I would find the magical words on one of the pieces of paper. The paper I was lying on was blank except for one word: Lucas. The rest was a jumbled mess. I couldn't give up, though. *It's a new day,* I told myself. *I'm going to shower, get some coffee, and figure this out before I head back to TLC this afternoon.* It wasn't my day to go in, but I couldn't handle Lucas being mad at me. I hate when anyone is mad, but for whatever reason this was eating at me even more than usual.

When I finally arrived at TLC, it was quiet. Eerily quiet. I eventually found everyone hanging out in the lounge. As I walked in taking in all the faces sitting together, panic quickly set in. Lucas wasn't there. I walked over to Trevor and took a seat.

"Hey, what's going on?" I asked, trying to be casual.

"Steve is worried. He doesn't know where Lucas is."

I felt like my stomach fell all the way to my feet. *Shit, Drea, what did you do?* I got up and went over to Steve and whispered in his ear, asking if I could borrow him for him a minute. He got up and followed me out into the hallway.

"Drea, it's not really a great time right now. Lucas is gone." He sighed deeply and shifted his weight uncomfortably between his feet.

"That is what I wanted to ask you about. What do you mean he is gone?"

"No one has seen him since last night. He has never left without at least telling someone where he went."

I swallowed hard as I felt vomit begin to crawl up my throat.

"You have no idea where he would go?" I asked.

"Aside from his parents, not really. You know he wasn't one for sharing personal information."

"What about his cronies, did you ask them?"

"Cronies? Are you trying to make me laugh? But they insist they don't know either."

"You care if I ask them?"

Steve looked at me confused but shrugged. I walked away quickly toward Lucas's two buddies. I only knew the one guy's name was Rob. I didn't remember the others. They never really spoke or participated, so I never bothered either. Bad on my part. I slid down next to one of them on the wall and took in his shock.

"Uhhh, can I help you?"

"Yeah, you can. Tell me where Lucas is."

"Why the fuck do you care?"

"Look, I don't have time for this, just please, tell me where he is."

He must have sensed the concern in my voice. Looking over at this buddy, they exchanged a few glances and finally looked back at me.

"We have an idea of where he could be."

"Great! Where??"

"We aren't going to tell you. You have to earn it."

They have to be kidding. I looked back and forth between the two of their faces and realized quickly they weren't joking.

"Earn it how?" I asked, trying to contain my annoyance.

"You have to help us."

What could I possibly do for these two hooligans?

"Can we stop playing games and you just tell me what you want? Time's a wasting."

"We want you to make it so we don't have to stay here

permanently anymore. We want to be able to come and go as we please."

Stay here permanently? As far as I knew, Steve didn't make anyone stay, so what on earth were they talking about?

"Make you stay here? I thought everyone was here voluntarily."

"Eh, wrong, princess. Some of us were sent here. Lucas included."

What is with all the royalty comments? Did I start acting conceited recently? It did make more sense why Steve was worried, but I couldn't imagine he kept them under lock and key. It must just be a "Keep me in the loop" type arrangement.

"OK, OK. So, what do you expect me to do?"

"That you have to figure out."

I wasn't liking these games, but I had to figure out where Lucas went. What if he was going to do something stupid, all because I was scared? I wouldn't be able to live with myself. Getting up from the wall, I went back to Steve. He had returned to the circle. I went to interrupt him, and he stopped me.

"Aundrea, whatever it is, it is going to have to wait until tomorrow. This is important."

Tomorrow?? This can't wait till tomorrow. When I tried to speak again, he waved me off. I looked desperately to Trevor, and he shook his head. There was no way to get through to Steve now. I was going to have to wait until tomorrow, but that didn't mean I couldn't do something.

I drove around town looking anywhere I thought Lucas might even slightly consider. Parks, stores, bowling allies, even the VA. Nothing. The longer I looked without success, the bigger the rock in my stomach got. I drove around until my vision started to blur and I knew I had to head home.

When I got home, I went straight to my bed and curled up in a ball. I wanted to cry, but the tears wouldn't come. I felt sick, stressed, worried, sad, and mad all at the same time. Where could he be? I wanted to be hopeful and think he was just with a family member. Just needed some time away from TLC, but I couldn't stop the negative thoughts from creeping in too. Tigger came and curled up in my arms. He could always sense when I was distressed. As the tears finally started to stream down my face, I had the most terrifying thought. *What if I never see him again?*

FIFTEEN

I woke with a start. Not sure if I was coming out of a dream or if it was the clap of thunder from outside. I peeked out the window, and it was pouring. I prayed that Lucas was at least somewhere safe and warm and went to the shower. Letting the hot water run over my face, I fought back more tears. Crying wasn't going to solve anything. I needed to get myself together if I was going to find Lucas. I just hoped those guys weren't messing with me. I stood in the shower until the hot water was gone and then found a pair of pajamas. As I was headed back to bed, I noticed the notepad on the ground next to my bed. Picking it up, I grabbed a pencil and sat in bed. It was time to turn these raw emotions to words on paper. I just started writing. Writing anything and everything that came to mind. I didn't worry about forming perfect sentences or if it all flowed, just wanted to get it all down. When I was done, I set the notepad and pencil on my nightstand. Didn't even reread it. Whatever I wrote was going to be exactly how I felt. Even if it wasn't movie-worthy, it was real. The night was starting to lighten, but the rain had not let up. I could still hear its pitter-patter on the roof. Sliding down into the blankets, I closed my eyes and tried with all my might to think of where Lucas would go. What he would consider a "refuge." Instead, sleep found me.

When I woke again, my room had lightened a little more but not much. It was still raining. Peeling myself out of bed, I went to start the coffee machine. Coffee was going to be a must today. As the smell started to fill the house, I grabbed my cell phone. It was only 7:30 a.m. I must have only slept for a few hours last night. I decided to send a quick text to Trevor before getting dressed.

"Morning. Any news?"

He responded instantly.

"Unfortunately, no. I was just going to call you. You coming in today?"

"I'll be there in thirty," I replied.

I resisted the urge to feel panic and run for my closet. I got dressed. Doctored up my coffee and drove over to TLC. Trevor was waiting out front on one of the benches. He looked like he hadn't slept either. I motioned for him to stay put as I walked by him. Going into the kitchen, I grabbed a disposal cup and went back out to Trevor. I handed him the empty cup as I unscrewed my coffee container. I poured half of the sweet liquid into his cup before sitting down beside him.

"How did you know I needed some coffee?" he asked.

"You look as bad as I do, and the only solution for that is coffee."

We both took a sip, knowing we were delaying the inevitable.

"So, why were you going to call me this morning?"

"Honestly?" he asked.

I nodded. "Wouldn't expect anything else from you."

"I was gonna call and ask if you found Lucas."

"Awww, Trevor has a heart."

"And if you tell anyone, I will kill you."

We both laughed.

"I wish I could say I had, but no such luck." This reminded me about what Lucas's two buddies had said. "Hey, Lucas's gang said they would help me but only if I could make it so they don't have to stay here permanently anymore. Are some people here by force?"

"I wouldn't call it by force, but some families do send their loved ones here. Kind of like you can send someone to rehab. Except Steve is pretty lenient. Long as you tell him where you are going and when you will be back, he is fine letting people leave. Lucas is the first person to leave and not say anything."

"So his buddies, Rob and whoever, can't leave and not come back. They have to come back at some point."

"Yes. Sam. The other's one name is Sam, that is all I know about the two of them." He paused and took a sip of coffee. "So they said they would help you but they want out?"

"Yup."

"Well, Steve adores you, so I doubt that will be that hard."

"Unless Rob and Sam haven't talk much about themselves for an even bigger reason."

"Don't go there, Drea. C'mon, let's go talk to Steve. I'll help."

Trevor got up from the bench and offered me his hand. I found myself even more thankful for his friendship in this moment and took his hand. We found Steve pacing in his office on the phone. We sat outside waiting and watching him aggressively stride back and forth. He was on edge. If only Lucas could see this, he would realize how many people did care about him. When he was finished on the phone, he looked over at us with tired eyes.

"What's up, you two?" he asked.

"We have a proposition for you," Trevor said.

"Normally I would be intrigued, but now is not the time, guys." He went to leave his office, but I stopped him.

"Steve, it has to do with Lucas." I replied.

"What? You know where he is??" There was a slight amount of hope in his voice.

"No, but we know two people who say they do."

"Well, what are we waiting for?" he asked, throwing his hands up in the air

"They want something in return," Trevor said.

"It's Rob and Sam, isn't it?" Steve asked.

Trevor and I both nodded. Steve muscled his way in between us and sighed. This was not a good sign.

"They want to be able to come and go as they please?"

We nodded again.

"Shit."

I knew this wasn't going to be easy.

"What, Steve?" I asked.

"They are ordered here by the court. They have to spend a designated amount of time here or until I say there are rehabilitated."

"Shit is right," said Trevor.

"Can't you just say they are rehabilitated?"

"I could, but if something else happens after they are out it can fall on me. Plus that would be falsifying an official document."

"Shit," I said.

"Now you know why I said it," Steve replied.

"They told me the only way they would tell me where

Lucas is, is if I make it so they don't have to be here permanently. They want to be able to come and go."

"This situation just got even hairier."

"What are we going to do?" asked Steve.

"We lie," I said.

Both Steve and Trevor turned to look at me.

"The three of us will go tell them they have a deal."

"They aren't just going to take me at my word," Steve said. "They are going to want the documentation."

"Then write up the documentation. You don't have to send it over. Tell them you won't send it over until we find Lucas, but once he is back you will."

"I can't lie to them!" Steve replied.

"You have to," I said. "Lucas's life may depend on it."

I was the first person to say the actual reality out loud, but I knew we all felt it. He had never disappeared before and there had been no peep from him since. It wasn't an outlandish thought, it was a real possibility.

"I am a terrible liar. Just ask my wife. They are going to be able to see it on my face."

"Steve, we have to do this," Trevor said.

I nodded in agreement.

"OK, OK, you two win, but don't be mad if they don't believe me."

"Let's start the paperwork. We can't let another day go by," I said.

I resisted the urge to run out and tell Rob and Sam that it was done and to take me to Lucas. I know they would want to see proof, and having Steve with me would make all the difference. All I could do was pace the floor. With each hour Lucas was gone, my anxiety rose. I didn't think I could go another night not knowing where he was. Trevor grabbed my hand mid pace.

"Drea, can you sit? You are giving me anxiety."

I shook my head no and went out to the hallway to pace. I felt like if I stopped moving it meant I was giving up on Lucas. I was the one who started this whole thing. I had to fix it, and quickly. What felt like days later, Steve and Trevor finally came out of Steve's office. Steve was holding the paperwork, and Trevor nodded to me it was time. The color must have drawn from my face, because Trevor came over and took my hand and we walked together over to where Rob and Sam were hanging out today. They both turned to look at us as we closed the distance.

"Well, well, well, to what to we owe this great pleasure?" Rob asked.

Steve handed over the paperwork without speaking a word. My guess was he thought if he spoke, he would blow the whole thing. Rob looked over the paperwork and handed it to Sam.

"Woah, no way," said Sam.

Taking a deep breath and forcing my voice to stay as calm as possible, I spoke.

"Please, tell me where Lucas is."

"Have to hand it to ya, dance lady, I didn't think you could pull this off. Are you sleeping with him too?" He asked, pointing at Steve.

The raw lioness inside me exploding, I jumped on Sam and knocked him back onto his ass. I started punching him anywhere I could while screaming, "TELL ME WHERE HE IS NOW, YOU PUNK ASS HOLLIGAN." Steve and Trevor grabbed both my arms and pulled me off. I was still swinging at nothing when Trevor's face came into view. He was holding up both his hands. My arms were frozen in the striking position, breathing heavy as if I had just run a mile. I could feel the anger pulsing through my veins.

"Drea, look at me."

Swallowing hard, I forced myself to actually look at Trevor and not just over his shoulder.

"You want to find Lucas, right?"

It took a moment for my neurons to make the connection before finally letting me nod yes.

"Then you have to calm down and stop punching Sam."

"I'm not telling you shit now, you pyscho!" Sam yelled.

Here comes that anger again, but before I can unfreeze myself Steve steps in front of me.

"Then I tear up the papers and I keep you here for as long as I want," Steve replied.

Sam, holding one hand to his head, looked over at Rob. They were realizing this wasn't just their game anymore. They didn't hold all the cards and were going to have to help.

"FUCK!" Sam yelled in frustration.

"You are the idiot who instigated her," Rob said angrily.

"I didn't think she would fucking hit me," Sam replied, still rubbing his head.

"Look, let's just stop this nonsense. I will submit this paperwork as soon as we have Lucas back. So please, just tell us where he is," Steve said in a nice but firm voice.

After several beats, Rob finally spoke.

"Give me a pen and a piece of paper. I'll write it down."

I wanted to yell out, "Victory!" but I could not chance messing this up again. Trevor moved closer to me and motioned to put his arms around me. I was afraid if he did this I would break down, so I just signaled to him that my sanity had returned. I moved away from the group and went to the bench in front of TLC. Trevor came shortly after with two glasses of water. Handing me one, I took it and began sipping as he sat slightly beside me. It was almost creepy how well Trevor knew me. How he knew what to say and when, and how he knew when to say nothing at all. Sometime later, Steve finally appeared. I half smiled at him, waiting to hear the news.

"Well, we know where to go look. Hopefully he will be there, but you owe me an explanation," he said, looking at me.

I resisted the urge to roll my eyes.

"Look, I'm sorry I let my anger get the best of me..."

"No, no. Not that. When the hell did you start sleeping with one of my vets?!?" he asked.

Shit. He caught on to that.

"Can we do this in the car, please? We are wasting more time."

"We can, but you better talk or I will pull over and wait for the story."

I held out my pinky and he instinctively hooked his pinky in mine and we kissed the pinky swear to lock it in.

Before Steve even had his truck in reverse, he started grilling me.

"You better starting talking, young lady."

Who did he think he was, my mother?

"I am more impressed you knew what a pinky swear was," I said, trying not to laugh.

"I'm old, not dead. Who hasn't done a pinky swear before? Now talk."

I took a deep sigh and began to give as brief of an explanation as possible.

"It just... happened. It wasn't planned. It wasn't expected. It just happened."

"That literally tells me nothing, Drea. Did you sleep with Lucas?"

"Yes."

Steve let out a deep sigh.

"Why?"

Did he really just ask me why? Why does anyone sleep with someone? A deep electric attraction? A mutual appreciation? An animal-like need? What the hell could I say to this?

"A deep electrical attraction?" That seemed like the best option.

"Well, that is one hell of an explanation. Not," Steve said.

"I can't explain it, we were dancing, he kissed me, and before I knew it we were lost in each other."

"Drea, you two hated each other... I... I... I am so confused," Steve said.

"You and me both."

Steve smiled. I could tell even though I was looking at the back of his head. Then he stepped on the gas. Apparently, my explanation was a good enough reason to find Lucas, and fast.

"Those papers may not end up being a lie after all," he said.

"Really? You feel safe doing so?"

"If you can find and bring out the good in Lucas, maybe letting Rob and Sam have their lives back will do the same."

Lucas running off was having some positive effects. I was feeling better. Sam and Rob were potentially going to have a second shot at life. Steve wasn't going to be a liar.

As we cruised out of town, we headed toward the mountains. They were tall and ominous around us. I usually loved going into the mountains, today they felt much larger than usual. I watched the trees go by, trying to count them to keep my mind occupied. The sun was warm coming through the window, and my muscles slowly began to relax. As I reached well into one hundred trees, sleep found me.

When I opened my eyes the next time, the sun was much lower in the sky. I wondered how long we had been driving and if Rob and Sam were sending us on a wild goose chase.

"Where are we?" I asked stretching the best I could in the back of the truck.

"We are almost there," Steve replied.

"I would hope so. How long have you been driving??"

"Couple hours."

"Are you sure they didn't send us on a wild goose chase?"

"Yes, I am sure," Steve said.

"How?"

"Just trust me, OK."

I nodded even though Steve couldn't see me and went back to trying to count trees. Steve exited the highway and started following a small two-lane road up deeper into the mountains. As he wound around the road, Trevor turned on the GPS for him. After just a few more turns, Steve pulled the truck up to a small cabin. It was all alone surrounded by woods. Smoke was coming from the chimney, and a lone beat-up orange truck sat in what could barely be called a driveway. The truck was not one I recognized. It was not what Lucas was driving the night he showed up at my house.

"This is it," Steve said.

"Are you sure? That isn't Lucas's car."

"Yes, it is," said Trevor.

"It is? That's not what I have seen him drive."

"I'm positive, Drea. Now go."

I reached for the handle and paused. *What if he is mad*

that I am here? Maybe Steve should be the one to go in. Break the ice first.

The boys must have sensed my apprehension. They spoke in unison. "Go."

I looked at both of them, worry pulsing through my body. I felt so strong up to this point, but now that I was actually faced with seeing him, my fear returned. What if I went in there and he wasn't alive? I couldn't handle seeing that.

"Drea, it's going to be OK. We will be here until you tell us otherwise."

I nodded and exited the truck. Slowly walking toward the door, I unknowingly started to fix my hair. I shook my head and told myself to knock it off. I patted my front pocket to make sure my note was still there. I heard the crinkle of the paper that let me know it was still tucked away safely. As I come face to face with the door, I heard something from inside. Sounded like TV or maybe a radio. I said one final prayer before knocking on the door. Relief flooded me instantly as I heard rustling from inside the small cabin. The curtains rustled in the window, but I never saw who looked out. Hoping that he didn't see it was me and just went back to what he was doing, I heard the bolt flip. The door opened. There he stood, Lucas. He was wearing a T-shirt and jeans and was barefoot. His hair was messy and he had growth on his face. His blue eyes really popped from under his dark hair. They looked somewhere in between stunned and mad. He looked incredible, and I had to resist the urge to smile and bite my lip. I went with something much simpler.

"Hi."

"Hi, yourself."

"Can I come in?" I asked, swallowing hard.

He stepped aside, and I walked in. As I was removing my shoes, he spoke again.

"How did you find me?"

"Rob and Sam," I said, looking up at him as I slid off my second shoe.

"Wow, some friends they are," he replied, running his hands through his hair. How did he make something so simple look so sexy?

"They blackmailed me for it. If that makes you feel any better," I replied, smiling slightly.

"Oh ya? What did they get out of you?" He smirked back, taking a seat in a chair at the table in the kitchen.

"Freedom."

He sat upright, trying to hold back the shock.

"But you don't have the authority to do that, do you?"

"No, but Steve does. He's out in the truck."

Lucas got up from the chair and went to the window. Moving the curtains out of the way again, he looked out at the truck. After a moment he waved. Releasing the curtains, he turned and looked back at me.

"Is that Trevor in the truck too?"

"Yes, we were all worried about you."

This brought out a laugh. He still didn't believe any of us cared about him. I didn't really blame him at this moment. He sat back in the chair and leaned back.

"I have to admit I am impressed. I never thought anyone would find me."

This stung a little. He honestly thought I was just going to let it go, forget about him like it never happened?

"You can tell them to come in," he continued.

"Or I can tell them to leave..." I said, my eyes locked on the floor. I couldn't look at him, fearing his rejection.

"You trust me to take you home at some point?" he asked.

I forced myself to look at him. He was smirking again. I think he was enjoying the thought of torturing me.

"Yes," I said, keeping my eyes locked on him.

"Then tell them to go."

Like an obedient child, I got up and walked out to the truck. Trevor rolled down his window and I walked over to his side.

"Well?!"

"He's OK. You guys can go."

"We aren't..." Steve reached over and cuts him off.

"Call us if we need to come back."

I nodded, and Steve put the truck in reverse and backed out. Trevor had a look of terror on his face. He would just have to handle it. I had to do this. I walked back to the cabin and closed the door, now realizing I walked out without my shoes on. Good thing it wasn't winter.

"That was quick." Lucas was still in the same chair. I decided to be bold and go sit on the couch. I knew I was not going anywhere, so why not get comfortable? Lucas made no move to come near me. The question now was how do I start this. *Do I just bust out my note and start reading? No, that's too unoriginal.*

"The hamster is running really fast on the wheel over there. Why don't you try and say out loud what's on your mind? Or did you come all this way to just sit here."

"No, I just... I don't know where to start."

"I find simple is best. Something like, 'I can't do this. It's over.'"

What? He thought I came all this way to tell him that it's over? Is he for real? As I watched him shift uncomfortably in his chair, I quickly came to terms with the fact that he was being real. He was so, so damaged that he thought no one could possibly care for him.

"I was thinking more along the lines of 'I'm sorry.'"

"Sorry for what? Showing your true feelings? No reason to be sorry. I'm the one that should have known better. To think that you would be different."

I laughed. Couldn't even keep it in if I wanted too. He looked over, disgusted, thinking I was laughing at him, and I slapped my hand over my mouth to silence myself. I couldn't fuck this up. I stood up and took the crumpled piece of paper out of my pocket. Sitting back down, I unfolded the paper and saw all the words I wrote down what felt like months ago, when in reality it was just yesterday. The words seemed foreign and over the top, but I wrote it from the heart so I started reading.

"I am scared. Scared to fall for you. Scared you will leave. Scared it will end before it even gets started. I didn't take into account that I wasn't the only one involved in this. I let the fear of being left alone again take over and ended up hurting you. I never wanted to hurt you, I was just so lost in my own emotions. My own head. I lost sight of you. I lost sight of what I really want..."

"You were doing so well... What do you really want?"

The hot tears were forming behind my eyes. It was now or never, and I couldn't hide anymore. Look what happened last time. Locking my eyes with him I said, "You. I want you."

The fear was bubbling up. I swallowed it back down and one tear fell down my cheek. His eyes were on me. His expression was unchanged, and he hadn't moved.

"This is low, Drea."

What is low? He thinks I'm kidding?

"I'm not messing around, Lucas. I want you."

He stood and went to grab his shoes.

"C'mon, I'll take you home."

The fear was overtaking me. As the panic rose, I quickly moved to the front door. I flung it open and began running away from the cabin. I had no idea where I was going, but I had to get away. As I reached the hill going down the far side of the property, I caught too much speed and slipped and tumbled down the hill. I finally came to a stop just before the tree line. Lucky for me, the tree didn't have to stop me. I put my hands over my eyes as the tears flooded my vision. I was gasping for air and could feel warm liquid dripping down my leg. I felt something warm on my arm and jumped, expecting to see an animal. Lucas was kneeling beside me. I tried to roll away. As I rolled, a sharp pain ran up my side. I cried out in pain as I continued to push myself up on my arm and away from Lucas.

"Drea, stop, you are hurt. Let me help you."

"NO! Leave me alone."

He went to reach for me again, and I forced myself to stand up and started walking away. The helpless feeling I had been fighting since Ryan died had completely overtaken me, and I just wanted to be alone now. Where no one could see my hurt and I couldn't hurt anyone. I was totally lost in my panic attack. I found myself limping slightly but kept moving.

"Drea, please."

I stopped, feeling like I was going to puke, but I managed to find words.

"I have no reason to stay anymore." And I begin to walk again but after only a few steps the world went black.

SIXTEEN

I *see him. Ryan. He is smiling. His smile was always my favorite. He is reaching for me. I reach out but he is too far away. I try to get closer but no matter what I do the distance between us never gets closer. I am trying to call to him for help but he just keeps smiling. Smiling and saying something. What is he saying? I turn my ear and hold my breath hoping this next time I can hear him. In a very faint voice I hear. "Aundrea, you have to wake up."*

My eyelids fluttered before finally opening. There was a small ray of light coming from a window to my left. I tried to turn to look, but my neck was stiff. Letting out a soft groan, I closed my eyes again. As I felt myself start to drift back to consciousness, I felt a hand in my hair. I opened my eyes again and as the world around me came into focus, Lucas was standing over me. I went to move, but my entire body ached.

"Lucas?" I managed in a soft voice.

He let out a giant sigh and sat next to me on the bed, letting his head fall into his hands. Instinctively I started to rub his back. My fingers were filthy. I had a flashback to falling down the hill and was surprised I was still at the cabin with Lucas.

"Why am I here?" I asked him.

"What, you thought I was going to leave you outside?"

I forced myself to sit up and stretch. As I moved my neck and arms, the achiness got a little better.

"You could have drove me home."

Lucas turned to look at me, shocked. "Like you were? People would think that I raped you or something?'

"No one at TLC would ever think that of you," I said, getting myself up out of bed.

Lucas panicked and ran over, expecting me to fall over.

"What are you doing? You need to lie down."

"No, I need a bath. Then I am going home."

I moved past him and into the bathroom. Luckily, just as I hoped, there sat an old claw foot bath tub. I turned on the water and started to pull off my dirty clothes to assess the damage. There was no explanation for my hair. My face was a streaky mess of dirt and old tears. My arms seemed for the most part to be unharmed except for a few bruises. As for my lower body, not as lucky. My butt had a big bruise and a nice cut running down the side of my hip. This would explain the hot liquid I felt. All things considered, though, it wasn't bad. The hill didn't win. Lucas was standing in the doorway observing. He looked horrified.

"My hair looks as horrified as your face," I replied, trying to be funny. Holding on to both sides of the tub, I stepped one foot in. The water was so hot I could barely stand it, but that is exactly how I like it. I stepped my other foot in and slowly immersed my entire body, sliding down up to my neck. It was hot but felt so good. I took my hands and started rubbing the dirt off my arms. Lucas moved from the doorway and walked over to a small closet. He opened it, rustled around, and then closed the door. He walked over to me and handed me what he had fetched out of the closet. A washcloth. He reached up above me and grabbed soap, handing that to me as well.

"I'm horrified by how much you hurt yourself, not your hair."

"I'm fine."

He leaned both arms against the wall next to the tub and sighed again. This wasn't going at all as planned.

"I'm sorry."

He started to speak, but I continued.

"I have been holding back so much emotion that I finally snapped and went into a full-blown panic attack. I made a fool of myself and I'm sorry. I can call Trevor to come get me."

He went to speak again and stopped himself. *He must be thinking of a nicer way to reject me since I went full pyscho on him last time*, I thought to myself.

"You don't need to say anything. I did this to myself," I continued. It was true. This whole situation was happening all because I couldn't be honest with myself. We wouldn't even be here if it wasn't for me.

"Please don't," he finally said.

"Please don't what?" I asked.

"Go."

I didn't know what to say, so I opened the soap and squeezed it onto the washcloth. My nose was filled with his scent. My lady parts responded instantly just from the scent and I had to control myself. I moved the wash cloth down my arm and farther away from my nose to slow the reaction.

"You OK? Does it hurt?" *Oh baby, that's not the reaction I was having.*

"No, it doesn't hurt."

"What then?" he asked.

"Please don't make me say it..."

"Why not?" he was now smirking.

"Because I am tired of making an ass of myself."

His smirk widened.

"Please..."

What else did I have to lose? I already rolled down a hill in front of him and looked like I had hair from *The Croods*.

"Just the smell of your bodywash turns me on..." I said, trailing off, realizing how stupid it sounded out loud.

He moved away from the wall and pulled the T-shirt over his head. Now not only did I have his scent engulfing me, his was teasing me with his godlike body. I thought he was done until he reached for his top jean button. Undoing the button and unzipping, he let his jeans fall to the floor. I was surprised to see he has no boxers on underneath. I gulped hard. My face would have flushed if it wasn't already red from the hot water. He sat on the small edge of the tub and I resisted the urge to pinch his butt as he took off his prosthetic. Swinging himself over, he stepped in and slid down into the water across from me. He let out a soft moan in response to the hot water and closed his eyes. Talk about pure torture. I had no words, so I continued my cleaning as I drank him in. Working my way down to my legs, he sat forward and took the washcloth. I let go and watched him take it down my leg the rest of the way and around my foot. Once he was done with one leg he went over to the other. I felt like I could pant but refused to give him the satisfaction. Once he was done, he rung out the washcloth and hung it over the edge of the tub. As he went to sit back, he pulled me into the space in between his legs. He twirled his finger over my head telling me to turn around. Doing as requested, I spun in the water so that my back was facing him. Now that I was facing the other way, he pulled me all the way into him. My back pressed against his chest. He smoothed my hair down the best he could and tucked it behind my ear. I found myself unknowingly relaxing in his arms. Letting my head fall to his shoulder and closing my eyes. His fingers were gently stroking my arms. I was somewhere between turned on and incredibly relaxed. His mouth gently touched my ear and the turned-on portion started to win when he said softly in my ear, "I want you too."

I sat up quickly, causing the water to create a wave and slosh over the sides of the tub. I turned to look at Lucas and he was smiling ear to ear.

"What?" I managed to spurt out

"You heard me." His smile somehow managed to get bigger, and man did it look good on him.

"Is this just because I almost killed myself?"

This got a boisterous laugh out of him.

"No, that part made me feel terrible. I've wanted you since day one. I told you that already."

Now it was my turn to smile like a fool.

"Say it again," I said, bringing myself back to his lap and leaning into his chest looking up at him.

"I want to be with you too," he said in a soft, sexy voice.

I sat all the way up and turned myself to face him, straddling him. Taking his face in both hands, I brought my lips to his and kissed them softly. Just gently teasing his lips with mine. It didn't take long for one of his hands to end up in my hair and the other at my lower back. Our kisses deepened as his tongue found mine and all of the pain and stress exited both of our bodies. Pulling away before we got too carried away, he looked up at me with a deep want in his eyes. I slid back to my side of the tub and dunked myself completely under the water. The warmth flooded around me and my hair released all the dirt, returning it to semi-normal status. As I came back up and took a breath, Lucas's eyes had not changed and I even sensed a slight annoyance.

"Way to leave me hanging." He smirked.

"My apologies, dominus, but I figured I should get my hair clean and under control before I let you have your way with me." I had been watching too much *Spartacus*.

"*Apologies, dominus?* And that is not what I meant?"

I crawled back over to him, pulling myself up to the point that our lips were just barely not touching.

"I need to wash my hair," I said as I went to kiss him, but at the last moment pushed myself back to my side and grabbed the shampoo.

He bit his lip in frustration, running his hand through his hair, and dunked himself under the water. I couldn't help but smirk. I couldn't remember the last time I had this kind of sexy power or whatever the hell this was. Whatever it was though, I liked it. A lot.

"My restraint isn't going to last much longer if you keep doing stuff like that," he said as he resurfaced.

"Doing what?" I said in my best innocent voice as I lathered up my hair.

He rolled his eyes and reached for the bodywash.

"You are on."

SEVENTEEN

After just escaping the bath, I stood in front of the mirror in the bathroom towel drying my hair. I doubted this little cabin has a blow dryer, so this would have to do. I also become very aware that I was standing naked, totally uninhibited. Even when Ryan and I first got married I rarely just stood naked in the bathroom. I always had a towel wrapped around me. It took a good year before I felt comfortable enough to just be... naked. Yet here I was, with a man that in all reality I barely know, completely exposed. As I was looking at myself in the mirror, Lucas appeared in the reflection behind me. He drank me in before kissing the top of my head.

"Most beautiful sight I've ever seen," he said, planting another kiss on my head.

"I was just thinking about Ryan."

"And that's not what I want to hear..." He turned to walk away, and I grabbed his hand.

"That's not all. Let me explain I started that off on the wrong foot."

He sighed but didn't move. I let go of his hand and went about fixing another error my mouth had made.

"I was just thinking how I didn't feel this comfortable with Ryan. Not right away anyway. I always wore a towel after getting out of the shower. Yet here I am. With you and it didn't even cross my mind."

Lucas closed the distance between us and took me into his arms, kissing the top of my head and shoulders.

"You should probably start with what you ended with next time."

"I'm sorry, this is just all so..."

"Crazy," he said, filling in the blank for me.

"Yeah, it is crazy but it's also... incredible."

In one swift move he swept me up into his arms. He stood just holding me, looking down at my completely naked self. Naked not in just the actual sense but emotionally too. He kissed my lips deeply, causing a soft groan to form in the back of my throat before carrying me off to the bedroom.

When I woke up the room was completely dark except for a soft light coming from the fireplace. I was twisted in a mess of sheets with an arm tucked around me. Lucas was sound asleep. He looked so peaceful again. I couldn't help but reach out and touch his face. I ran my fingers softly down the side of his face and into the scruff that had formed on his chin. I like the scruffy look on him, he wears it well. I continued across the bottom of his chin, letting one finger graze over his lips. As I started to go up the other side, I felt his lips press into my wrists.

"Now that is a nice way to wake up," he said, smiling slightly, eyes still closed.

"I didn't mean to wake you, you just looked so peaceful and I wanted to touch you."

"You can touch whatever you want." His slight smile turning into his sexy-time grin and he opened one eye.

"I need to eat and rehydrate," I said, planting a kiss on his lips. "How does some breakfast sound?" I asked.

"Delicious."

I got out of bed and saw one of his T-shirts slung over a chair in the corner. I went over, grabbed the T-shirt, and slid it over my head as I headed to the kitchen. Opening the fridge, I was surprised to find it well stocked. Good to know when he runs away he doesn't skimp. I took out some eggs and bacon and went to work in his little kitchen. *Wait, is this his kitchen?* Not long into my scrambling, he came and sat at the stool in front of me.

"I have to say I was surprised to see the fridge fully stocked."

"Hey, I gotta eat." He shrugged.

I decided to ask him the question I was just contemplating.

"Is this your cabin?"

"It belongs to my family."

I stopped stirring, having a brief moment of panic that his parents could walk in the door at any moment.

"Relax, they know I am here. They aren't the pop in kind of people."

"You bring girls here often, huh?" *Way to be jealous for no reason, Drea.*

"No, actually. You are the first. Well, the first anyway since I..." he stopped.

"Since what, Lucas?"

"Since I lost my leg."

"Anyone who would dismiss you because of your leg isn't worth your time anyway."

He forced a kind of smile and I decided to change the subject.

"So, does your family know why you are here?"

"Yup," he said simply.

"You told them about me?"

"Sure did. After that first night I had to tell someone. You were such a breath of fresh air. My brother wants to meet you immediately."

I felt a slight sting of remorse as I had not told anyone in my family yet. The only people who knew outside of TLC were Victoria and Tara.

"I can't wait to meet him either." I was surprised by how honest this statement was. When you think about ever dating again, the thought of not only having to start over with a new mate but a new family is really intimidating.

"Have you told your family about me?" *Shit, of course he would ask that.*

"No, I haven't yet. I don't talk to my family as regularly as I used to. They couldn't tolerate my... depression."

He didn't seem to approve, so I continued.

"I have told my neighbor and my best friend, though. If that counts for anything."

"Is that what you were doing that night I showed up at your house?"

I nodded and poured the eggs into the pan with one hand and tended to the bacon with my other, making sure it was cooking evenly. Going back to the fridge, I found orange juice and cheese. Holding up the juice, I started pointing at random cabinets. He pointed to the correct cabinet. I set the juice and the cheese on the counter and got two glasses. I poured one glass and hand it to him while I filled mine. He downed the entire glass before I was even finished pouring mine. Apparently someone was thirsty.

"More?" I asked.

He nodded and I refilled. He took another big sip but didn't empty the glass.

"Why does OJ just taste so good sometimes?" he asked.

I laughed because I knew exactly what he was talking about.

"I don't know, but I know what you mean."

He held up his glass. I grabbed my glass and held it out to his.

"To many more nights like this," he said and we clinked glasses. I was smiling like a damn fool. If you would have asked me a few months ago if I thought I would be sitting in a tiny cabin with Lucas in his T-shirt making breakfast in the middle of the night, I would have died laughing. But I do like how the story changed.

"What are you thinking?" he asked.

"That I can't believe we are here," I said as I served everything out onto a plate and set it in from of him.

"Crazy. huh?" He got up from his chair and went to a drawer to grab forks and knives. I knew I had forgotten something. As he repositioned himself on the stool he kept talking. "I used to dream about you all the time."

This took me by surprise, but I guess at this point nothing should surprise me anymore.

"Really??"

"Yeah, it use to piss me off," he said, laughing, "I wanted to hate you so bad but even my dreams wouldn't let me."

This piqued my interest and my lady parts.

"Oooo, so you were having sexy dreams about me?" I said as I sat on the stool next to him.

That beloved smirk came to his face, "I plead the fifth." And he dug into the eggs and bacon.

I decided not to poke at him anymore and eat. When

we were finished, he got up and started the clean-up duty. I sat and watched him. He moved fluidly just like he does when he dances. As he sets the dishes on the small counter, I spied the towel hanging from the stove. I started drying the dishes, which then gave me a delicious idea. I dried both plates and did my best sexy sashay over to the cabinet. Lucas was watching out of the corner of his eye. Opening the cabinet, I rose onto my tippy toes to be able to reach and put the plates away. As I rose onto my toes, the T-shirt rises up my back and showed the round outline of my ass.

"Tread lightly, sweetheart, or I will have you right here," Lucas said over his shoulder.

Lowering myself back onto flat feet, I purposely dropped the towel on the floor. Bending over to grab the towel, his T-shirt went all the way up my back, exposing my entire backside. Before I could even grab the towel, his hand met my ass in a swift spank. My face flushed as my entire body felt like it was lit on fire. Lucas hadn't moved, his hand still firmly planted on my ass. I was surprised by my desire for another. Lucas seemed to be trying to gauge what I was feeling. I'm guessing his instincts kicked into full gear.

"Again," I said. That sexy smirk returned to his face and he did it again. That fire in my body got hotter. Standing up, I turned and kissed him hard, biting at his lower lip. He picked me up and set me on the edge of the counter as he slid down his sweatpants, his lips never leaving mine. I pulled him toward me, my nails digging into his ass. I had to have him right away. He responded by thrusting into me deeply, and I wrapped my legs tight around him to hold him there. He wants to move, but I wouldn't let him. He growled through clenched teeth. He wanted this as bad as I did. I loosened my grip and he began going in and out of me, using every inch. Slow at first then faster and faster. I felt my body quickly building, and in response he deepened the kiss. Just as he did, I totally lost myself in him and he did the same.

We were panting. I was leaning into him, unable to hold myself up. I had never lost myself that easily with anyone. Ever. He kicked off his sweat pants the rest of the way and then picked me up again. I completely relaxed in his arms as he carried me to the bedroom. He laid me down and covered me with the sheet before crawling in next to me. He stroked my hair out of my eyes as I got lost in his.

"You are so beautiful. My goddess," he said softly and with satisfaction. I smiled at him. I was starting to get use to the "goddess" word. "I told you I would take you right there if you didn't knock it off."

"I had to hold you to it."

He kissed my forehead.

Can I tell you something?" I asked.

"Anything."

"I have never been able to let go that quickly with anyone until you."

The moment I said, it I could see his ego growing.

"Oh really? Let me see if I can do it again."

I tightened the sheets around me.

"Stop it, we can't just do... that... all the time. We need to get to know each other."

"Oh I know you, alright," he said, kissing me through the sheets.

I resisted the urge to moan "No, you can wait."

"Alright, alright, what do you want to know?"

We spent the rest of the evening actually getting to know each other. I found out we share a love of pizza, but who doesn't? He hates olives. He spent a summer working at a country club and one of his duties was taking the red pimento out of the olives and replacing it with blue cheese. He said ever since then he couldn't stand them. He has never been married but thought he was close once. He skated around the details, so I decided to wait until later to probe him about it. I told him about how I drifted from my family after Ryan died but Tara and Victoria really stepped up to the plate. If I didn't have them, I'm not sure I would be here. I started dancing at six, he started around eight. He said it took him longer to convince his dad it had nothing to do with his sexuality. Which is one reason why he went into the Marines, the other reason being his brother. He did say joining was one of the best decisions he ever made. The brothers he gained joining were worth it alone, even though he lost his leg.

"What was it like losing your leg?"

"Honestly, the hardest part was the first time I woke up. Seeing the missing lump in the bed fucking terrified me."

"I can't even imagine."

"What about walking and stuff?"

"It took a lot of practice getting use to the prosthetic, but now that I am use to it I forget it's there sometimes."

"Did you have to learn to dance again?"

"Not completely, but I did have to relearn certain things. I was meant to dance though, so it's almost like my body taught my leg." He laughed. "Wow, that sounded better in my head."

I reached across and rubbed his arm. "No, I totally get what you mean." I found myself wanting to know everything about him. Including who or what caused him to become so guarded. "Can I ask you something that you have been avoiding?"

"Only if I can do the same back to you."

I nodded in agreement. Only seemed fair.

"Did a lot of women treat you badly because of your leg? You have hinted at it a lot and I just... I want to know how you..."

"How I became an asshole?"

"Your words, not mine."

"Well, you know how I said I was close to getting married."

"Mhmm."

"Well, that was after my leg. I met this girl out with the guys one night and we just hit it off. Kind of like you and me, but not so intense. We danced, had a good time. She tried to take me home, but I wouldn't. I had women literally kick me out of the bedroom the moment they see my prosthetic before. So since we never talked about it, I just never brought it up. Until things got really serious. I thought I was in love. So did she. So before I wanted to propose I had to tell her about it. I took her out. Had a great time and when we got home before things got compromising I sat her down and told her. She thought I was lying. Using it as an excuse not to sleep with her and I must be gay or something. That is, until I took my pants off and showed her. She ran out of my apartment and I never saw or heard from her again."

My mouth was hanging open. How could someone do that? To anyone?

"Don't act so shocked," said Lucas, closing my mouth. "Not everyone is so accepting as you. You are a rarity."

"I shouldn't be. That's... that's... horrendous.

He shook his head and I could tell it still stung. I leaned forward and kissed his forehead.

"Her loss, my gain."

He managed a small smile.

"Well, it's your turn. Ask away." I figured this would

cheer him up, especially if I was more willing to participate even though I was afraid of what he would ask.

"Why did you start ignoring me? Is that the same reason you don't talk to your family right now?"

Wow, that was a loaded question.

"I started ignoring you because I was terrified. Losing Ryan... and I'm sorry to keep bringing him up, but it's a part of the story. But losing him was the hardest thing I have ever been through. The thought of losing anyone else is unbearable at times. My depression was so dark and deep no one could handle being around me. I see a therapist weekly because of it. So as a result I keep everyone at arm's length. Where they can't hurt me and they don't have to deal with my depression. At least according to Dr. Cox. Which when you think about it, it isn't a very logical solution because I am still losing them. Just not to death."

"So you knew you wanted to be with me, before I disappeared."

"Yeah, I did, and it scared me. Which I get is cliché or whatever you want to call it, but I couldn't bear the thought of telling you and you laughing in my face."

"Why would I laugh at you?"

"A small part of me thought you only slept with me to brag to your buddies about me. A very small part of me."

"What convinced you otherwise?"

"You know you are over your questions limit, right?" I chuckled. "Tara. When you showed up at my house and I wouldn't let you in. She called me to tell me you were still sitting outside. She told me you wouldn't still be sitting there unless you cared. I knew she was right."

"I better buy Tara a beer."

I leaned in and kissed his lips. "I owe Tara a lot more than a beer at this point."

"Why don't we have a party?"

"A party? For what?"

"For you. For you becoming yourself again. Invite your friends, the guys from TLC, your family. Make amends and honor who got you through."

"Then why not make it for us? You have come a long way too. I bet you once we get back you can 'graduate or whatever you guys call it from TLC."

"You know I'm not there voluntarily?" he asked, sitting upright.

"Yeah, Steve told me when you went missing."

"Did he tell you why?"

"No, should I be concerned?"

"No."

"Lucas..."

"The short answer is my attitude got me into a lot of trouble."

I nodded, knowing this attitude from previous experience. He really had shown a completely different side to him. I was guessing this was the real Lucas. The one I originally met was angry Lucas. The Lucas that hated the world. He must have started getting worried as he asked me another question.

"And you still want to be with me?"

"I just told you I have a therapist. C'mon now."

He pulled me into him and wrapped me tightly into his arms.

"You really are a rarity, Aundrea," he said, kissing the back of my neck. "Hey, we did all this talking and I don't even know your full name."

I turned to look him in the eyes. He was beaming. I had never seen him like this. I swear each day as more of him came through, the better looking he got.

"Aundrea Rose Conte."

"Conte... Italian?"

"My dad, yes."

He mulled this over as I waited for him to answer.

"Well..." I said, motioning with my hands. I expected him to answer the same question.

"Oh, what you want my full name? Sorry, that's classified."

I rolled my eyes and he tried to tickle me only to quickly find out I am not ticklish.

"Shit, OK, so much for that. Need an explanation for that later. I am Lucas Adam Parks."

"Does anyone call you Luke?" I asked.

"Just my dad. No one else has been allowed to."

"Allowed to?"

"My mom insisted that she name me Lucas, nothing else. I think my dad does it just to irritate her, honestly."

"I think I am going to like your parents," I said, smiling

"I think they are going to love you."

EIGHTEEN

When morning finally broke and we both had gotten a few hours of sleep, I helped him pack up his stuff and the cabin. He suggested we come back that weekend so we could eat the rest of the food in the fridge. I joked with him that we could only come back if Steve allowed it. He only found my joke mildly funny. On the way back, he let me control the radio and he frequently took my hand, weaving his fingers in and out of mine. He would occasionally bring it to his lips and kiss each knuckle. Every time he did it, I felt the heat rise in my body. How he had such an effect on me I still had no idea, but I liked it. Maybe the sleeping giant was just asleep for so long it didn't take much to release anymore. I laughed to myself thinking about it. Lucas reached over and turned down the radio.

"What's so funny?"

"Nothing." I smiled.

"You really don't think I am going to buy that, do you?"

Damnit, now I was going to have to explain myself.

"I am just amazed at how easily you can turn me on,

OK. I don't know if it's because I went so long without or if it's just... you."

"Is it selfish if I hope it's me?"

"Ha! No, of course not. I wouldn't expect anything less."

Lucas reached down and took my hand in his and began kissing my knuckles again. Oh shit. This was exactly why I didn't want to tell him. His kisses traveled as far down my arm as his seat belt would let him when I had a realization. *I have more control over this situation than he does.* I undid my seatbelt and slid over the bench seat until I was right next to him. The truck was stick shift, but we were cruising along the highway and he shouldn't have any need for it. Tilting my head up, I started to kiss right where his neck and shoulders met and slowly trailed them up to the base of his ear. I heard a soft groan escape from his lips and took it as a sign to continue. I licked up the base of his ear and then softly blew air back down before taking a nibble at his earlobe. This caused him to really squirm.

"Drea... I'm trying to drive and this is really distracting."

"Are you complaining?" I asked, whispering in his ear.

"I wouldn't say complaining, but I don't want to crash either."

"I guess I shouldn't do this, then..."

I continued nibbling on his ear while I unbuttoned and unzipped his pants before he could stop me. He started trying to rezip it, but it was too late. I freed his erection and stuck it straight into my mouth. Cupping my lips around him, I slid down slowly and came back up feeling him grow inside my mouth. His hips instinctively lifted as I went back down and soon he has one hand on the back of my head holding my hair. I knew it wouldn't take much to convince him. I sped up and he let out an uninhibited moan and tightened his grip on my hair. I could feel him building, and it was so sexy. I couldn't wait to unravel him. Just like he had done to me so many times. I tightened my lips and took him all the way back in my throat. He was shaking trying not to explode, but I was not going to stop until he did. He pulled back on my hair trying to stop me, but I sped up and looked up at him and he came undone. Holding tightly to my hair with one hand and the steering with the other, he was done, enjoying every second while trying to keep the truck in a lane. I licked my way up his shaft making sure nothing was left, which caused him to shudder, before tucking him back into his pants and rezipping him. I slid back over to my side, redid my belt, and wiped my thumb across my lip.

Lucas was now hanging on to the steering wheel with both hands, his eyes glued on the road. He wanted to say something but he was clearly at a loss for words. I slipped off my shoes, pulled one knee into my chest, and looked out the window. I figured he would talk when he was ready, but I couldn't help the smirk that came to my face with utter satisfaction. He finally broke the silence.

"Pleased with yourself, are we?"

"Yes, yes I am. I owed you."

"Owed me? Owed me how?"

"Are you kidding?"

He finally found his sexy smirk. "Baby, you haven't seen nothing yet."

"Well, good thing I took my chance then."

"I can't believe I didn't crash the truck!" He practically shouted.

"Good?" I asked.

"Good, that was the best fucking head I've ever gotten."

It was my turn to smirk.

"Like I've said, you are a damn goddess."

Since we were on the topic, I decided to ask the question that I have been wondering.

"Are you a dom, or whatever they call it?"

"Is that why you called me dominus the other day?"

"No, I just watch too much *Spartacus*. I ask because of the kitchen spank."

"Says the one who asked for another one."

We exchanged heated glances.

"No, I am not a dom," he finally answered. "I don't want someone to be at my beck and call, but I do enjoy playing with the lines of pain and pleasure."

"Hence the spanking?'

"Mhmm, and from what I can tell you liked it. Have you never been spanked before?"

"Nope."

"Oh sweet goddess, we are going to have some fun together."

A short time later we arrived at my house. As I was getting out of the truck and walking to the house, he called after me.

"Hey!"

I turned and look at him.

"No kiss?"

I smiled and ran around to his side of the truck. Climbing up onto the step, I planted my best "I'll miss you, come back soon" kiss on him.

"I'm going to go check in with Steve and the gang. If I'm allowed, can I come back?"

I guess my kiss worked.

"I told you I wanted you, didn't I?" I winked and walk to the house.

NINETEEN

As I walked in the house, I got a very upset greeting from Tigger. *Shit. He is probably hungry.* I turned on the light and started to walk over to his bowl when I noticed a note on the table.

"Notice you didn't come home. Yes I am creepy like that. I fed Tigger. Expect deets later. Love ya."

Seriously, I needed to do something big for Tara. I reached into my purse for the first time in a few days and saw I had over fifty text messages. More than half of them were from Trevor. He must have been freaking out. Opening his text thread I read through all the messages. He went through a wide range of emotions. Mad. Worried. Sad. Mad again, and eventually the last text just said "Please text me when you are home." I would say Steve must have talked some sense into him. I knew he didn't trust Lucas, but he certainly couldn't honestly have believed my life was in danger. I sent him the following text. "Hey, I'm sorry I sent you on such an emotion filled journey. I'm fine. I am home. Thank you for caring about me." The other messages were a mix from Tara and Victoria. I sent them short messages letting them know I was safe and would update them soon. Before putting my phone away for the night, I decided to send one last text to each of my family members. They all differed slightly but had the same underlying message. "I miss you. I love you. I'm sorry I've been so lost for so long. Let's get together soon." Hopefully they hadn't completely written me off.

OK, time for a shower. My hair, even though I had it tied back, looked like a lion's mane without a hair dryer. I was also ready for some new clothes, pajamas to be exact. I was still donning one of Lucas's T-shirts. Not that I didn't like it, it was just time for something... fresh. It no longer had Lucas's patent scent.

Soon I was curled up in my bed between a Tigger and a book. I felt very content but was missing having Lucas beside me. That was one of the hardest adjustments when I first lost Ryan. The thought of never having him beside me in bed again. When you have it, it seems like such a minute thing, but when it's gone forever you would give anything to have it back. Maybe that was one of the reasons I was thinking farther ahead about Lucas already. It all goes back to that fear of being alone, never having another to share your bed with. *Sounds like a conversation I need to have with Dr. Cox.* I had finally progressed to biweekly sessions. She wasn't 100 percent on board but was happy with my progress so she went along with it. She also promised to be on call when and if I ever needed her. Said it was "a part of the job." I think she was still worried I had suicidal tendencies. Can't say I blamed her after some of the stuff I said to her. I would be interested to read what I said to her back when we first started. I honestly don't even remember those first few weeks. Everything just seemed so... unnecessary. *I guess I have come a lot farther than I thought.* Compared to what everyone else is doing with their life, I constantly felt twenty steps behind. No wonder they say comparison is the thief of joy. Lucas was right. *We should have a party. A welcome back to life party. I just hope my family will come.* We used to be so close. I called my mom almost daily. I absolutely was a daddy's girl. My brother taught me to fight and to never take crap from anyone and my sister, she was my best friend. I had to fix this. Fix it and celebrate it.

My eyes snapped open and I was sweating. I had no recollection of what I was dreaming, but it wasn't pleasant. I surveyed the darkness as I took a few deeps breath until my body slowly started to relax one muscle at a time. As I rolled over I ran into a giant lump and screamed. Scrambling out of the sheets, I grabbed my ASP and turned on the light. Just as I was about to strike, the lump yells.

"DREA, IT'S ME!"

Still holding the ASP above my head and blinking a few times, I saw Lucas sitting in my bed, his hands up in the air as if being arrested by the cops. I dropped the ASP to the floor, grabbed a pillow, and started hitting Lucas with the pillow.

"What the hell is wrong with you! I thought you were a kidnapper?!?!" I asked in between blows.

"Why would a kidnapper be asleep next to you?!?!" He quickly wrapped both arms around me and pulled me into him. I was wiggling like a fish on a hook trying to get away. He scared the shit out of me. *Bad enough to have a bad dream but I have to roll over to unexpected company. I guess this is what I get for thinking I miss having someone to sleep next to every night.* I eventually stopped squirming and he released me.

"Holy shit, you scared me," Lucas said, lying on his back, his breath labored.

"ME?!? Me scare you?!? How the hell did you get in here?"

"I can't tell you." He smiled up at me.

"You can't tell me how you got into MY house."

"Nope."

"I hate you," I said, climbing back into bed and lying down with my back to him. He pressed up against my back and said into my ear, "I know that's a lie."

I elbowed his stomach half as hard as I wanted to and he let out a groan but backed up slightly.

"Why the hell do you have an ASP next to your bed anyway?"

"You never know when some crazy person is going to break into your house and get in bed with you. I need to get a dog."

"OOoo that's a good idea, let's get a dog."

"Let's?!" I said, turning back to look at him. He had his big shit-eating grin on his face. I wanted so badly to stay mad at him, but he was making it really difficult. He pulled me into him and kissed my nose.

"I'm sorry I scared you. I was going to wake you when I came in, but you looked so comfortable and when you didn't wake up when I climbed in bed I knew you needed the sleep."

"I can't believe I didn't wake up. I can hardly sleep most nights."

"You too huh?" he asked.

"Yeah, unfortunately."

"Well, together we seem to do better."

I nodded and curled up into his chest. His intoxicating aroma filled my nose and calmed me. I closed my eyes, breathed him in, and before I knew it, I was asleep again. When I woke up the next morning, I smelled a completely different aroma. *Is that... pancakes?* Getting out of bed, I walked to the kitchen. I paused in the doorway and took in the sight. Lucas was making pancakes. The coffee machine had also just roared to life and was making its delicious elixir. I stood and admired him. Even in just athletic shorts and a T-shirt, he looked sexy. It then dawned on me he was wearing shorts. I had never seen him wear shorts before. Ever. I walk over and sat down at the counter.

"A girl could get use to this," I said.

He turned and smiled. "Stealing my lines, huh?"

"What can I say, it's a good line."

"Coffee?"

"Yes, please."

After breakfast I drove us over to TLC. Even after everything we had been through, it still felt weird to be driving there with Lucas. To walk in together. As we were coming in, Rob and Sam were walking out of Steve's office. Lucas looked at me, to them, and back again.

"What? You don't need my permission to go talk to them."

"Just making sure, the blackmail and all."

He strode over, they did some bro type handshake, and then they started chatting. I decided to go take refuge in my office. Surprisingly, Steve didn't shout for me to join him in his office. I guess he figured he would leave the whole cabin situation alone. I wouldn't even know where to begin. *Hopefully Trevor did most of the talking for me. Shit. Trevor. I haven't talked to him since being back.* I left my stuff at my desk and went looking for him. It didn't take me long to find him sitting by the pond.

"Mind if I join you?" I asked at the edge of the bench.

"Please," he replied and motioned for me to sit.

We sat in silence. I think we were both searching for the

right words. I doubt Trevor ever thought he would have to talk with me about an intimate relationship with Lucas. I never thought it would happen either. Hell, I never thought I would be intimate with anyone ever again. Which is crazy. I'm young, but in my darkest days with my dark cloud, it was my truth.

"Is he good to you?" Trevor finally asked.

"Yeah, actually. He is. He made me breakfast this morning."

"He spent the night at your house?"

"Trevor, we were in a secluded cabin for a few days, are you really that surprised?"

"No, I guess not, but that was a very uncomfortable situation for me..."

"Why?"

"I have known him longer than you, I've seen his shitty attitude for years, let's just say it's harder for me to accept this newfound 'Lucas,'" he said, putting air quotes around Lucas's name.

I can understand Trevor's worry. The old quote says a tiger can't change his stripes, but I was never one to believe that. I think you can change, become better, learn. Some people just choose not to.

"All I can say is I promise to be careful."

"I don't know, Drea, you are already in pretty deep."

Again, he wasn't wrong, but there was no backing out now. I had to trust that he had changed and that we had something here.

"We are going to have a party, and I hope you will come."

"Please tell me you aren't engaged."

I laughed. "C'mon, Trevor, give me more credit than that."

"OK, OK, I'm sorry. What's the party for?"

I told him all about the "Coming to Life" party and how the whole thing was actually Lucas's idea. Trevor hated to admit it, but he loved the idea and thought it was well deserved on my part. He wasn't ready to give Lucas complete credit for turning over a new leaf. At least I knew someone had my back if for whatever reason it took a turn for the worst. Now that I had talked to Trevor it was time for me to tackle my family. Kissing Trevor on the cheek, I told him I had an important errand to run and if anyone else asked, I would be back that afternoon.

I pulled up to my parents' house a short time later. The entire ride over, I was trying to remember the last time I was here and when it was hard to remember I knew it had been way too long. I was scared but also very optimistic. My mom always told me growing up she would love me no matter what, so here's to hoping that would ring true. In normal circumstances I would just walk in, but today I rang the bell. I could feel my heart beating in my throat as I waited for someone to answer. It wasn't long before my mom's face was on the other side of the threshold.

"Aundrea? My sweet baby, is that you?"

"Hi, Mom. Can I come in?"

"Of course you can, would you like some coffee?" she called over her shoulder. "Tony, Tony, you'll never guess who is here! It's Aundrea!"

"Aundrea's here??" I heard my dad say from his den.

It didn't take long for my dad to pop his head around the corner.

"Aundrea!"

"Hi, Dad." He pulled me into him for a giant hug.

This was not the welcome I was expecting after being MIA eight months. They refused to leave me alone the first few months after Ryan passed. I'm not a parent, but I am sure one day I will understand why. Dad released me from his hug and held me out at arm's length.

"You look great! You look like my daughter."

That simple statement warmed me to the depths of my soul. The change in me was visible, and my dad was ecstatic. I sat in the kitchen with them and told them all about my last eight months. Every boring, horrible, and amazing detail. They sat quietly for the most part, reacting appropriately when necessary. They of course wanted to meet Tara and Trevor, or as they dubbed them, Team T. Now you know where I get my nerdy sense of humor. I had saved Lucas for last, telling them how when I started at TLC he felt like my mortal enemy. Until one day dance brought us together and before we both knew it, it became so much more then that dance.

"You always loved to dance. It doesn't surprise me it would bring you a soulmate," my mom said.

"I didn't say anything about him being my soulmate, Mom, and what about Ryan?"

"Oh honey, anything you do from now on isn't an insult or a dishonor to Ryan. Actually I am pretty sure he would be proud and want you to be happy."

"He did love me, didn't he?"

"To his core," my dad said.

"I'm sorry I was lost for so long..."

"Honey, we always knew you would come back. You never give up," Mom said.

"And don't think we weren't secretly keeping an eye on you." My dad winked at me.

"Dad, that's creepy."

"It's called being a parent. You'll find out one day."

"So, when we going to meet all your new friends?" Mom asked.

"Actually Lucas had this great idea to have a 'Coming to Life' party, so if you guys come to that, you can meet everyone."

"We wouldn't miss it for the world."

I asked about my brother, Michael, and my sister, Gabriella. They both had been super worried and a number of times my dad had to stop them from just showing up at my house. He was worried an unannounced visit would put me into a tailspin. Good ol' Dad always watching out. They also said they were thrilled to get a message from me the other night. I decided I would three way call them on my way back to TLC. Just like my dad said, they were excited to talk to me and hear how I was doing. I didn't give them as much boring detail as I gave Mom and Dad, but did my best to fill them in. I had to sit in the parking lot for a while because getting through eight months of information took much longer than twenty minutes. Yes, all this time my family lived just a short trip away. I just couldn't handle seeing the pity in their eyes. I don't do well with pity, but I am guessing most people don't. My heart felt completely quenched after talking to my family. The guilt had disappeared and the fear of them writing me off was long gone. I just had the party to look forward too. The only other person I hadn't talked to in a few weeks was Victoria but I had the perfect fun solution to that. As I walked back into TLC, I sent her a quick text: "sleepover my house tonight? I have beer." She responded before I even reached the door. "Hell yes!" Looked like I would be doing more storytelling later. The difference was I could give Victoria all the sexy details. Right now, it was time to do what I loved most. Dance.

TWENTY

As I was packing up to leave, I heard a soft knock at my door. Lucas was standing in the doorframe.

"Leaving so soon?" He smirked.

"Yeah, I gotta get back to the house. Victoria is coming over tonight."

"Does that mean I can't crawl in your window tonight?" he asked, sticking out his lip, attempting a pout.

I chuckled. "No, no breaking in tonight."

"Man, I was looking forward to a good night's sleep."

Walking over to him, I pressed my body against his and kissed him, sweet and tender at first before I parted his lips with my tongue and had him wanting more.

"See you tomorrow."

"Way to leave a guy hanging."

"I doubt it's hanging," I said, winking, and headed out the door.

As I drove home I was so excited to have a girls' night. Victoria and I used to do these all the time. Even before I lost Ryan. He would go over to a buddy's house and leave me and Victoria to our own devices. There was always beer, popcorn, sweets, and a bad movie involved. I got to thinking if I should invite Tara but figured it was better to have my own time with her. These two ladies kept me alive, that is for sure. In preparation, I got on my best jammies, set up a comfy floor bed fort, and scrolled through Amazon Prime looking for a really good bad movie. Why a bad movie? Because most of the time we didn't pay attention to the movie anyway. We were too busy chatting, or making fun of whatever random scene we happened to catch. Unless it was *Magic Mike*. We watched the entire movie. When she arrived I hugged her for what felt like ten minutes. I didn't want to let her go. I only did when she finally complained that she couldn't breathe and I was hurting her boobs. We got comfortable in our bed fort and cheersed to our friendship. It didn't take long for Victoria to start asking questions.

"So, where were you for two days? I came by when I didn't hear from you, and Tara told me you hadn't been home."

"I was in a cabin in the woods."

"That is a really bad movie."

Beer shot out my noise. Victoria always knew how to get me. She was laughing but managed to hand me a napkin.

"Trust me, my cabin in the woods wasn't bad."

"Please tell me you were there with sexy dance guy, what was his name, Lucas?"

"How do you know he is sexy?!"

"OH MY GOD, it was him!! I told you guys named Lucas are usually hot. Well…"

"We have been sleeping together."

"And and anddddd…"

"It's fucking incredible," I said, falling onto my back

"Man! I'm so jealous. Can I come up to this TLC place?"

"Of course you can, but I'm not sure who else is single. Most of the other guys I can think of are married."

"Yeah, you would get the only single guy with this body," she said, attempting to slap the side of my butt.

"Yeah, he does that too," I said without thinking.

It was Victoria's turn to spit out beer.

"He spanks you?!?"

"He did, twice."

"You dirty bird. I love it."

"Have you been spanked before?" I asked, rolling onto my stomach to look at her.

"Girl, you don't want to know half the shit I do." She grinned, taking a big sip of beer

"Victoria, you have been keeping secrets from me!"

"I didn't want you to think I was some pervert."

"I already think that, but c'mon, we talk about everything."

"Touché. It was a fairly recent development for me too."

"Do tell."

We spent the rest of the night not watching a single scene of the movie but rather swapping sexy stories. Her experimentation had of course happened during my year of darkness. I was starting to think I needed to just remove that year from my life, but without it I wouldn't be where I was now. Lucky for me, my amazing friends and family were willing to wait out the storm. They knew long before I did that the sun would shine again.

When the sun was shining the next morning, I had another surprise. Victoria was in my kitchen making breakfast. This was the second time in a week I had woken up to someone cooking breakfast in my kitchen. It was definitely something I could get used to. The debate was who would I pick to be my kitchen slave. Victoria or Lucas. I needed to try the food before I could decide.

"What can I do to help?" I asked.

"Nothing. You sit your butt down and admire the view," she said, passing me a cup of coffee. So far Victoria was winning. This was first class service. I took a sip of coffee as Victoria moved about humming and cooking a delicious meal. She had two burners going. One with hash browns and one with eggs.

"Where did you magically find hash browns?"

"Girl, you just shred potatoes. It isn't hard."

Now I was really impressed. I had never even thought of doing that before. Shred cheese, yes. Potatoes, no. I guess you never stop learning in the kitchen. Before I knew it, I had a steaming hot plate of breakfast placed before me. If it tasted even half as good as it looked, Victoria would be making the clean sweep in the kitchen slave contest.

"This looks amazing," I said as she sat down next to me.

"Enjoy, darling." She was smiling ear to ear.

"Why are you grinning like the Cheshire cat?"

"I am just so happy you are back to your old self. I was really worried there for a while if I am being completely honest."

"I would have been worried about me too," I said, taking a bite. "Mmmm, can I keep you?" I asked.

"I'm not going anywhere. I have to make sure this Lucas guy is as good as he seems."

And there it was. I knew she was worried. She was worried that if I got hurt again I would go back to that dark place and my dark cloud would engulf me forever. How did I get all of that out of one sentence? Years and years of friendship.

"I think it's going to be OK."

"Are you sure? You don't know everything about him. You never got the full answer of why he is at TLC."

"Yes, I am sure."

But I wasn't really sure. She was making a valid point. Lucas did dance around what had brought him to TLC, no pun intended. I definitely knew I didn't want to fight with Victoria about it. We'd had a great night together and now a great morning. I decided I would at least appease her.

"OK, you've got a point. I'll see what I can find out."

"I wouldn't expect anything less from you."

"In the meantime, what would it cost to keep you as my kitchen slave?"

"For you, baby, free 99."

She always knew how to make me laugh. I personally think that is one of the keys to life. Having people around you who can make you laugh.

Victoria also demanded she get to meet Lucas. Which led me into telling her about the party. She of course thought it was a perfect idea but still insisted on meeting Lucas before then. This would also be the perfect time to include Tara. I was pretty sure at this point that I owed her a year's worth of dinners. *Do I invite Liam too? Would this be an include husband situation? Maybe I would just ask Tara instead of spending the next few days debating what the appropriate action would be.* It just so happened that following morning as I was enjoying my coffee, Tara and George were going for their morning walk.

"Hey, neighbor," I called to her.

"Have I been downgraded to neighbor now? No more name?" she said back, teasing.

"You know better, but I do have an offer for you."

"Oooh, pray tell."

"I want you to come over for dinner and meet Lucas. Plus you could formally meet Victoria."

"I am so in. I can't wait to meet mystery man."

"I have to ask though cuz I am not sure what is appropriate," I said, putting air quotes around "appropriate."

"You know you can ask me anything."

"Do I invite Liam too? Is this a bring the husband situation? I owe him dinner too, not just you."

Tara laughed. "You don't owe us anything, and I am thinking this is a no husband situation."

That was so much easier. Instead of stewing and wondering for two days if I should invite him or not, I just asked directly. Why didn't I start doing this sooner? Now I just had to figure out what I was going to make for dinner. I hadn't made dinner for anyone in a long time. I did make breakfast for Lucas the other day, but this seemed more important. Probably because I was worried Victoria and Tara wouldn't like Lucas. Only time would tell. I decided to just focus my attention on what I was going to cook. I went back inside and starting flipping through my recipes when someone knocked on the door.

"Come in," I shouted, assuming it was Tara.

I was pleasantly surprised when Lucas strolled in the door.

"Do you always just say come in?"

"I assumed you were Tara. She and I were just chatting."

"Never assume, baby," he said, kissing the top of my head. Spoken like a true Marine. Always worried about safety. "Looking for a certain recipe?" he asked.

"No, just looking to see what I want to cook for you all."

"Who is you all?"

"You, Tara and Victoria..." I said, looking at him with my best grin.

"Wow, I'm meeting the girlfriends, huh? You going to tell your parents about me next?"

"Actually I did that already," I said, casually going back to my recipe book.

He closed the book and waited for me to look up at him.

"You did? Really?"

He seemed shocked. Did he really think I wasn't going to tell my family about him?

"Yes, I did. They look forward to meeting you at the coming back to life party."

"I have to say I am shocked."

"Lucas, I get you have been hurt in the past, but I am here to stay."

"Touché. I'm glad you patched things up with the fam."

"Me too, thank you for encouraging me. Soooo, you are OK coming to dinner with my two best girlfriends."

"Anything for you, my goddess." He smirked.

"Not now. I'm busy," I said, opening my book and trying to find the page I was on.

Lucas swooped me up and carried me to the bedroom before I could utter another word.

After getting lost in Lucas, and several text messages later, dinner was set up for next week. I was feeling nervous, but Lucas assured me he would be on his best behavior. I was more nervous about all the questions the girls were going to ask him than I was about him behaving, but it was cute he cared. Lucas wanted to stay the entire day but had promised Steve he would be back. Apparently Steve was cracking down on Lucas more about being at TLC. I found it kind of curious, but Steve always has the best interest of his guys at the top of his list. It must be a part of the "getting well" process. I did finally decide what to make for dinner. Stuffed shells and garlic bread. Being part Italian, I figured you can never go wrong with Italian. Plus, I had my grandmother's recipe. I would call that a win win.

When I went to bed that night I found myself not overthinking the dinner but why Lucas would have to go back to TLC. Did he really have to go back, or was he just trying to get away from me? Or even worse, was there something that I didn't know about? He hinted that he didn't have the best past, but who does? His family probably just sent him to TLC to make sure he got everything he needed. I knew if Ryan had come back and needed help I would have done anything for him. At some point I did finally fall asleep and I must have done so much thinking that I didn't even have a nightmare.

When I woke up in the new day I knew I had overthought the Lucas situation. Plus it's not like I would never see him. He did live where I worked. Which was where I was headed this morning, coffee in hand, feeling very happy and optimistic about life. I'd never thought I would feel that again. I was still surprised I hadn't gotten the million questions from Steve, but I was starting to think he didn't want to know the answers. As long as Lucas was no longer being a pain in his ass, all was good. I then had a good idea. Victoria had mentioned wanting to come to TLC anyway, and maybe having some more estrogen around was what some of these guys needed. So I called up some of my lady friends and asked them to meet me in the TLC parking lot. I was going to sneak them in the back so hopefully no one saw until it was class time. I always loved surprises as long as they weren't done to me. The pure joy you see on people's faces when they are surprised is the best. I did have to call Steve. At least give him a heads up.

He must have stared at the phone and answered on the last ring, because I was just about to give up when he answered.

"Hey, Drea."

"Steve, I'm bringing a bunch of ladies to dance class today," I said, straight to the point, hoping to avoid whatever awkward conversation he thought was coming. I might have made it worse as he sat on the other end completely quiet. Only reason I knew he hadn't hung up was I could hear him breathing. "Steve..."

"You are bringing a bunch of ladies around a group of horny military men."

"Yup."

"I'm going to print out some waivers."

"Steve, these are my friends."

"I'm going to print out some waivers."

"Steve!"

"What?!?"

"Just trust me, OK." And I hung up.

Once we had all gathered in the parking lot, I called Steve to keep everyone occupied while I snuck them all in the back door and had a little pre-class meeting. I wanted them to know the plan and to not be alarmed if something popped up. I then set up chairs around the room and had each of them sit in one. I sat on a chair in the middle as we waited for our unsuspecting victims. Steve came in first and stood against the wall. As the rest of them came in, their paced slowed and they looked around the room very confused. Lucas was in the back trying to see what the fuss was about.

"Come on in, don't be shy," I called to them.

Lucas pushed his way to the front and looked around. A smirk came to his face, and I am pretty sure he had figured out my plan as he shouted out, "The one in the middle is mine." This got a laugh out of the others as well.

"Who said you guys would be doing the picking?" I said.

Lucas's smirk deepened. Trevor on the other hand looked slightly panicked. Ahh, sweet Trevor. So considerate of his wife. I hoped he would bring her to the party. I had been dying to meet the woman behind the man.

"Ladies. Pick your poison," I said.

My friends all got up from their chairs and headed over to the group. If I did this right there should be perfect numbers. I was quite impressed I had so many friends willing to drop in without much notice to help me with a pet project. I guess I had more friends around me than even I realized. Victoria was in heaven. Walking slowly, teasing them about who she was going to pick. All these hardy military men looked very... concerned. Victoria finally stopped in front of Sam and held out her hand. Sam's eyes looked like they were going to pop out of his head, but he took her hand without hesitation. As the rest of them paired off, Lucas walked halfway over to me before coming down to his knees and sliding across the floor until he landed at me feet. It was very suave, if I am being perfectly honest.

"Sweet goddess, will you please pick me as your partner?" he asked, holding his hand out to me.

"It looks like you are the only option, so I guess my answer is yes," I responded, putting my hand in his. As he came to standing, he pulled me into him and pressed his lips to my ear.

"Only option?" he growled.

"Apologies, dominus, it is only a joke."

He nibbled at my ear before releasing me. Such a tease. I looked up to find everyone looking at us. Time to get things moving. Turning on some music, I give them all three very simple Bachata moves they could do together. The rest they were just supposed to feel. My hope was everyone would let go and have some fun. Just like that scene from *Dirty Dancing* when Baby goes into the staff dance party. Everyone is free of inhibitions and just dancing. It might not be as sexy as that scene, but I hoped it would be as satisfying.

It did not start that way. Everyone was stiff. They just kept repeating the three moves in the exact some order and the amount of space between them could fit a small car. This was not going to do. I quickly went into intolerant dance teacher mode. I turned off the music.

"No, no. This is not going to do. This is not how you Bachata." I grabbed Lucas's hand and took him to the center of the room with me. "This is how you Bachata. Music, Steve."

Steve hit the music right on que and Lucas and I began with a basic step, the first move of the three moves. We then moved into a forward back and the music was starting to fill us. I could feel it in our fingertips. The last move of the three was a hammerlock. He did it twice and as I went back to repeat one more time just for demonstration purposes, Lucas pulled me in close and started to do waves. I start to wave and roll with him and before I know it we were in perfect harmony. Dipping, rolling and moving our hips around the room. When the song was done, I was panting. I was not sure if it was from the dancing or if I was turned on, but either way, I liked it. As we peeled away from each other and looked around the room, the looks on their faces were priceless.

"Lucas, do you have your phone?" I asked him under my breath.

"Yeah, why?"

"Can I see it for a sec?"

He shrugged and dug into his pocket. I took a quick photo. This seemed to annoy them, but I had to document their looks. Apparently they had no idea how sensual Bachata was.

"I am not doing that..." Rob said.

"What, you scared?" asked Victoria.

This of course got the intended results and everyone got into position.

"You have to get close. I am not asking you guys to get married, this is just a dance. Have fun with it. Enjoy it."

"I am going to enjoy it, all right," Victoria said, winking at Sam.

I nodded to Steve to turn the music back on, and Lucas and I walked around the room correcting and motivating them. Slowly, as the music played on, everyone started loosening up. Hips were shaking, heads rolling, and bodies twirling. It was beautiful. I would have brought my gal pals in here a long time ago if I had known it would have this sort of effect. As I was admiring my handiwork, I felt lips pressed to my ears again.

"Care for another dance?" his hot breath trailed down my neck, causing the little hairs on the back of it to stand up. Even if I wanted to, I didn't have the willpower to say no. For several songs, everyone in the room lost themselves. To the music. To the connection. To their demons. I had found my place and not just in Lucas's arms.

I said goodbye to everyone and on my way out Steve stopped me.

"I have to admit I thought that was a terrible idea... But I was wrong. I haven't seen that many happy faces in forever."

"I agree, I wish I had thought of it sooner."

"I told you you would be an amazing mentor."

"She is a genius. Healed us all with the power of the pussy," Lucas said, joining the conversation.

"Way to keep it classy, Lucas. Goodnight, you two." And Steve disappeared into his office.

"Can I give you a ride home?" he asked.

"My car is here."

"I know, but I figure if I give you a ride home there is less of a chance you send me away."

Gosh, he can be cute sometimes, I thought to myself. I nodded and he put his arm around me and walked me to his truck and opened the door for me to climb in. Once he was in beside me, we were off. He was holding my hand doing the usual winding and unwinding of our fingers when red and blue lights came up behind us. *Shit.* Was he speeding? It hadn't felt like it. Lucas eased the truck to the side of the road and waited patiently for the cop to come to the window. He had not released my hand.

"Good evening," the cop said at the window, shining his flashlight inside the truck. I looked up and smiled while trying not to be blinded.

"Do you know why I stopped you, sir?" he asked Lucas.

"I honestly can't say, sir. I was slightly distracted by this beauty beside me."

Not really the best answer, Lucas, I thought, but I smiled. The cop seemed slightly amused as well when he asked for his license and registration. Lucas motioned to me to get the registration out of the glove box as he went into his pocket for his ID. The cop strolled back to his car to run everything. Lucas was looking at me. I was completely lost in his eyes. I wanted to kiss him but I didn't think making out while at a traffic stop was a good idea.

"Sir, I am going to need you to get out of the car," the cop said, startling me. I had not seen him return. The amusement was long gone from his face. What on earth was going on? Lucas didn't speak a word and did as requested. Once outside the car, the office put him in cuffs. I resisted the urge to jump out of the car and stop him.

"Sir, you are under arrest for violating probation."

"What?!?!" I shouted. "What probation?"

"Ma'am, I need you to stay calm, please."

Lucas finally spoke. "Drea, it's OK. I will explain. Just stay calm, OK."

Stay calm? How the fuck was I supposed to stay calm when he was being arrested. The officer and Lucas went to the cop car and I was left with my runaway thoughts. *What could Lucas possibly be on probation for?*

"Ma'am?" The cop was back at the window. "Usually I would impound the vehicle, but I am willing to let you drive home since your friend has been so cooperative. Can you handle a stick?"

Did he just make a perverted joke at me?! Just as I was about rip him a new one, I realized he meant the truck.

"Yes, sir, I can. Can I ask you what is going on?"

He half smiled at me. "I'd love to tell you, ma'am, but that is his place. You be careful getting home, OK."

And just like that, the officer and Lucas were gone. The hamster on my wheel couldn't run any faster. Pretty soon the wheel was going to catch on fire. I was going over possible reasons he could be on probation, but nothing stuck. What I did know was I couldn't keep sitting here on the side of the road. I had to drive home. Pulling the truck into the driveway, I could feel the anger welling up inside me. At least I was able to hold it back until then. I wasn't sure if I was more upset because he was arrested or because

I didn't know the reason why. Maybe this was his past coming back to get him, and Victoria was right. It would also explain why he never talked about it. It was something serious. I wondered if I could get answers out of Steve. Still sitting in the truck, I dialed his number. He answered on the first ring.

"Drea, are you OK? You never call this late."

"Lucas just got arrested."

"Shit."

"My hope is you know why."

The phone was dead silent.

"Hello?"

"Drea, it's not really for me to tell you."

"Well, someone better tell me something before I fucking freak out."

"OK, how about this. I come get you and we go down to the police station together. Maybe we can bail him out."

I nodded.

"Drea..."

"I'm nodding."

"You know I can't see you nodding, right? I'll be right there."

Twenty minutes later, Steve was at my house. I got out of Lucas's truck and into his. The tension was so high you could cut it with a knife. I knew Steve knew and him not telling me was progressively making my anger rise.

"Steve, I need to know what is going on."

"All I can tell you is it's my fault he got arrested."

Now I was really confused.

"How could it be your fault?"

"He was violating probation by not being at TLC. He is my responsibility."

Well, this just got even more interesting. It explained

why Rob and Sam needed permission to leave. Steve had to report to their probation officer and sign off in his name that they were suitable to be back with society. If something went wrong, part of the blame would fall back on Steve.

"Why did you let him?"

"He has been doing great, you know that, and I was going to submit his paperwork next week anyway so I didn't think there would be an issue. It didn't even cross my mind he would get pulled over."

"You going to get in trouble?"

"I'm not sure, Drea."

Steve looked extremely worried. I wasn't sure if it was for himself or Lucas, or maybe it was both. I was thankful he offered to do this. I was mad at Lucas but I didn't want to leave him in a jail cell either. The idea of bailing him out didn't even come to mind. Good thing I called Steve. When we got to the station, Steve did all the talking. I had a feeling this wasn't his first rodeo. Steve's passion for helping people ran deep even if it included a run-in with the police. He also had the power to make an impact. I was just the "friend." I sat watching Steve talk to the cops. The conversation started off very serious but seemed to relax as they went on. I crossed my fingers and hoped this meant he was getting somewhere. When Steve walked back over to me, his face was flat. I couldn't tell one way or the other what the verdict was. He sat next to me and put a hand on my knee.

"I can't bail him out tonight."

"Why?"

"It's not easy to get someone out on bail when violating probation. They usually make you sit in the can until your trial."

"What!?"

"Relax, because I'm the one in charge of him and I

explained what happened. They said they would probably let me bail him out tomorrow but would have to talk to the judge first."

I sighed. "OK."

"They are going to let you talk to him."

"I can?"

"Yes, the cop who arrested him said he has been nothing but a perfect gentleman and is OK letting you speak to him. He also knew you were confused and didn't want you to be worried."

I nodded. I spied the officer who arrested him. He was waiting to take me back to where Lucas was. I walked over and he led me to a locked hallway.

"Thank you for letting me talk to him," I said as he unlocked the door.

"My pleasure, ma'am. I am going to be standing right here by the door. I can't leave you alone with him, but I'll try and give as much privacy as I can."

I smiled at him and walked over to the only jail cell with someone inside. Lucas was sitting on the floor sunk against the wall. For the first time, he looked small.

"Lucas..."

His eyes shot up to me. He rose quickly and practically ran over to the bars. He reached out, and I found myself involuntarily backing out of his reach.

"Drea, I was so worried about you, please..."

"You need to explain yourself."

His eyes shifted to his feet that he was shuffling awkwardly back and forth.

"I really don't want to do this here..."

"You lost that privilege when you got arrested."

He looked back up at me and his eyes were filled with

regret and pain. There was a part of me that wanted to feel bad for him but there was a bigger part that was really mad.

"I used to get into trouble a lot, and instead of spending time in jail Steve offered his facility. I figured anything was better than jail."

"You are going to have to do way better than that."

"I was a drunken asshole, OK. I used to get wasted and get in bar fights regularly. Until one night I got into a fight with an off-duty cop who decided to press charges."

"Are you an alcoholic?"

"I'm sure some would say I am, but I don't think so. I thought I was drinking to have fun. When I was really drinking to forget. I can control it. I just didn't want to."

"Why? Why didn't you want to?"

"You don't want to hear why..."

"Yes, Lucas, I do. You owe me that."

"I was hoping I would eventually get in a fight with the right person. The person who would kick my ass so bad I wouldn't ever wake up again."

I didn't know what to say. I was mad, but I was also heartbroken. Heartbroken over the fact that he never bothered to tell me any of this, and over the fact that he ever felt so lost and alone.

"Why didn't you tell me?"

He sighed. "Why would I want to tell? So you could hate me?"

"Are you serious? Have you not learned anything? I could hate you now for not telling me. I told you all about my demons. Which is the point—we all have them."

"You hate me?"

"That is what you heard out of everything I just said?"

"Yeah."

"Lucas, I... I don't hate you, but I am not happy with you right now."

"I'm not happy with myself either."

"I'll be back tomorrow," I said, turning away and letting the cop know I was done.

"Drea, wait. Please let me touch you."

I wanted to let him touch me. I want to hug him and tell him it would all be OK, but right now, I couldn't.

Steve and I drove back in silence. I wanted to ask him more questions, but at this point I was exhausted. I think we were both exhausted. As I got out of the truck, there was one thing I needed to say.

"It's not your fault, Steve."

He half smiled at me. "See you tomorrow."

And just like that I was alone with my thoughts again. For a brief moment I debated a whiskey, but after what had just unfolded it seemed inappropriate. I was already wondering what drunken Lucas was like. What did he act like? Was he more aggressive then the catty interactions he had with me? Did it make the pain behind his eyes more visible? We tend to think drinking masks our insecurities when actuality it brings them to the surface. I decided a bath would be the best way to calm my nerves. I lit a few candles, put on some classical music, and turned on the water as hot as humanly possible. I slid into the hot water overflowing with bubbles and just let it overtake me. The beautiful music started to fill my soul when I noticed the candle flames go from completely still to dancing. I have taken many baths in this house and I never remember the flames moving. *Is there a draft in here?* As I was looking around the bathroom for a source, I remembered something my grandma use to say. She would always tell us when a flame flickers it announces the arrival of a spirit. She never noticed it around the house until grandpa passed away. She took it as her reminder that he was still with her.

"Ryan, is that you?" I asked the darkness.

Maybe I was hallucinating or maybe it was wishful thinking, but I swear the flames danced a little faster in response.

"I miss you. Every day."

The flames kept dancing and my heart swelled with happiness. There is a part of me that thinks it's all just coincidence, but I can't deny that part of me that thinks Ryan was with me when I needed him. I stayed in the tub until the water got too cold for my liking and without even dressing dragged myself into bed and went to sleep. The tub wasn't the only place Ryan would visit me tonight.

I am back in the hammock. Ryan's nose in the crook of my neck taking in my smell. It's a memory I don't actually have but my subconscious keeps bringing me back to. We may be in the same place, but the conversation changes.

"Are you mad at me?" This time I am able to open my eyes and look at him. He is just as handsome as I remember. I reach out and run my hand through the scruff on his chin.

"Why would I be mad at you?" he asks, kissing the top of my hand.

"I'm falling for someone else. I'm cheating on you. Us."

He smiles my favorite smile. "No, you aren't. You could never cheat on us. This... will always be here but you need something real and I can't give that to you anymore."

"I'm scared."

"Don't be scared. Our memories can never be replaced, but it's time for you to make some new ones."

"I love you, Ryan."

"I know. I love you too, but I'm not the only one."

I awoke to someone knocking on my door. I felt like I

had just gone to sleep but the sunlight coming in the windows suggested otherwise. Getting out of bed I had forgotten I went to bed naked. I scrambled for some clothes before finally opening the door to Steve. He looked at me confused.

"I thought for sure you would be up and ready to go back to the station this morning."

"I'm not sure I am ready to face that again, to be honest. Coffee?"

"Why would you say that? And yes, please."

"Good, because I need some and because what if he is hiding something else?"

"Drea, you have every right to be upset with him, but he didn't do it maliciously. I can promise you that."

"How do you know that?" I asked, scooping coffee into the filter and pressing the brew button.

"Because he is crazy about you."

"He told you?"

"No, I can just tell. You should have seen him when he first got to TLC."

"A drunken asshole?"

"He told ya, huh?"

"He told me the very basics, yes."

"He was a mess. He didn't know how to handle the loss."

"Of his leg?"

"His girlfriend, his brothers, his leg. It was all too much."

"You guys have all lost brothers."

He looked at me very seriously. "Not like Lucas has."

This stung. Not only because again this was a story I didn't know, but that he had to experience such substantial losses.

"What happened?"

"He needs to tell you, but what you do need to know is that as much as you feel that he brought you back to life, you did the same for him. I have never seen him like this. Ever. And he has been with me for three years."

And I thought my one year was long. I felt my heart starting to soften. I mean we really had known each other deeply for only a few weeks. How many stories did I expect him to tell me in such a short period of time.

"You have done more for him in these last four weeks than I have in three years. That's something, Drea."

"Thank you, Steve."

"I'm the one who owes you a thank you. I was starting to think I would never get through to him."

"I am sure you did. I was just the cherry on top," I said, pouring him a cup of coffee and passing it to him.

"I will cheers to that," he replied, holding up his coffee. I poured myself a cup and clinked his glass.

As we went out the door, I decided I would bring Lucas a cup of coffee and a bagel. I had a feeling he didn't eat or sleep much. Plus, I figured it would be a good way to break the ice. Even after all this, I felt very connected to him and I wanted to know more about him. Everything about him, the good and the bad. I thought he deserved a little break. The only real wonder was if he would open up his bag of dirty secrets. When we got to the station, I decided to stay in the truck. Lucas would be initially disappointed that I wasn't there but surprised to see me in the truck.

It felt like I waited forever until I saw them bust through the door. Steve was trying to crack one of his jokes, and Lucas... Lucas was lost in his own thoughts. Until he saw me sitting in the truck. He stopped in his tracks and a half smile came to his face. A half smile to show his happiness to see me but the worry of my potential anger. This was of course quickly followed by him running his hand through his hair, as he always did when he was uncomfortable. As he came to the truck I leaned out the window, gave him my best grin, and held out the coffee and bagel along with my cheesiest line.

"A brew, a bagel, and a broad."

This got a full grin.

"Babe would be more accurate."

"I felt broad was funnier."

He reached up and took the bagel and coffee. "Well, thank you, broad." And he kissed my cheek. At least he knew better than to go for the full kiss. Steve drove back over to my place and we ambled out of the truck.

"As much as I would love to let you stay here, you need to drive right over to TLC, Lucas."

Lucas saluted Steve and he laughed and drives away.

"You heard the man, baby. I gotta go."

"That's fine. I need my car anyway."

"Oh yeah, that's right, I had hoped to get lucky but instead got hassled by the law."

We got into his truck and as we backed out of the driveway, Lucas had a sudden thought.

"Did you drive this here?"

"Mmhmm."

"A girl who can drive stick. I like it."

"There is a lot I can do." I winked.

"Oooh, baby."

"Don't get too excited there, bub, you owe me an explanation."

"I had a feeling you would say that," he said, looking disappointed, but he had to know that it was coming.

He parked and went to check in with Steve as I headed

out to the pond. The morning was quiet aside from a few ducks on the pond. I wished I had something to fed them and made a mental note for next time when Lucas sat down.

"I know you are mad, but you certainly look beautiful sitting here."

"I'm not mad, Lucas. I'm... disappointed."

"That is what my mom use to always say."

"You did not just compare me to your mom."

"I wasn't comparing, just brought back memories."

Looking over. I could tell he was lost in a memory. It seemed to be a good one.

"You close with your mom?"

"Very. Well... I used to be. Hopefully I can fix that. Like you did."

I put my hand on his. "I'm sure you can. Moms usually always find a way to forgive."

He rubbed his thumb across mine before bringing my hand to his lips to kiss the top.

"What happened?" I asked.

"I told you. I was out of control. Drinking every night. Starting fights with anyone and everyone. I had to prove I was tough. That nothing could hurt me."

"What about in Afghan? What happened to your brothers?"

He looked at me. His eyes had changed from his usual turquoise to an almost grey and his face had lost all color. This really wasn't an easy subject for him. He took a hard swallow and squeezed my hand.

"Remember how I told you I took heavy machine gun fire and that is how I lost my leg?"

I nodded, keeping my responses simple so he could tell the story his way.

"While I was under fire, two tried to provide cover fire while two ran in to get me out. One of the two was my buddy Mark." He stopped and closed his eyes. Like he was seeing it all again. I moved closer and tilted my head onto his shoulder. I heard him stammer slightly as he continued.

"Mark was hit fatally as he dragged me to safety. I held him until the helicopters arrived. Even when the corpsman told me they needed room to work on my leg I refused... I watched Mark take his last breath... because of me."

The tears welled out of my eyes and down my cheeks. Not just because I couldn't even imagine watching my friend die, but because someone else had that same memory with Ryan. One of his buddies had to watch him take his last breath. Lucas wasn't only stuck with the loss, he had the memory and the guilt to go along with it. I pulled him into my arms and held him as tightly as I could in my small frame. I felt his tears fall onto my chest as we cried together. Cried for his brother lost in the grip of war. Cried for the heavy burden he had been carrying all these years. Cried for the guilt.

When I finally felt like I could speak without stumbling over my words but without releasing him, I said, "That is not your burden to carry." He tried to pull away, but I would not let him.

"It is my burden, Drea. If I didn't get into that situation, he never would have been put in his."

"Lucas, he was just doing what he was trained to do. What you would all do. That is why you call each other brothers. When one is down, you pull him out. Are you telling me you wouldn't have done the same for him?"

He took a moment before answering.

"In a heartbeat."

"Then it's not your burden, and I doubt he would want you to be walking around with that."

"You know what's funny?"

"Hm?"

"His wife told me the same thing."

"He was married?"

"Yes, her name is Carrie."

"Do you still talk?"

"Yes."

"Can I meet her?"

He sat up and looked at me. "I think she would love that."

I reached up and wiped away what was left of the tears on his face. The color was starting to return to his eyes. As I pulled my hand away, he took it in both of his and kissed my knuckles.

"Your touch is everything," he said. "When you wouldn't let me touch you last night, I..."

"I'm sorry, I just..."

"I know," he insisted. "I'm sorry."

"Don't be. I mean, I was mad at first but when I got to thinking about it, we have only been doing... whatever this is... for a few weeks. I couldn't expect you to tell me all your secrets in a few weeks."

"What is this?" he asked.

"Ha! Clearly I don't know, but whatever it is, I like it."

"I want to say something but I feel like this is the wrong time."

"No, saying this is the wrong time is the wrong thing." I laughed.

"No, it's the wrong time but when I know, you will be the first to know."

"Way to leave me on pins and needles."

"It will be worth the wait, trust me."

I wanted to stay in that moment, but Lucas had just inspired me to do something I had been putting off for a year.

"I have something I need to go do. You OK?"

He looked are me with a mix of surprise and confusion but nodded. As I got up to walk away he grabbed my hand.

"Can I know where you are going?"

"I'm going to see Ryan's brothers."

He nodded with full understanding now and I kissed his hand before releasing it.

TWENTY-ONE

Several of the guys from Ryan's old unit met up every week on Thursday night at one of the local bars. I know this because they told me if I ever changed my mind I would know where to find them. Tonight just so happened to be Thursday. Between Lucas telling me his story and the fact that it was Thursday, I took it as a sign that it was time to go talk to them. On the drive over, the anxiety bubble in my stomach was growing but I did my best to ignore it. There was even a small part of me wondering if they would remember who I was. It's not like we hung out regularly. As I parked I took one final deep breath before getting out and walking to the door. At the door I paused, said a small prayer to Ryan asking if I was doing the right thing and if I was to give me the strength, and I walked in. It didn't take me long to locate them. If you haven't ever been around a group of Marines, they tend to stick out like sore thumbs. They have this... aura about them. I walked over to the table they were crowded around and paused. I honestly couldn't tell you all their names and even some of the faces seemed unrecognizable but I think that had more to do with me trying to contain my pain then not actually knowing or remembering them. Someone was mid story and they were all listening intently. Until one on the far side of the table caught me eavesdropping.

"Holy shit."

By his reaction I took it he remembered me. As I focused on him, a memory came back. I saw him with a baby at a barbecue. A beautiful woman whispering in his ear. I closed my eyes for a moment to take it in and his name comes to me.

"Greg," I said. "It's good to see you haven't lost your way with words."

He smiled. "Drea. I didn't..." he looked around the table at the others. "We didn't think you would ever come."

"I honestly didn't either, but here I am."

Greg got up and came around the table. Before I know it, he was embracing me and I was fighting back tears. This was going to be a long night if I couldn't get my emotions under control.

"Come. Sit. Have a beer and tell us what brings you here."

As he went to release me, I held him at arm's length and said a sentence I never thought I would be able to. "I want to hear all your Ryan stories. Including... that day."

He wrapped an arm around my shoulder. "Lucky for you, we got a fuck ton of those."

On my drive home I caught Victoria up on everything. She told me I was better than any movie or TV show and needed to write all of this down. I told her I would think about it and let her know in the next episode. She also told me she thought Lucas was a keeper. This was a huge comment from Victoria, especially since she hadn't even met him yet. Victoria was very protective over me and was also very picky. She also told me she was proud. Proud that I went and heard all the memories of Ryan that I never got to hear from the people who loved him like a brother. Before I hung up, I had to ask her one question.

"How can you say he is a keeper without even knowing him yet?"

"The smile you get on your face tells me everything I need to know. Now go get some sleep. You must be emotionally exhausted."

And she hung up. I needed to see this smile. Knowing Victoria, she would get a picture at some point. She was all about capturing candid moments. Just not of herself. Maybe she could get some good ones at the party. I had forgotten all about the party while dealing with the whole run-in. Now I could focus on actually planning it. The first step would be picking a date. *A date? Wait a second, that is something Lucas and I have never been on.* Maybe that could be the start to figuring out whatever "this" was.

As I was getting ready for bed, curiosity got the best of me. I sent Lucas a text.

"How about a first date? To figure out what 'this' is?"

His response came just a few minutes later, as I was getting under the covers.

"I'll pick you up Friday at 7."

I decided to be "cute."

"Are you sure the warden will allow it?"

"I'll make sure to get the proper paperwork approved."

And just like that I was excited. When I imagined my first date after Ryan, it horrified me. To think about going on a date with someone I barely know after an amazing marriage that was cut off too soon. This was the complete opposite of how I imagined it. I felt excited. I felt revived. I felt... something.

Several mornings later, as I continued party planning on my patio, Tara appeared for her usual walk with George.

"Morning!" I said cheerfully.

"Good morning, what you got going on over there?"

"Oh, I am just planning this brought back to life party for Lucas and me."

"Sounds wonderful. Am I invited??"

"Of course you are. You and Liam."

"I can't wait to hear all about it when I come over for dinner tomorrow."

Shit! I had forgotten all about that. Good thing Tara said something. She must have been able to read the sense of panic on my face.

"You forgot, didn't you?"

"Guilty," I said.

"You are welcome." And she took off around the block with George.

Closing up my notebook and collecting my computer, I rushed inside to get dressed. I had to go to the store to get all the ingredients I needed for dinner tomorrow. Once dressed, I brushed my teeth, tossed my hair into a messy bun, and swiped my lashes with mascara.

First stop was my favorite little Italian shop. I use to come here all the time, especially with my mom. I hadn't been cooking like I use to when Ryan was still around, so Gina, the shop owner, was thrilled to see me. "Oooh, Aundrea, it's so good to see you!" she said, followed quickly by, "What do you need? What can I get you?" She scooped up everything I needed and then some but would never let me pay for then some. She pulled me into a giant hug before finally allowing me to escape with my goods. Which reminded me why I hadn't gone in a while. In my depressed state I would have never been able to handle that. I would have broken down right in the middle of the store, and Gina wouldn't have known what to do. She may be chatty just like most Italians but unlike most, she never asked too many questions. She always waited for me to be willing to give it up. Which is why I did love her shop. All the Italian love without all the prying. Next up was the liquor store. I needed a good red wine to pair with my shells. I wondered briefly if Lucas would drink, but he never said he was in AA. I picked out a higher-end Pinot Noir and then went to my last stop: the grocery store for the stuff to make cheesecake. I had decided while picking out wine that I wanted to make dessert too. I loved making dessert. Not to toot my own horn but I wasn't just a good cook, I was a good baker. Again, I thank my family for this. My mom and grandma were always cooking or baking something. When I got home and everything was stowed away, I sent out a reminder text to my guests plus a time to arrive. I couldn't have been the only one who forgot, right? I of course knew Tara hadn't forgotten and based on the text I received back from Lucas and Victoria, they hadn't forgotten either. Thank God for Tara. They all would have shown up and I wouldn't have had anything to feed them. I guess I could have ordered pizza. I thought briefly about actually ordering pizza but knew it would feel good to be in the kitchen preparing for my best friends and my... boy toy. God, I had to think of a better name for him. Boy toy felt too juvenile and we definitely weren't just friends. Does Google offer solutions for this? Could I type in what to call a guy who I have sex with and get a proper answer? I vetoed googling for now, afraid of what response might pop up, and went back to focusing on the big party. The truth was, the big party felt like so much more than a party. It felt like the official start to a new and much happier life. I would never forget Ryan, but I would no longer let his loss stop me from living again. Especially after the chat last night with his brothers. I would be going back to see them again soon. Instead of it being a burden like I thought it would be, it was the exact opposite. I lifted the giant guilt off my shoulders. I had even more people on my side to get me through.

The following night, I quickly found myself back in my elements. Moving fluidly around the kitchen. I baked the cheesecake earlier and it was cooling on the counter before I moved it to the fridge. I had decided last minute to add in a salad and was in the process of cutting everything up. My true Italian side was coming out, making way to much food for a small amount of people. The only element I was missing was the "Eat, eat! You need to eat." I promised myself that I wouldn't go there. Taking a break from chopping, I stirred the sauce and checked to make sure the noodles were cool. It is no fun to stuff shells when they are hot. I took a final taste of what was going into the middle. The garlic bread was waiting to go into the oven, and the only thing I had left to do was set the table. Just as I took my place back at the cutting board to finish the salad, there was a knock at the door.

"It's open," I called.

The door opened. I was expecting to see just one person, but all three of my guests walked in the door together.

"Well, hi there, everyone."

"Isn't it funny, we all showed up at the same time," said Victoria.

"Sure is." I said taking my focus back to the salad.

"It smells amazing in here Drea," said Tara. "I should have asked you to repay me dinner a long time ago." And she handed me a plate of delicious-looking chocolate chip cookies.

"You didn't need to bring anything," I said, placing the cookies next to the cooling cheesecake.

"You know me, can't show up empty handed."

"Me neither," said Lucas, kissing the top of my head and setting a bottle of wine on the counter. He actually brought over a very nice-looking Noir himself. *He knows wine? This man never stops surprising me.*

"Thank you." I smiled at him.

"My pleasure, beautiful," he said in my ear, kissing it gently.

Victoria was also holding a bowl. What did she bring?

"What's in the bowl?" I asked her.

"Salad." She blushed.

Oh shit. Now I felt like a jerk. When I texted them I didn't say anything about a salad. I dropped the knife.

"Good, now I don't need to finish this," I said, smiling at her. "Why don't you put the salad on the table?"

"I can set the table too."

The house felt so alive and warm. Having three of my favorite people over and the joy of being back in the kitchen, all my anxieties about the dinner were drifting away. I stood for a minute and watched Victoria set the table as Tara made pleasant conversation with Lucas. I assumed it was pleasant, anyway, because they both were smiling. After taking in my wonderful surroundings, I checked on the sauce. Taking a small taste, I deemed it worthy and went to work stuffing the shells. Lucas came up behind me and wrapped his arms around me and kissed my neck.

"A man could really get used to this," he said.

I couldn't help but smile. "Even with two other females watching you for any error?"

"I like your friends. They are nice and are just watching out for you."

I still couldn't believe this was the same Lucas. The Lucas who use to make rude comments and never compliments. Even though I knew that was just a front, it was still hard to believe how much he had come out of his shell.

"What are you thinking?" He asked, kissing my neck again. I felt the heat slowly showing its head.

"That you really have come out of your shell."

"I'm a turtle now? Am I at least a Ninja Turtle?"

"Ha! You know what I mean."

"It's all thanks to you."

"What are you two doing over there?" Victoria asked, wandering over with Tara close in tow. They had opened the wine Lucas brought and poured themselves large glasses. The table looked perfect.

"I was just stuffing shells, minding my own business."

"Lucas, are you bothering our host?" Tara asked.

"I highly doubt this is bothering her."

Both Tara and Victoria laughed.

"Touché," said Victoria.

I finished the shells and got them into the oven. As I was taking off my apron, Lucas walked over with two glasses and what was left of the bottle of wine. I nodded before he even asked and he poured and handed one to me, filling the second glass with what was left. He was about to cheers to me when he turned to the ladies.

"What should we cheers too?" he asked.

"To amazing friends," I said.

"Friends?" Lucas looks puzzled.

"Is that what you two are? Friends?" Tara asked.

"I want that kind of friend," Victoria added.

"I thought we were dating," Lucas replied.

"You know what I mean. Amazing people. You guys are the amazing people in my life that keep me together."

"OK, I can get in on that," Lucas said.

And we clinked glasses.

"Speaking of sexy friends, Lucas what can you tell me about Sam?"

He laughed. "Be careful."

"Oooh he's a bad boy, huh? Just what I like. He said anything about me?"

"Honestly, Victoria, we don't really talk about stuff like that."

"Lies," I said.

They all turned and look at me, surprised.

"You told them about us."

"Only because they saw what was going on," Lucas replied, running his fingers through his hair. Shit, it was supposed to be a joke.

"Lucas, I was only teasing."

"I just don't want you to think I go around telling private business. They don't know any details. He didn't know we actually slept together, he just took a stab in the dark based off your reaction."

I went over to him and rubbed his back, kissing his temple. "I know," I whispered in his ear.

"Gag me," Victoria said, making the gagging motion with her finger.

"I will make sure to tell Sam he has an effect on your panties, though."

And he was back. He wouldn't be prepared for Victoria's answer, though. I sat back and waited.

"Please do. If you want, I can provide you with proof."

There it was. Lucas froze, jaw on the floor, Tara laughing, and Victoria looking serious just as if she had asked an everyday question. I continued to sip my wine. Lucas turned to look at me and his shock deepened by the fact that I wasn't shocked. He finally managed to say something.

"I'd prefer not to run around with dirty panties that aren't my girl's."

Good response, babe. I liked hearing him say "my girl's."

"Victoria. I like you," Tara added.

"I knew you two would," I said, taking another sip of wine.

"Let's have a threesome," Victoria said, "and by threesome I mean a threesome sleepover party."

"You just wanted to say threesome," Lucas said.

"You may be right."

Just as I felt a standoff coming, the timer went off for dinner. It was time to eat. I asked that everyone sit down and I brought everything over to the table. Once we passed everything around and started enjoying dinner, Victoria decided to make it interesting.

"So, Lucas, what are your intentions with our girl?"

I coughed, trying not to choke on my food. Lucas and Tara both started patting my back.

"To take her out on a date," he replied.

Not really the answer I was expecting, but it wasn't wrong. We did have a date set for Friday.

"That's it? What about this mind-blowing sex I've heard about?"

"Victoria!" I snapped.

"What? I got to make sure you are taken care of on all levels." She winked.

"Well, if I already told you it was mind-blowing, wouldn't you say that's taken care of?"

"I'm not sure if I should be mad you gave me hell for talking private stuff to my friends or proud," Lucas said, trying his best to hide his satisfaction.

"I would say proud." Tara makes the decision for him. "I might be upset though that I wasn't included in this mind-blowing sex conversation."

I finished off my wine and went to grab the new bottle as the three of them laughed at their wit. I felt very teamed up on but was very glad they were all getting along and having fun. Returning to my chair with the open bottle, I filled my glass and passed it over to Victoria.

"See how well she knows me. Handing me more wine without me even asking."

"She is good at remembering stuff like that," Tara added.

My cheeks blushed at the simple compliment.

"She is an amazing woman," Lucas added.

"OK, guys, you don't need to butter me up now after embarrassing me."

"Mind-blowing sex is embarrassing?" Victoria asked.

Well, that lasted all of ten seconds. I decided to turn things toward Victoria.

"Lucas, would Sam be able to provide mind-blowing sex to Victoria so she can knock this off?"

"I'll be sure to ask," he said, patting my leg.

"Ask him about the panties too."

"I had just gotten that image out of my head," Lucas replied, shaking his head. He quickly changed the subject. "This is absolutely delicious, Drea."

Victoria and Tara nodded and mumbled in agreement. Tara took the conversation in a more useful direction.

"Lucas, where are you from?"

"I grew up about twenty minutes from here. Forever a Colorodoan I love it here."

"Sexy," Victoria added. "Why did you join the military?"

"My brother did and we were always close. I wanted to be just like him. Plus I figured it would give us another way to bond."

"How old is your brother and does he look anything like you?" Victoria asked. Never fails.

"He's three years older than me. I would like to say we look alike. I'll show you after dinner if you want."

"Only if he is single." She winked.

"He is actually. Just recently. Some bitch broke his heart."

"What happened?" I asked.

"I don't know. He won't tell me, which means it was bad."

"Want me to try?" I asked. I am not sure why I asked this, as I hadn't even met his brother yet, but I knew it was obviously bothering Lucas.

"Why don't you meet him first?" he said coyly.

"Yeah, good idea." I made a mental note to apologize to him later and explain it was just because I could see it was bothering him.

"You need to have dinners more often, Drea. I have been months without any men in sight and now I have two potentials."

"Let's not get too far ahead of ourselves."

"What about you, Tara? Are you from here? How did you meet your husband? Liam, right?" Lucas was steering the conversation away from his brother.

"Wow, you know my husband's name, I am impressed.

Yes, I grew up here. I feel the same, I love it. I met my husband at the grocery store, of all places."

"This sounds like a good story," Lucas said.

"Not really." Tara laughed. "We were standing in line together complaining about how long the line was. As I was leaving, he asked me for my phone number. The rest, as they say, is history."

Before Victoria could interject another dirty comment, Lucas turned his sights on her.

"Why aren't you married, Victoria?"

She pushed the food around her plate. She liked to have fun, but this was a semi-sensitive subject for her.

"I haven't had the best of luck," she finally replied. "I don't know, maybe there is something about me that drives them away, but I haven't found Mr. Right yet."

"I'm surprised. You seem like a real catch," Lucas said, holding out his wine glass. This brought Victoria back around and she clinked glasses with him. This made my heart sing. Everyone was letting their walls down and being very open and honest with each other. I couldn't have asked for a better outcome. We sat around the table until we finished off the bottle of wine. Victoria managed to find my stash of whiskey that I had hidden away and we moved to the living room. I put on a movie and we drank the whiskey and swapped all kinds of stories. Stories from when we were kids. Including the good ol' "game," what's that scar from? We talked work, hobbies, family, and even love. When I fell in love with Ryan, I thought that would be my last love. When I lost him, I still thought he would be my last love. Now I wasn't so sure.

The ladies left first, dawdling in the driveway together. I called Victoria an Uber as there was no way she could drive and she refused to stay at my house. I think she was being too kind leaving room for Lucas to stay if he so desired. Tara was keeping Victoria company until the Uber came. Or perhaps she was just holding her up. I was standing in the doorway beaming at both of them when Lucas came and wrapped his arms around my waist.

"I have to say, those two are pretty great," he said, pressing his warm lips to the soft spot behind my ear. *Shit. He finally found my spot.* I tried my best not to groan. "Oh, is this a turn-on button?" Now I had to resist giggling.

"Button? As far as I know I am all flesh and blood."

"Well, from what I can tell the blood is rushing to one location." And he kissed the spot again, trailing it down to my collarbone. There was no containing the groan this time.

He spun me around, my back now pressing against the door frame. His eyes were filled with desire and the look alone could send me over. The only thing keeping me from letting him take me right here was the door being open and my two best gals in the driveway.

"They would have no idea," he said, taking my face into his hand. "They are too drunk and preoccupied." And he kissed me softly but finished by biting my lower lip. Before I could respond, he picked me up, kicking the door closed with his foot. He sits on me on the edge of the bed and before I could push myself back, he held both of my legs to stop me. Reaching up between my legs he uses one finger to push my underwear aside while he slides the other inside me. Another one followed as he starts to twirl and dance his finger inside of me in all the right places. Leaning my head back, I moaned softly. Just as the heat started to rise, he stopped. I sat up to look at him, and his face was filled with a devilish grin. He moved his fingers to the top of my panties and slid them down. I raised my hips so he could get them over my butt and stepped out as they came to my ankles. He pushed my dress up to my waist, revealing me. I tried to shy away but he would not let me. Kissing the inside of my thighs he said, "I believe I owe you one, my goddess." He trailed all the way up my thighs and planted a soft kiss on my clitoris. I tried to squeeze my legs together to stop him, but he used his hand to press my leg into the bed. As he continued his affections, the two fingers found my spot and I was quickly lost in him, no longer stopping him but lost in his touch. Each finger and his mouth knew exactly what I like. It wasn't long until I climaxed for him. He held his place, taking in my high before kissing all the way back up to my collarbone and the soft spot behind my ear.

"I am not done with you yet," he whispered, kissing the soft spot again.

He stood and went to unbutton his shirt. Standing, I moved in front of him. His eyes locked on mine. Reaching up, I put his hands to his side and began to unbutton his shirt, our eyes never losing contact. When I reached the last button, I opened his shirt. The view was perfection. His breath was calm but ready. I ran a finger from the base of his throat through his abs to the top of his boxers. I stuck one finger into the top and pulled him closer to me. I slid his shirt off his shoulders. He shrugged the rest of the way out of it and gripped the back of my neck, pulling me into a deep kiss. His kisses were full of hunger and want as his other hand found my bare ass under my dress. My hands made quick work of his jeans button and they fell to the floor. Before I could get his boxers off, he released me. Looking down at me, he twirled his finger for me to turn around. Doing as he requested, I turned away from him. He unzipped my dress and I was in my glory.

"Mmm, no bra. I love it," he said, kissing the top of my shoulder.

When I turned back around, he was nude. He pulled me into him again, pressing his forehead to mine.

"I never knew I could feel this way," Lucas said.

And before I could respond, I was lost in a sea of deep kisses, his tongue intertwined with mine, our hands in each other's hair. Making it to the bed, he made quick work of his prosthetic before climbing on top of me. Our lips had not left each other as he entered me slowly. I groaned deeply into his mouth, taking in every inch of him. He responded with a soft moan of my name. As he began to pick up speed, I slowed him and pushed him back slightly as I sat upright. We ended up in a modified Lotus. My legs were wrapped around him as I sat in his lap, which gave me the control but also the closeness. He had one hand at my back, surprised by the new position, but as I rode him slowly, he gave in. His other hand found the base of my neck and he brought me back into his kiss. As he held me close, I wrapped my legs around him tighter until we reach the heavens together.

TWENTY-TWO

As I lay watching the sun just starting to come up, I felt a body press against mine and kisses being trailed down my arm.

"We need to sleep at some point," I mumbled.

"But why, this is so much more fun?" he asked in between kisses.

"As much as I agree, I have to work today and the sun is already coming up."

"I'm sure with one call to Steve we could have the day off," he said, going to kiss lower.

"Lucas, you can't always distract me with your sexiness."

"You think I'm sexy?" he asked, looking up at me.

Sitting up, I let the sheet fall so my breasts were exposed to him.

"Just as you think I am. My first thought when I saw you that first time was that you were molded from rock. A god."

"I'm sorry, I didn't hear a word you said. I seem to be distracted by something," Lucas responded, crawling up toward me, kissing my breasts and rolling my nipple between his thumb and forefinger. My body gave in to him and we were lost in a sea of sheets. Lucas was dozing in the new morning light and as much as I wanted to stay right here, I decided to take a shower. I was tired, but I am not one to blow off work. Hopefully the adrenaline of the night's activities would get me through the day. As I was drying my hair, Lucas came into the bathroom.

"I am sorry I missed the shower, but I am glad to have made it before you got dressed." He closes the distance, kissing the top of my head. "Do you really see me as a god?"

"I thought you didn't hear a word," I replied, smiling.

"Small white lie, but I was very, very distracted."

"Yes, I do."

"Even without my leg?"

"Even more so because of it. Nothing has stopped you."

He cracked a sideways smile. I pulled on some panties and a T-shirt. Putting my hair in a messy bun, I noticed Lucas sitting on the stool in the corner of the bathroom. He seemed to be lost in thought. I turned to face him, leaning against the sink.

"A penny for your thoughts?"

"Remember how I told you there was something I wanted to say to you but it wasn't the time?"

I nodded. He ran his hands through his hair looking nervous now. It sent a shiver of panic down my back.

"I love you, Aundrea." He was looking at the floor, his knees shaking slightly. I went to him and kneeled in front of him. It took him several moments before his eyes found mine. He was searching, waiting for the answer. My panic was gone as I reached for one of his hands and brought it into both of mine. Kissing the top, I looked him directly in the eyes and said, "Say it again." He took a breath and tried hard to stop the shaking in his knees. Without breaking from my eyes, he said it again. "I love you, Aundrea." I kissed his hands again and fought back the happy tears welling behind my eyes.

"I love you too, Lucas."

Apparently we had both been fighting the urge to say those three little words that mean so much.

He pulled me into his embrace and kissed me. Still holding me tight, he said, "I was fucking terrified you would say something like thank you when I said it." He laughed slightly.

"Is that why you didn't say it before?"

"That, and it felt like it was too soon, but it literally hurts to hold it in. When you pulled me into you last night and had... made love to me in that hot sitting position... I wanted to say it so bad. It felt like it was burning a hole in my lips..."

"I wanted to say it too."

"You are the girl I always dreamed of but thought would never come."

Touching his face I said, "You don't have to dream anymore, but speaking of dreams, you want to hear something kinda crazy?"

"Kinda crazy is my specialty."

"I had a dream a few nights ago that Ryan came to me and told me he wasn't the only one who loved me."

"So the ghost of your husband beat me to the punch is what you are saying?"

"Yesss..."

"Even in death he is one-upping me," he said sarcastically.

"It was more to tell me that it was OK I move on," I said, beaming at him.

When we finally made it into work, Steve had already moved on to another project. He had everyone outside painting. Yes, painting. You could tell most weren't happy about it, but they were appeasing him. He told them they could paint whatever they wanted as long as they painted something. Not surprisingly, there were some odd paintings. I'll leave it to your imagination. I went over and talked to Trevor as he painted. He actually had a really great picture of a tree coming together. Lucas was catching up with Sam and Rob.

"So, are you going to fill me in on what is going on with you two?" Trevor asked.

"He loves me," I said without even thinking.

Trevor almost fell out of his chair and knocked over several paint containers onto the grass.

"Excuse me?"

"He loves me, Trevor."

"What about you?"

"I do too."

"Are you sure? Or is the sex just that good? Never mind... forget I asked that. I don't want to know," he said, rubbing his eyes.

"I know it's... weird, but... it happened."

I was looking over at Lucas but could see Trevor looking at me from the corner of my eye. I couldn't bring myself to look at him.

"Shit."

"What?"

"You do fucking love him."

"How do you know?"

"By the way you two are staring at each other while in two totally different conversations. Like two magnets."

"It feels that way too. I can't get enough of him."

"OK, that really is enough."

We moved the conversation to an easier topic and Steve brought me an easel and paint. He said as long as I was sitting here I might as well participate. I figured why the hell not. I used to love to paint when I was a kid. Steve did the same move with Lucas, and he obliged as well. I loved seeing Lucas more relaxed and willing to participate. Hopefully he wouldn't paint anything too obscene. Trevor and I made bets about what he and his buddies could be painting. We decided to make it really interesting. The loser had to jump into the pond. Naked.

We both sat waiting. Staring at them. Lucas caught on that we were up to something, not that it was hard to tell, and came over to see what was going down.

"OK, what are you two up to?" he asked.

Trevor couldn't contain his smile. "Drea is going to jump into the pond naked."

This changed Lucas's face completely.

"Why on earth would she do that?"

"We have a bet going, and she is going to lose."

Lucas rubbed his eyes. "Drea, can I talk to you for a second?"

We walked away from Trevor and Lucas was doing his best to contain his anger.

"Why the hell would you make a bet that would involve you getting naked?"

"It's all in good fun, Lucas."

"That is not fun to me. I don't want everyone seeing my girl." He was almost growling at this point. Maybe the dominus comment wasn't as far off as I thought.

"I am not going to lose anyway," I tried to reassure him.

"What is the bet?"

"Which one of you three painted the most obscene painting."

"You are joking, right?"

I shook my head.

"Please tell me you didn't pick me."

I shook my head again.

"Good girl. Did you pick Sam?"

Another shake no. Now Lucas was smirking. I knew it! Sam showed that he could be a little shy when he was dancing with Victoria. The old Lucas I wouldn't put it past, but now, not so much. So that only left Rob.

"See, I told you I was going to win." And I went back over and sat down next to Trevor.

"No cheating now, Lucas. You better not go over there and start covering shit up."

He laughed and walked over to his painting, picked it up, brought it over, and handed it to Trevor. His mouth dropped open.

"Fuck, I should have known better." And he showed the painting to me.

It was a painting of me, and it was beautiful. No Monet, but beautiful nonetheless.

"Wow, Lucas, I didn't know you could paint."

"Not well, but I do my best. Doesn't do justice to the real day." He winked.

I hugged him. "I love it."

"That is all that matters."

Looking over at Trevor, I smiled. He knew what to do.

"I hate you." And he stripped off his clothes and ran for the pond. It took everyone a moment to realize there was a nude man with a prosthetic running by. Steve debated chasing after him, but the thought of tackling a nude amputee must have made him change his mind. As Trevor reached the pond, he shouted, "Cowabunga!" and jumped in. Ducks and birds took flight as he cannon-balled in. We all ran over to wait for him to surface. He came up quickly and was flaying around like a crazed chicken.

"Get me outta here! There are things swimming near things that I am not comfortable with."

Everyone laughed before a few brave souls decided to help the crazy naked man out of the water.

As Lucas and I left TLC that night, an idea came to my mind.

"Hey, do you think Sam would be willing to go on a double date with you and me and Victoria?"

"I do, but actually, I was thinking my brother might be a better fit for her."

This took me by surprise. Especially since he said his brother wasn't in the best state right now.

"I know what you are thinking, but I think Victoria's fun personality and sense of humor could bring him back around. Kinda like you did me for me."

OK, I could see his point, and I agreed to let them meet at some point. In the meantime, tomorrow night was our first official date. It felt weird to get excited about a date considering all the times he had already been over and spent the night, but it made it feel like what we were doing was more than just sexual. What was I going to wear? I would have to have the ladies over tonight to help me decide. I was sure they were going to say it was ridiculous since we had already been seeing each other, but I figure there was never a reason not to try. He liked to call me goddess. I wanted to show him goddess. The true question was if I had anything goddess-like in my closet.

I decided a *Sex and the City* evaluation was a must. Even complete with champagne. Instead of the signs saying take or toss, they said yes or no. I would walk out in a dress, and the ladies would vote yes or no.

"This is such a fun idea," Tara said, pouring champagne into the three glasses.

"You can thank Carrie Bradshaw," I replied from inside my closet.

"You know, I never got into that show," Tara said.

"Really?!?" Victoria and I said in sync.

Note to self for next girls night: bust out the Sex and the City *seasons DVDs.* Not that I would really have to bust them out. I watched them on repeat. Often. I picked a cream-colored one-shoulder dress to start. I quickly received two no's. The light color might be why? As I moved through my closet, I get several no's mixed with a few split decisions. Just as I was starting to lose hope, in the very back of the closet I find some old dance dresses. Anyone who has danced knows how sexy they can be. Maybe this was what they were looking for. I selected one that was dark-grey sequins with a V neck. The moment I walked out, both their mouths dropped open.

"Holy shit, where has this dress been all night! This is a hell yes!" Victoria said, holding up her yes sign.

"I completely agree," Tara said, clinking her champagne glass with Victoria's.

"Are you sure it isn't too much?!" I asked, turning in the mirror and feeling very exposed.

"Sweetheart, you got a killer body. All that other stuff was too frumpy. Not you. This. This is you," Victoria said.

"If it's not me what is it doing in my closet?" I asked, perplexed.

"I'm not sure. I guess that happens when you get married? Tara?"

Tara nodded. "Yes, those are 'I am married, don't look at me' clothes."

"Wow, OK then. My clothes suck."

"No, no, your clothes don't suck. I shouldn't say they are married clothes. They are 'I am getting older and I don't want to just be looked at anymore' clothes. You know what I mean? When you are twenty you want to look hot and you want men to look at you. When you are thirty you still want to look hot but not as whorish. Am I making any sense?" Tara asked.

I smiled. "Yes, you are making some sense. Now help me pick out what shoes."

After my ladies left, I sat on my bed staring at this outfit they had help me pick out. There was still a part of me that found it outside my comfort zone and then the part of me that remember ed the other me. The me that loved to get dressed up and go out dancing. *Hey! That's a great idea. After dinner Lucas and I could go dancing.* It may have been forever and we may have been older, but that didn't mean we couldn't enjoy what we love anymore. Even if that included getting sexy. They teach sexy at any age, at any point in life, and I was going to embrace it. What I really wanted to embrace was Lucas's reaction when I walked out in that outfit. I sent a quick text to Tara.

"Tomorrow will you take a picture of Lucas's reaction when I walk out?"

"Absofuckinglutely."

TWENTY-THREE

I realized the next morning I had no idea what to do with my hair. I love to wear it down because it's long and sexy, but dancing with your hair down can get sweaty and irritating. The simple solution would be to wear it down to dinner and bring a hair tie for the club. Or I could do it half up half down. No no, that was too young. Here we go with young again. Wearing down to dinner and bringing a hair tie it was. Done and done. I was supposed to go into TLC today to work, but conveniently Steve had said there was work being done to the studio. I was not sure what work could possibly be done, but I left it be. I could be wrong. This meant I had all day to sit around and wait for dinner. Drinking coffee and reading the paper only took an hour of my time. What else could I do? I could go for a run. Get out this anxious energy. I hadn't gone for a run in years, so why not now?

It didn't take long to find out why I hadn't been running in years. I suck at it, it's hot, and I just feel weird doing it. The only time anyone should run is if they are being chased. I forced myself to get a couple miles in before completely giving up. Just had to keep reminding myself it was taking time off the clock even if it sucked. Once back, I polished off a glass of water, had lunch, and watched several episodes of *Sex and the City*. Now I had given myself permission to start getting ready. I am not sure about other women out there, but I am never satisfied with my hair the first go around. Now, I am not saying I shower and start over from scratch, but there are usually strands that are misbehaving that require extra love. Lucas had never seen me dressed to the nines and I was determined to give him a sight he wouldn't soon forget. I knew he thought I was a goddess. It was my time to feel like one with clothes on. As I styled my hair, I contemplated makeup. Lucas had never seen me with much on. All I ever wore on a consistent basis was mascara. I was blessed with long, beautiful lashes. I did want to put on more, but not too much. I opted for some eyeliner and lipstick along with the usual mascara. Nothing on my face or eyes. That way it was still fairly natural, just a little spruced up. I love a good lipstick. Just putting on lipstick for the first time in a long while made me feel sexy. I picked a color called Spicy Red. It felt suitable for both our previous conversations and for going dancing. Since our last dance at TLC, it was clear Lucas had done Bachata before. So I picked a club that was dedicated to Machata dancing and couldn't wait to take him there. Hopefully he would like the idea. He did still get self-conscious about his leg sometimes. After sliding into my dress and strapping on my shoes, I took a look at myself in the mirror. I couldn't argue with the ladies any longer. I looked good. My hair was behaving, and the dress and the lipstick sealed the deal. I even had ten minutes to spare before Lucas was supposed to show up. I shot a quick text to Tara.

"Don't let him come to the door. Have him stay by the truck."

"You got it. Can't wait to see his face. I'll let you know when he is here."

Ten minutes to the dot, Tara came in my door.

"He's here." She was smiling as big as her face would let her.

"Why are you smiling so big?" I asked her.

"I feel like I'm sending my two babies off to prom or something. I know it's ridiculous. I'm just so happy."

She hugged me, and I held her for a few moments before letting her go.

"Give me a sec to get into position before you walk out." And she was out the door. Hopefully Lucas wasn't weirded out by wherever Tara had positioned herself. When I got to the door I saw Tara had cleverly placed herself on her own porch. The phone appeared to be set up on something, and she was pretending to read. I highly doubt Lucas bought her act, but she got an A for effort. Taking a deep breath, I stepped out the door. Lucas was standing by his truck momentarily distracted, trying to figure out what Tara's agenda was. and he looked... amazing. He was wearing a dark-colored pair of nice jeans, a button-up shirt, and dress shoes. Not underdressed but not overdressed either. It was perfect. The steel-blue shirt he had on was pulling the blue color from his eyes and making them pop. If I wasn't concerned about my lipstick, I would be drooling. Once his eyes caught me, he seemed stunned. I did my best sexy walk over to him and planted a soft kiss on his cheek, careful not to leave any lipstick. When I looked up at him, he is sucking on his lower lip and his eyes were taking in every inch of me.

"Good lord, are you trying to kill me?" he asked, leaning down to kiss my cheek in return.

"You wanted goddess." I winked.

He opened the door and I took a seat. He closed the door. Waved at Tara and her camera and took his place in the driver seat.

"Why was Tara videotaping me?" he asked, gliding us into traffic.

I felt my cheeks flush as I answered, "I asked her to."

"Should I be concerned?"

"No, I just wanted to remember your face when you saw me."

He smiled and focused on the road. A short time later we arrived at what looked like an Italian restaurant. He opened my door and took my hand.

"I figured we have good luck with Italian."

"We sure do." And I hooked my arm into his as we walked to the front door.

When we sat, Lucas took control. He ordered us a bottle of wine and an appetizer. He seemed to like having the control but had been doing his best to let me have my say as well. This prompted me to question him.

"So, Lucas does like having control," I said as the waiter left with our order.

"I can't lie, I do, but I am trying to be better about it."

"Have you always been this way?"

"Yes, but it became more prominent as I rose in my military career. It felt like the more control I had, the better things went. That was, until I met you."

The waiter came back and poured us each a glass of wine. He set the bottle on the table and quickly disappeared off to his next task. Lucas held up his glass, and I did the same.

"To the dress that may kill me." He smirked.

"So, you don't like my dress, Lucas?" I asked, taking a sip. The wine was delicious.

"Oh, I like it and so do many others in the room. That is what I don't like."

"You have nothing to worry about," I tried to assure him.

"They are still looking at what is mine."

"Oh, I am yours now?" I asked.

"I would like you to be..." He trailed off. Apparently I was not the only one not using girlfriend/boyfriend over thirty. He started again. "I would like you to be my better half."

Oh, I like that, Lucas. Good job.

"I would like that too."

Everything about dinner was wonderful. The wine, the food, and especially the company. As we walked out the door back to the truck, it was my turn to take control.

"Can I drive, dominus?" He gave my butt a good smack and I let out a small yelp.

"Yes you can, if you stop calling me that." He tossed me the keys and got in. Without skipping a beat, I fired up the truck and started in the direction of the club. He kept looking down at my feet and back up to me. Did my shoe break or something?

"What is wrong with my shoes?" I asked.

"I can't believe you can drive stick in those things."

This made me laugh.

"There are a lot of things I can do in these."

He covered his mouth with his hand and I brought my focus back to driving. I was surprised he hadn't asked where we were going, but pleased he was letting me surprise him. A short time later I found a parking spot on the side of the road and turned off the truck. Lucas was looking around trying to figure out where we are.

"Is this where you kill me?" he asked.

"Sorry to disappoint, but we are going there," I said, pointing to the club.

Lucas smiled.

"Oh you are on, baby," he said, getting out of the truck and coming over to open the door for me. I hopped out and took his arm as we crossed the street to the club. As we pushed through the doors, we were surrounded by music. The room was filled with rhythm and sticky air from body heat. I could hardly contain my excitement. Lucas leaned down to talk into my ear, "Would you like a drink?"

"Is it lame I just want to dance?" I asked.

He shook his head and led me to the dance floor. As usual, we instantly fell into sync with each other. Side stepping, rolling, waving, and spinning all over the dance floor. I was in complete heaven, and I was there with Lucas. When I looked up, the crowd had parted away from us. They had been watching. We'd been completely oblivious. As the song ended, we parted and the crowd clapped. I blushed, and Lucas took a goofy bow. The crowd went back to dancing and Lucas bent down to ask if I wanted water. I nodded, and he disappeared to the bar. I found a stool off to the side of the floor and took in the scene. I had forgotten how much I loved to do this. Maybe we could make this a regular thing. Looking over to the bar to find Lucas, I find him talking to a beautiful blonde. My temperature rose and I decided to go over and find out who this blonde was. I walked over and tapped Lucas on the shoulder. He spun around and so did the blonde. I was worried Lucas would look caught, but instead he looked relieved. My mood instantly changed, and I reached up to take his face into my hands and gently kiss his lips. His hand found the back of my neck and he deepened just before the edge of us losing control. He looked at me almost telling me telepathically to save him, so I introduce myself.

"Hi, I'm Drea," I said, holding my hand out. She looked at it momentarily before taking my hand.

"Hi, I'm Brook. I was just telling Lucas how surprised I was to see him. It is making more sense now."

"Oh yeah? Why is that?"

"Never mind. Good to see you, Lucas." And she stalked off.

Lucas couldn't even look at me as she walked away. Whoever she was, she had an impact on his entire demeanor. It was my turn to distract him. I took a big drink of the water he ordered me, put it back on the bar, and went back to the dance floor. I stared simple. Side stepping to the music, letting it slowly take control. I started rolling my hips and took my arms overhead so that my dress pulled up just enough to show Lucas some extra thigh. When I looked over to him, he was watching intently. My plan was working. I added in some turns, waves, and more hips but from the corner of my eye I sensed another set of eyes on me. There was a guy inching his way toward me. *Oh please tell me Lucas sees this.* Sure enough, before the stranger could close the distance, Lucas pulled me into his arms and dipped me slowly. My hair drifted down as Lucas brought my leg up just far enough to not flash anyone. He swung me back up to his shoulder and we started dancing together again. The strange guy was still debating a way to step in until I looked at him directly as I bit Lucas's neck. He got the message and disappeared into the crowd, but he wasn't the only one to respond.

"Don't do that or I will have you right here," Lucas growled in my ear.

Apparently it was my turn to find his button. I debated doing it again but I believed him and instead planted a kiss in the same spot. We danced for a few more songs before heading home. When I got into the truck I was sweaty and tired but happy. Really happy.

"What's with the big smile?" he asked, starting up the truck.

"That was really fun."

"Yeah, it was." But he didn't sound as convincing. I decided to ask about the blonde as I took my shoes off.

"Are you going to tell me about the blonde?"

"That's Brook."

"I got that part. Who is she?"

"That.... was the girl I was going to marry," he said like it was no big deal.

"The same one who ran out when she saw your leg?"

"One and the same."

"Go back so I can kill her."

This broke the ice a little and Lucas seemed to relax.

"As much as I appreciate you saying that, it isn't worth your time."

"It obviously still bothers you."

"That was just the first time I have seen her since it happened. It was a... shock."

"I'm sorry."

"Don't be. I'm just glad I didn't need to kill that guy."

"Yeah, my plan kinda backfired."

"Only kinda. Thank you."

He pulled up to my house and I was surprised he left the truck running. He came and opened my door and helped me hop down.

"Thank you for a great date."

"The pleasure was all mine."

"I am guessing you aren't staying," I asked, pointing to the truck.

"What kind of gentleman would I be if I expected to get laid on the first date?"

With that he kissed me, got back into the truck, and drove off into the night. I had to give it to him. He could still surprise me.

TWENTY-FOUR

As I lay in bed enjoying a slow morning, Tigger purring on my chest, there was a knock at the door. Dragging myself out of bed, I went to the door.

"Coffee?" Victoria asked, passing me a cup.

"God, I love you," I replied, taking the coffee and inhaling its sweet aroma.

"Now if I could just get a guy to say that to me," she said, crashing onto my couch.

This brought back the memory of a discussion Lucas and I had.

"I may have a solution for that, actually."

"God, I love you! Do go on."

"Lucas mentioned the other day that he thought you might be good for his brother."

"Shut up, you are fucking with me."

"Nope, I'm sure not."

"Damnit, and I forgot to ask to see the picture."

"I'll work on that too."

"I'm so happy you met Lucas."

"Ha! Just because of his brother. I am sure I could help you find someone in other ways."

"Well yes, but not just because of that. It's so great to see you so happy again. You two... just work."

"Yeah, we do, don't we?"

"OK, enough about you, give me all the deets on the bro."

I didn't have much else to give Victoria but promised I would work on it later, picture included. I had to go up to TLC anyway. I hadn't been working as much and figured it would be a good idea to check in. I did my usual messy bun but wore a T-shirt and shorts today. It was a gorgeous summer day, and everyone was outside. I plopped myself down next to Steve, who was inconspicuously trying to read by a tree.

"You know everyone can see you, right?"

"I guess I should get the camo back out."

I laughed.

"I feel like I haven't seen you in ages," Steve said.

"I know, me too, and it's only been what, like two days? Glad to know you missed me though."

"Ditto, doll."

"Doll?"

"I'm trying to increase my vocabulary."

"I would try something else besides doll."

"Doll no good?"

"Doll no good."

I scanned around and didn't see Lucas anywhere.

"Where is Lucas? He in the studio?" I asked, going to get up.

"He's at work."

Did Steve just say Lucas is at work, or am I losing my mind?

"Excuse me, what?"

"He didn't tell you."

I shook my head and pressed down the anger, knowing it would not be directed at the right person.

"Yeah, he went to his old boss and got his job back."

"Old job?"

"You guys don't talk much, huh?"

"Shut up, Steve." *Relax, Drea, he is just trying to be funny.* I let out a deep breath. "I'm sorry, I just don't get why he wouldn't tell me."

"Well, he hasn't told anyone yet. I only know since I am the warden but only for a few more days."

"Where is he going to go?" I asked.

"Probably to the house he just bought."

I must have passed out, because the next thing I knew Steve, Trevor, and several others were standing over me. As I blinked trying to regain my focus, Steve told everyone to step back and give me some room. Steve helped me sit up on the ground.

"Did I faint??" I asked Steve, confused.

"Like a limp noodle. You went so quick I didn't even have a chance to catch you."

"I have never fainted before in my life."

"Come sit back on the bench."

"You can sit in the middle," Trevor said.

Steve helped me to my feet and sat me down next to Trevor before sitting on the opposite side of me. Trevor handed me his water bottle. I took a few sips and wondered why Lucas hadn't told me anything of this. I was just starting to trust him again after the whole arrest thing.

"Why didn't he tell me any of this?"

"I don't know," Steve replied.

"But maybe he has a reason," Trevor added.

"I don't know what reason he could have for not telling me two very important things in his life."

"Why don't you wait and find out before you get mad?"

"Too late."

I debated going home but knew I would just be pacing my floor waiting to hear from him. At least here I could hang out with Steve and Trevor. Steve did get bored of me after a while, but Trevor, tried and true, stuck by me. Even when his wife called and asked when he would be home. This did leave more questions in my mind though.

"Your wife isn't mad that you are sitting here with me instead of at home with her?"

"Nope."

"Wow, that's a good woman."

"Very. She knows I would do anything for her and only her... and if I am staying it must be important."

"So she knows the whole story, huh?"

"She can't wait to meet the Lucas-tamer."

"Lucas-tamer! I like that one but maybe it needed to change."

"Drea, you have to trust him. This won't work without it. You know that. That's why Paige isn't mad at me right now. She trusts me."

"He blew it once already."

"Did he though? Or was he just embarrassed by his past?"

"Why are you always right?"

"Someone has to talk some sense into you, and speak of the devil." I looked up and saw that Lucas was walking toward us. "Let me know how it goes," Trevor said, patting my leg as he got up from the bench. As he and Lucas crossed paths, they shook hands and exchanged a few words. When Lucas got to the bench, he sat down. We both watched as Trevor disappeared into TLC.

"Why didn't you tell me?" I asked him, breaking the silence.

"It was supposed to be a surprise."

How was him getting a job and a house supposed to be a surprise for me?

"Why?"

"I wanted to show you I was getting my act together. That the arrest, the fights, all that was in the past. "If... If this goes somewhere serious... I want to be ready."

"Serious? Serious how?"

"I don't know..."

"Don't lie to me, Lucas."

"Marriage maybe."

It was my turned to be freaked out. I knew I would date again at some point after Ryan, but I never considered getting married again. I never wanted to. Just felt like I had my one chance and that was it.

"Now is when you say something," he continued.

"I don't want to get married again."

"Ha!"

"I'm serious."

Lucas's face changed completely. He looked somewhere between ankle-breaking mad and peed-your-pants embarrassed.

"Then what are we doing?"

"We are getting to know each other. Having fun."

"So let me get this right. You wanted to know where this was going a few weeks ago and now you tell me you don't want to get married again."

"I mean we can be together, but..."

He cut me off. "But not get married. What? I'm not good enough. I don't hold a candle to your precious Ryan."

I stood up and looked at him, trying my best to hold back the tears.

"That is not fair, Lucas."

"No, it's not fair."

And he got up and walked away. I could hardly breathe, but I didn't want to cry. I was afraid if I started crying it wouldn't stop, and I had to get home. *Did Lucas just break up with me? Why can't we just be what we are?* I didn't figure Lucas was the marrying type anyway. I know he told me he almost did before, but after a hurt like that I didn't think he would still want to. *Don't most people feel like I do? You get one great love. One great marriage and then everything after that just gets you by?*

I managed to get home and to the couch. I even managed not to cry, but my thoughts would not be quiet. Eventually I fell asleep because the next thing I knew there was knocking at my door again. "What now?" I asked myself out loud, peeling myself from the deep crevice of the couch. At the door for the second day in a row with coffee was Victoria. Without saying a word, I took the coffee and went back to my crevice in the couch. Victoria lifted up my feet and sat, returning my feet to her lap. She waited several minutes before finally speaking.

"You going to tell me what's going on or we just going to keep looking at the wall?"

"I think Lucas broke up with me..."

"What?!" Victoria shouted, spilling coffee all over herself. "Shit." She threw my legs off of her and went for some paper towels. "What on earth happened? I came over to see when our double date was, only to find out there is not only not a date but you are single?"

I nodded, doing my best to sip my coffee while lying down.

"Aundrea. Sit up. Tell me what happened."

Reluctantly, I sat up. She took the paper towel wet with coffee and used it to wipe my face. I could only assume my eye makeup was a hot mess. Now my face was sticky, smelled like coffee, and still looked like a hot mess, but she got a thumbs up for caring.

"C'mon, Drea. I don't care about the double date. I was just being funny."

"Well, he got a job and a house without telling me."

"Now I am really confused. He has to ask you permission to have a life?"

"No!" I shouted. "I just can't believe he didn't tell me."

"So because he didn't tell you, you broke up with him?

"No..."

"Then what, woman??"

"He brought up marriage and I told him I don't want to get married again."

"He asked you to marry him?!"

"No. When I asked him about why he didn't tell me about the job and the house he said he wanted it to be a surprise. That he was getting his life together in case it got serious. I asked him what serious was, and he said marriage."

"Oh, honey."

"Don't oh honey me like I fucked up!"

"But you did fuck up."

"How did I fuck up? I don't want to get married again."

"Drea, listen to me. You may feel that right now, but you may not feel that way forever."

"Yes I will, Victoria. I can't do it again."

"Can't or won't?"

"Both... I was just trying to be honest."

"I understand you were trying to be honest, but he wasn't asking you right now. He was thinking about a possible future. With you. And you don't know how you are going to feel in the future."

"It is not going to change."

"Oh, you are a stubborn ass sometimes."

"Did you just call me an ass?"

"Yes! Yes, I did. All I want to do is go on one good date, and you have a potential life in front of you that you are pissing all over before it can even really get going."

With that, it was Victoria's turn to walk out and slam the door. Apparently I had a knack for making people so mad they couldn't even look at me. I pulled the blanket off the back of the couch and curled myself back up into my crevice.

I'm not sure what time or what day I finally came to, but Tigger was vigorously meowing at me, which only meant one thing. He was out of food. I forced myself off the couch to fill his bowl and water. He thanked me with a couple of leg rubs. I went back to my spot and hoped I could just fall back asleep, but I was not that lucky.

My mind is running. I knew that Victoria was right, because she isn't the first person to give me a similar speech. Dr. Cox had tried to tell me many times not to nix marriage. It's not that I didn't want to get married. I loved being married. Having your person to wake up next to everyday. Who reminds you what is good about life even when they Dutch-oven you. It was the thought of ever losing that person again. It took me so long to just feel normal again, I couldn't imagine it being easier the second time. Hell, it would probably be worse. The problem was, though, instead of having it now and possibly losing it sixty years from now, I was losing it right now. I would have no new memories. I wouldn't sleep as good. I would just be left with Ryan's memories and nightmares. Ryan's memories were good, great actually, but could they get me through the next thirty, forty, fifty years? I didn't think so. I had to get out of this rut. First thing was a bath. I had been in the same clothes for I didn't know how long.

I started the bath and grabbed some bubbles—you can't have a bath without bubbles. I also found a few candles and some music. I soaked in the tub until I had sung my heart out and was a wrinkled prune. Tigger lay on the bath mat the entire time either enjoying the show or wondering if his human had lost her mind. I got out and checked my phone. It had been a few days and several calls and texts later, but currently it was 1 a.m. Time for bed. Tomorrow I would do full damage control. I couldn't keep crying. I made this mess and I was going to clean it up. I guess I just had to wallow for a few days first.

The next morning it was my turn to show up at Victoria's with coffee. I just hoped she would be home. She is a freelance writer and lives on her own terms. Lucky for me, when I knocked I heard rustling. She opened the door.

"Coffee?" I asked, holding it out to her. She thought for a moment before half smiling at me and taking the offer. So far so good. I walked in the door and took a seat at her kitchen table, where she had clearly been working on something. She sat back in her spot and went back to work.

"You were right. I am a stubborn ass." This brought out a full smile, and she stopped working.

"Please go on," she said, looking at me.

"I couldn't admit that I am scared to lose someone again."

"That is a hard thing to admit."

"Good thing I have you to remind me."

"Hey, what are friends for? To stubborn asses," she said, taking a giant sip of coffee.

"To stubborn asses," I repeated, taking a big sip.

I promised her I wouldn't be such a stubborn ass and I would do my best to keep an open mind. I also promised that no matter what happened with Lucas, I would be sure to get the downlow on the brother situation. Victoria deserved to be happy more than anyone I knew and if I could even have the slightest chance of helping that happen, I was going to do it. Victoria and I could never stay mad at each other. Even when we were in college and got into a huge blow-out over god only knows what, we made up two days later. We needed each other, including those fights, because they reminded us when we were being stubborn asses. I didn't know if Lucas and I would be the same, but even if we really were over, he deserved an apology.

I went over to TLC only to find out Lucas was at work again. I wanted to ask Steve what his new job was but decided I would prefer to hear it from Lucas. I stayed and did my work and when Lucas didn't show up, I went home. I did that every day until his last day at TLC. He no longer would have to "report" there. He was free to have his own life now that he was rehabbed. I bought a bottle of the same wine he ordered on our first date. I couldn't wait to give it to him. Even if this was over, I wanted him to know I would cherish the memories we had and I was so proud of him. As I waited on the bench out front, the time just kept ticking by until the sun set and it was dark. Steve walked out and was locking the door when he turned and realized I was still sitting there.

"Drea. What are you doing out here? It's late."

"I was hoping to catch Lucas," I said, turning the bottle in my hands.

"His goodbye party isn't until tomorrow. Didn't he tell you?" Steve asked, concerned.

"No, he didn't."

"Drea..."

"Steve, don't. Please. Will you just give this to him, please?"

Steve nodded and I got into my car and drove away. Victoria was right. I fucked up.

TWENTY-FIVE

I texted Steve the next day to ask for Sam's number. He tried to give me the whole line about how he can't give out "patient numbers," but I said I worked there too and it was work-related. Which was a lie, but it worked. I was about to call Sam when I decided texting would probably be a better approach.

"Hey Sam this is Drea. I was hoping you could do me a small favor."

He sent back a simple response: "Shoot."

"Can you give this number to Lucas. Tell him it's for his brother." And I typed in Victoria's number. It occurred to me as I typed it in that Sam also might be interested in having her number, but I didn't want to add any confusion.

"Whose number is it?"

"He will know."

"Will do."

I am guessing Sam knew what happened because he didn't ask why I didn't just do it myself. Word seems to travel fast around TLC. That was that. Probably the last time I would ever write or speak his name. The thought sent a sharp pain through my heart, but I was the only person to blame. I decided to invite Tara over for some wine and a movie. She showed up with chocolate. It was like she knew. As we watched the movie and enjoyed our wine and chocolate, I caught her up on everything that had happened. She comforted me, as always. She also insisted that we needed another movie and we should have Victoria come join us. I told her that was the best idea I had heard in a long time. She took my phone and called Victoria while I looked through Amazon for a good movie. All the suggestions I was getting were romance. Considering I don't watch many romances, I'm not sure if Amazon was fucking with me or sending me a sign. Either way I didn't like it, so when Tara got off the phone I had her look. When neither of us could decide, good ol' Victoria came in and saved the day. She knew all the good bad movies. I am not sure why Tara and I stressed over it anyway. We never really watched the movies. Victoria, of course, wanted an update too. I basically just told her I waited to talk to him and all week he never showed up. He couldn't even stand to be in the same place as me.

"Oh, I highly doubt that. He is just hurt right now."

"You are just proving my point."

Victoria rolled her eyes at me and takes a sip of her wine.

"I did however pass your phone number." This got her attention.

"You did? To who?"

"Lucas's brother."

"How the hell did you do that if you haven't seen him?"

"I texted Sam and asked him to pass it along for me."

"Oh, you are a good friend. Did you tell Sam he could keep it too?"

"I didn't tell him whose number it was. I didn't want to add any confusion."

"That will do for now." She beamed.

"So even though you blew things with Lucas you still made the effort to pass Victoria's number to his brother?" Tara asked.

I nodded. "Yup, no reason we both should suffer."

"Good for you," Tara agreed.

"Now, can we please change the subject?"

Just as we were getting off the topic and starting to pay attention to our bad movie, there was a knock at the door. Considering the only two people in the world who actually visit me were there already, I had no idea who was at the door. We argued about who should get the door when there was a second knock and they quickly reminded me this was my house. They did promise to be ready to knock anyone over the head if they tried to kidnap me. After several glasses of wine, I'm not sure how good any of us would have been at fighting anyone off, but I stumbled to the door anyway. When I opened it, there stood Lucas. The bottle of wine I had given to Steve was in his hands.

"Hi."

He opened the door just enough to hand me the bottle. "I don't want this," he said and turned to go back to his truck.

I started to close the door and the girls were telling me to go after him. I mouthed "Why?" and they told me to just fucking do it. Yes, I could tell they used that colorful word even without actually hearing it. I opened the door and made my best attempt to go after him but instead tripped and fell over my own two feet onto the driveway. He turned to look and raised his foot to go walk back toward me but instead continued back to the truck.

"Wait!" I shouted, picking myself up.

He stopped but didn't turn around.

"I fucked up, Lucas."

He still didn't turn around.

"Whatever this is. It scares me. It scares me how I feel about you. It scares me that you feel the same, or at least you used to. It scares me that I could lose you. But I let all those scared moments take over and instead of maybe losing you I did, and I'm sorry."

"This is the second time, Drea. I can't keep doing this. I'm sorry."

"So that's it…"

"That's it." He went to get into the truck, but I challenged him again.

"If that's it, then why can't you even look at me?"

He didn't respond and still hadn't looked at me.

"Is it because you know that if you look at me you won't be able to say no? Because what we have is real and that is why it is so scary? I know I fucked up. And I probably will again, but so will you. But that's life. And I am standing here probably bleeding underneath my jeans and ignoring the pain because I love you."

"You are drunk."

"So what if I am? Doesn't make it any less true."

He wouldn't turn around. Now who was being a stubborn ass?

"Lucas, look at me."

He wouldn't move. All he had to do was get into his truck and drive off, but he hadn't. I closed the distance, making it so I was only a person away from him. I wanted to touch him but knew if I tried he would pull away.

"Lucas… look at me."

He finally looked up. For the first time, I saw him

fighting back tears. I was not sure if they were tears of anger, regret, pain, or fear. Maybe all of the above. I moved so I was right in front of him. A tear rolled down his cheek as he looked away from me. I reached up and with my thumb wiped away the tear. He jerked away.

"Lucas, I love you, and if it means marrying you one day, then that is what it means, but right now in this moment, I can't lose you."

"It's too late, Drea."

"It's not too late." And I kissed him. He was fighting me at first but slowly he kissed me back. His hand brushed the hair off my face while the other was on top of my shoulder. I wrapped my arms around his neck and kissed him with everything I had to let him know I meant every word. When he finally pulled away he said, "That's not fair."

"Pretty sure this whole thing started with a kiss."

This got a small smile from him.

"Please forgive me. I can't promise I won't ever make mistakes again, but I can promise it will be worth it."

"Pretty sure I forgave you already. I gotta get back."

"Back to where?"

"My goodbye party."

"You left your goodbye party to come and give me my wine back."

He laughed. "It sounds crazy when you say it like that."

"That's because it is crazy."

"I was seeing red at the time."

"Wow, that bad."

He nodded.

"How about now?" I asked.

"I'm still seeing red but it's slowly turning. You and your damn kisses. Using them to make me change my mind." He winked and drives away

When I got back to the door, Victoria and Tara were pressed to it. I was not sure if they were stuck or just trying to make sure they didn't miss a moment. When they started wiggling and laughing to make it clear they were stuck, I stood there and watched them struggle. They were shouting at me to help but it was too much fun watching them trying to figure it out. I waited until they are red faced, teary eyed, and on the verge of peeing their pants before opening the door and separating them. Victoria fell to the floor and Tara made a run for the bathroom. I was dying laughing at them and it was exactly what I needed after that high-stakes conversation with Lucas. Once everyone has regained their composure, we took our spots back in the living room and watched the rest of the movie. Victoria was trying to take my pants off to see the damage I did to my knee and how she wished she had gotten it on video. I was not amused but I did let her take my pants off as long as she promised to clean me up and get me a pair of sweat pants. She obliged and, to my surprise, she didn't use the wine as antiseptic. The damage wasn't bad, which I expected since it didn't even tear a hole in my jeans. I don't know what it was, but I lost everything around Lucas. Including my grace. It was like I had two left feet, which isn't good for someone who is a dancer but was good for my heart. With my head in Tara's lap and feet in Victoria's, I felt so lucky. These two never left me, even when my dark cloud was lingering low over my head. Now they had me curled up in their laps like a child, even holding an ice pack on my knee. I enjoyed the warmth of their company until I fell asleep.

I was dreaming. Dreaming about Lucas. He was standing in a field and I was trying to figure out how to reach him but no matter what direction I went, he got further away. The only way I hadn't tried was across a rickety bridge over very turbulent water. Every time I stepped on it, it would sway dramatically and make horrible sounds. This was the only way I hadn't tried yet. I had to do anything to get to Lucas. So I closed my eyes and ran across the bridge. When I opened them again he was kissing my forehead. I made it. *Wait. This kiss feels really... real.*

When I opened my eyes, the house was dark except for some ambient light from the TV. There were soft lips pressed to my forehead that I was praying belonged to Lucas. As my eyes adjusted even in the dim light, I recognized his form. I went to speak but he placed a finger over my lips. He removed the now-warm ice pack from my knee and picked me up. I curled into his chest as he carried me off to the bedroom. He laid me down on the bed and moved the hair away from my face. He couldn't really see me, but he was looking at me. I couldn't take my eyes off him either. He got up and turned on a light on the far side of the room. He was still in the same clothes as before, and damn did he look good. When did he not, though? He shrugged out of his shirt and hung it over my armchair. He did the same with his jeans and came over and untucked the blanket. I scrunched up so he could get the blankets down and got in beside him. Lying on his chest, he ran his fingers though my long hair. We were out of words and just needed each other. Just as I was starting to doze off, he kissed me. Softly at first, but it slowly became more passionate as his tongue parted my lips. Pulling me into his body, his need engulfed me. I felt totally safe and wanted. I wanted to tell him over and over again that I was sorry, but this seemed better than words. I sat up and pulled my shirt over my head. He gently unclipped my bra as I took off my sweats. As I curled back into him, our lips found each other again and we were saying sorry the best way we knew how. He was cupping my face with one hand while the other was lost in my hair. I was holding his face with both my hands, keeping him as close as possible. His hand trailed from my hair down my back and pulled my entire body into him. I took my top leg and wrapped it around his back, giving him access, and he didn't miss a beat. Slipping into me, we made sweet love to each other. Breathing in every moment, every kiss, and every touch like we never had before.

The next morning I was still on his chest. I don't think I had slept that soundly ever. Lucas's breath was slow as he was still sound asleep. I closed my eyes and just listened to him breathe. His scent filled my nose and made me happy and erotic all at the same time. I needed to write a note to the company who makes this body wash. It's dangerous. My hand started stroking his chest. His skin was soft but firm. I couldn't resist the urge to kiss it, so I planted one just above his abs. This caused the sleeping beauty to stir.

"You are in dangerous territory there, lady," he said, eyes still closed.

"I couldn't resist," I said, planting another one. "I can't believe I almost let you get away."

He smiled a very sleepy smile as he ran his fingers through my hair and down my back before giving my ass a small pat. He got up and started to put his prosthetic back on.

"Where are you going?" I asked, pulling the blankets around me and feeling slightly panicked.

"I have to go to work. Glad you woke me up, or I would probably have been late."

"It's Saturday," I replied, trying not to pout.

"I work one Saturday a month and unfortunately today is that Saturday." He kissed my cheek. "I'll be back tonight. Promise."

As he got dressed, I found myself mad again. Mad at my own stupidity. How many chances did I think I was going to get? As he went to walk out the door, I called out to him.

"Lucas..." He turned to look at me. "I'm sorry."

"I know. Me too. But I think we proved that last night." He grinned. "See ya tonight."

I fall back on the bed with a ridiculous grin on my face. Pulling the blankets over my head, I let out a squeal. I felt like a sixteen-year-old girl who had fallen in love with her first boyfriend. He drove me crazy and challenged me but in a good way. It's what I never knew I needed. I guess it's true that you were given this life because you are strong enough to live it. I used to always ask why. Why did Ryan get taken so soon? Why was I given such a great love to only have it taken away? I never thought I would find another type of great love. There is no comparison between Ryan and Lucas. They are different, just like the love is different, but it doesn't make either one any less spectacular. Maybe now I could help Victoria find that great love. I wondered if Sam texted Lucas like I asked him to. I would have to find out when Lucas got home. For now, I was going to play the good girlfriend. Get the house cleaned up and organized and figure out what I was going to make for dinner. I sent Lucas a text just asking him when he had time to give me a rough estimate of when he would be home. I wanted to have dinner waiting. Even if we did make up last night, I wasn't going to stop trying to make it up to him.

In a few hours I got the entire house clean and sparkling. Next up was shower and clean clothes before heading to the grocery store. Tonight would be a "man's dinner": steak, potatoes, and green beans. Figure you can't go wrong with a classic. Plus I still had the bottle of wine that Lucas brought back. Perfect. Hopefully I would remember how to use the grill. It'd been a while. I decided if it came down to it I would ask Liam for help. Lucas wouldn't have to know I "cheated." As long as the food was good and hot, I doubted he would question it. I had to admit I liked feeling needed again. As much as I love work and my friends, there is something to be said about making a home life. An hour or so later, Lucas responded that he would be home around 6:30. Perfect time for dinner. When I went out to the grill later that night, it dawned on me that I didn't have any charcoal. *Looks like Liam will be helping me after all.* Knowing him, he wouldn't just let me borrow some charcoal but would insist on helping. I don't know what it is about a grill, but men can never resist the urge to stand over one.

True to form, Liam got the grill all fired up and before I could shoo him away, he was intently cooking. I couldn't break his heart, so I let him be and went back inside to check on the potatoes and get the green beans going. As I cut the beans and watched Liam in his element out the window, I felt like an ass. I had Liam out there cooking steaks for Lucas and I without having anything for him. *Way to be neighborly, Drea.* Or maybe I was overthinking it. I had only planned on asking him for charcoal. It wasn't my fault he took over. I sent Tara a text anyway telling her I owed them a steak dinner. She of course laughed it off and said I made his night, she hardly ever let him grill. Just as I was getting the potatoes out, Lucas pulled up outside. Well, so much for keeping Liam a secret. Lucas walked straight to Liam and, I assume, introduced himself. After a few exchanges, he came into the house. He went to the fridge, grabbed a beer, leans against it as he takes a sip while glaring at me. I'm about to ask what his deal is when Liam comes in steaks in hand. He handed them to me, nudged my shoulder, and disappeared back out the door. Lucas had not moved from the fridge, but now he was grinning

"What? I forgot charcoal," I said gingerly.

"And you can imagine my surprise to see another man outside your house grilling steaks when I pull up."

"Why would I invite you to dinner on the same night my other boyfriend is here?"

He was laughing but did not like the response as he took another sip of beer.

"You are going to be the death of me, woman."

"It's just Liam. You know, Tara's husband."

"I know that... now."

"Hungry?"

"Famished."

I had Lucas sit as I prepared the plates. I set them down and took Lucas's cue it was a beer and not a wine night and grabbed one for myself. I sat across from him and we both took a sip before eating. I wanted to say something inappropriate but figured it was a better idea to find out what kind of job he got.

"So, what's this new job?" I asked, cutting my steak.

"Construction. We are building a hospital right now."

"Oh wow, so big-time construction."

"Yeah, I have always loved it. I like working with my hands. Makes the work feel more meaningful."

"That explains a lot," I said, beaming. *Damnit, Drea, keep it PG. It's dinner time.* It didn't help that he smirked back, knowing exactly where my mind was going. I decided to keep the casual conversation going. "Where is the new house?"

"It's about ten minutes from here. I can take you by if you want after dinner."

"I would love that."

He caught me up on work and how he got involved in construction. Apparently his dad owns the company. He started working for him as soon as he was allowed to, and he loved it since day one. It isn't easy work, but he likes to be challenged. I listened intently as he told me all about it. When I went to clean up the dishes, he motioned for me to stay in my chair. He rolled up his sleeves and went to work. I enjoyed watching him. I never understood when I was a kid when my mom told me to embrace the little things. This is what she meant. Watching Lucas clean up my kitchen. After everything was done, we went out to the truck to go to his new house. I got in the truck and then he went and knocked on Tara and Liam's door. Liam answered and they had a short conversation that ended with a handshake. Lucas jogged over to the truck, got in, gave me a smile, and took off. I wondered what they talked about but left it alone.

Just as Lucas had said, in about ten minutes we were outside a beautiful house. A big beautiful house. That must have had something to do with the potential serious future. I would be lying if I said it didn't make me smile.

"Can we go in?!" I asked, excited.

"Sure can, I have a good relationship with the owner."

I laughed and clambered out of the truck to the front door. The front door was two wooden doors that came together to form a tree. It was beautiful and I instantly loved it. I ran my hands along the outline of the tree as Lucas unlocked the door.

"I had a feeling you might like the door." He smiled.

He was thinking about what I might like when he bought this house? This was serious. It still made me a little nervous, but I was doing my best to embrace it. The house was open concept. The living room, dining room, and kitchen all ran together and were surrounded by floor-to-ceiling windows. I couldn't imagine how beautiful this was during the day. The kitchen was perfection. Big island with lots of room to prep and cook, all topped off with a gorgeous dark granite. On closer inspection the granite had just a little sparkle in it. Manly with a touch of shine. The living room was centered around a large fireplace with doors leading onto a large deck. Out on the deck was the selling point that I can only assume hooked Lucas if the rest hadn't. Even in the dark I could tell it was a spectacular view of the mountains and a hot tub. I could imagine many mornings sitting on this deck drinking coffee. *Remember, Drea, this is not your house. It's Lucas's.*

"This is what sold you isn't it?" I turned and asked him.

"Yes. I pictured you standing there with that exact reaction on your face."

"Me? What about you?"

"That is what I want. Now you just have to promise to sleep over."

I ran over and hugged him. This was so much more than I could have ever asked for. He bought a house and not only that, he did it with me in mind. I would have never guessed we would be here after only a few short months, but I would not change it for the world.

After looking at the rest of the house, we went back to mine. He said I wasn't allowed back until it was finished. He didn't want to see it again until he had it exactly as he wanted it. I told him he better not take too long, and he promised not to keep me waiting. As I got out of the truck, he started it. *Wait he isn't staying?* I didn't get how he chose what days he stayed or didn't.

"You aren't staying?" I asked sheepishly.

"Trust me, I want to but I don't want our relationship to be all about... that."

Well, now I felt like a whore. I didn't want to tell him that I often thought about... that.

"Hey," he said, getting my attention back to him and out of my own head. "Don't overthink this. I love... that... but I love that it's you more. I won't last more than one night if I'm lucky. Can I come back tomorrow?"

He's so cute when he asks and doesn't just demand. We were really figuring this relationship stuff out. Just took a few fumbles first.

"You don't need to ask. Pretty sure you knew that already considering the two times you just materialized in my house."

"Give me a kiss."

There was the demanding Lucas I liked. I went over to his window, stood on the step, and gave him my best enticing "Are you sure you don't want to stay?" kiss. I stepped down from the truck. He shook his head and ran his hands through his hair before finally taking off. *Good to know I still got it.*

TWENTY-SIX

It was time to get back to party planning. We had told everyone about it but never set a date. After seeing Lucas's new house, I figured we could do a housewarming/coming back to life party in one. Plus, I wanted to show off his new house. His friends and family deserved to see how well he was doing for himself now. I did wonder where he got the money for the house as he had just started working, but being at TLC made it easy to save so it was not my place to wonder and I forced it from my mind. Lucas gave me permission to use his house in two weeks, so the party was set. Now to decide on food. Should we grill? Have a potluck? With all the previous military coming, I came to the quick conclusion that grilling would probably be the best option. They could all have manly bonding time over the grill and have plenty of meat. I would ask close friends and family to bring side dishes and I would make fruit salad and dessert. I loved a good excuse to bake. My mom offered to bring potato salad and deviled eggs. Tara said she would bring a salad and some rolls. Victoria offered beer. She's not really a cooker. Lucas assured me all his buddies would bring beer as well so we would have more than enough to go around. So much for the keg idea, but it was easier this way. My sister wanted to bring a Jell-O mold. All Lucas had to do was ask his family what they were bringing, and we were set. Easy enough. I didn't bother with invitations. Just sent out a text and made a Facebook event. I was excited for this party to celebrate Lucas. He deserved it. When I thought back on how he used to be, I didn't even know that person anymore. He was long gone. I couldn't wait to finally met his family either. Hopefully he felt the same about mine.

Just as I was debating what I wanted to cook for dinner, Lucas walked in the door with fried chicken. The smell filled the house, and I was famished. He set it all out on the table while I grabbed plates and silverware. He came over, wrapped his arms around me, and kissed my cheek so many times I lost count.

"Did someone miss me?" I asked, laughing and trying not to drop the plates.

"So much," he said, putting his nose to my hair and inhaling.

"You like my smell too?" He knew his smell brought me to my knees, but I had no idea he enjoyed mine as well.

"Drea... everything about you drives me crazy."

We sat and had dinner. He told me all about his day and I told him all about the party. He seemed to be excited too, which is an emotion I really like on him. It lights up his bright-blue eyes even more. After dinner, we retired to the porch and I brought out the dreaded bottle and two glasses.

"You up for some wine?" I asked.

He nodded and took the bottle. Opening it up, he poured me a glass, followed by one for himself. We both took a sip, and the delicious flavor filled my mouth.

"This wine is so good. How did you know about it?" I asked.

"My mom is a wine connoisseur. She taught me a few things."

"She taught you well." It hit me that he never mentioned anything about Sam texting him.

"Hey, did you ever get a text from Sam?"

"With Victoria's phone number? Yeah." He seemed a little perturbed.

"Did you give it to your brother?"

"No."

"Could we maybe try this again? Please?" I asked, trying to be very gentle. His expression softened slightly.

"I guess I shouldn't punish Victoria for your errors."

"Friday?"

"Sure." He still wasn't thrilled. I guess when I sent that text I didn't take into consideration Lucas's feelings. Getting a text from Sam that should have come from me probably sent him over the edge. Which also explained why he left his own party to come over and give me the wine back. I was sending mixed messages. Asking his friend to text him gave him the "we are done" message, but the wine said we weren't. Who knew being married for only five years would ruin your dating skills so terribly? That was my excuse, anyway.

"I'm sorry I suck at dating." This got a slight chuckle out of him.

"It's OK. I suck at it too." And he reached over and took my hand into his so he could kiss every knuckle.

"What is your brother's name, by the way. I feel weird just calling him your brother."

"Tyler."

"Oh, Victoria is going to love that."

When I told Victoria about the date, she said exactly what I expected. Tyler was the perfect hot guy name, and if he even looked half as good as Lucas, she'd be in heaven. She then went on about how I was the bestest friend ever. After her dealing with my miserable ass for a year, it was the least I could do. She made me promise to come over early that night to help her pick out an outfit. I of course promised and said I would bring Tara along. Two opinions are better than one.

The week droned on, and Victoria bugged me daily about the date. She was overly paranoid that Tyler might back out last minute. So when Friday finally rolled around and Tara and I showed up at her house, she was a hot mess. Clothes everywhere, running around like a chicken with its head cut off. Luckily, Tara was the smart one and brought a bottle of wine. She figured between the three of us it would be just enough to calm her down but not enough to make her inebriated. We told her to sit as Tara and I made our way through her clothes and picked out a few things that we thought were good options. Than all she had to do was try it on and we could give it either a yea or a nay. Victoria came out in the first outfit we put together, but it was a no-go. It just didn't suit. The second one had way too much cleavage for a first date and we agreed would give the wrong impression. The third option... holy moly. Victoria is a curvier woman with a killer booty and unforgettable boobs. The top and jeans combo we had her in was accentuating all her features without being over the top like the second outfit. Victoria did a little twirl and I am pretty sure Tara and I were both speechless.

"Well??" Victoria asked. "Not good, you guys aren't saying anything."

"We aren't saying anything because we are speechless," Tara replied.

"Speechless good or speechless bad?"

"Is there a bad speechless?" I asked.

"It's that good??"

"It's a 10, baby."

Needless to say, this little try-on with wine got Victoria back to her normal self. She was her sassy, sexy self. I couldn't remember the last time she and I went out together with boys. We had to have been teenagers. Just as we finished up the last bit of wine, there was a knock at the door. We all let out a little squeal just to relive our teenage years, but Tara volunteered to get the door. Victoria and I hid in the bedroom until Tara came back to get us.

"Oh, Victoria. You are a lucky lady," Tara said, coming back into the room and fanning herself.

"Tara, you are a married woman!" I replied.

"Married. Not dead. Now go have fun." And she was out the door. We heard her say bye and the door open and close. Victoria and I debated how long to leave them waiting but figured they might just give up after a while, so we went out into the living room where the guys were waiting. Tara wasn't kidding. Tyler is handsome, and you can absolutely tell he is related to Lucas. He has the dark hair and is built just like Lucas. As I walked out, Lucas beamed. He walked over to me and took my hand, kissing every knuckle.

"Good evening, my goddess."

"Hello, handsome. I am glad to see you in a good mood."

"I was worried until you walked out in this. Now I am worried for a different reason." I rolled my eyes but before he could respond, I went over to Tyler. As I went to introduce myself, Lucas did it for me.

"Tyler this is my girl, Aundrea."

"Aundrea, I have heard way too much about you," he replied, winking at Lucas.

"Drea, please. I'm glad to see you are sassy. You are going to need it." I took Victoria by the hand and pulled her over. "This is my best friend in the entire world, Victoria. Victoria, Tyler."

Tyler smiled at Victoria and again I saw Lucas. He wasn't kidding when he said they were close. Victoria's cheeks turned bright red as they got acquainted. Lucas came up behind me and wrapped his arms around my waist as he went to kiss the soft spot behind my ear. I caught on to his actions and leaned away so that he just grazed my earlobe.

"Don't start that shit now. We got all night ahead of us."

"You are no fun."

"I have to admit Tyler seems more into this than I thought he would be."

"We had the brother talk. I told him he had to be nice and be on his best behavior or there would be consequences."

"Oh, so you don't only threaten me."

He smiled his Lucas smile, and I made the decision to get everyone out the door. The guys actually had a plan. Picked out a restaurant and a movie. I'm guessing they figured it would be a good balance having dinner and a movie, one requiring conversation and one not. The restaurant tonight was steak and seafood. We ordered drinks and sat in silence. Everyone around the table looked like the wanted to start a conversation, but no one willing to take the initiative. Finally Lucas took the reins.

"Victoria, I don't think I ever heard what you do for a living at our last dinner."

"Uhh no, I don't think you did. I am a freelance writer."

"She writes fun, witty columns for the paper sometimes because she refuses to commit and she is working on some poetry," I added.

"That sounds like an exciting job," Tyler said.

Victoria nodded, and I gave her a nudge with my foot to keep the conversation going. She cleared her throat. "What about you, Tyler? What do you do?"

"I work construction with Lucas. We always seem to end up doing the same thing."

Lucas and Tyler laughed and smiled at each other, and in that moment they could almost be twins.

"That's gotta make it more fun," I replied.

They both nodded.

"Drea, I hear you are a dance teacher?" Tyler asked.

"Yes, I am. I used to also teach high school."

"Oh, the kids must have loved you." Lucas smiled.

"They did, she was voted the favorite teacher like three years in a row," Victoria said.

This made me blush. I hadn't thought about teaching in so long. When I was deep into my depression there was no way I could make it to school every day. Maybe it was time to go back. I did miss it, but I also loved what I was doing at TLC. We continued the get to know you conversation over dinner, and everything was going great. We even all split a dessert. Figured it was a way to indulge but not too much before getting more popcorn and candy at the movies. On our way the movies, I noticed we were near the dance club. I tried to suggest we go there instead, but I was out-voted by everyone, including Lucas. I am guessing he was worried about blondie again. Victoria claimed she had two left feet, which was inaccurate, but I didn't blame her for not wanting to grind against Tyler on her first date. While the guys got all the goodies, Victoria and I went off to the bathroom. I could tell she was busting to talk to me without them around.

"Oh my god, Drea, this is the best date I have been on in years!"

"Oh thank god, I was worried you weren't having a good time. You haven't been as fun and sassy as you usually are."

"I don't want to scare him away."

"Scare him? Are you kidding me? You are amazing. Fun. Witty. Who couldn't like you?"

"I am pretty sure I am sweating. You got some perfume or something??"

"Victoria. Relax. It's going great. But if it makes you feel any better, I do."

She nodded frantically. I figured anything I could do to ease her mind. As I was digging through my purse, the blonde from the club came out of the stall behind us. *You have to be kidding.* As she walked to the mirror, she recognized me and stopped.

"Aren't you that girl from the club?" she asked me.

"Mhmm, sure am. Brook, right?"

"Does that mean Lucas is here?" she asked, rolling her eyes.

"Yeah. He's in the lobby with his brother waiting for us."

"You leave first then, please. I don't want him to see me." Why would she care if he sees her? She's the asshole that ran out on him.

"I doubt he wants to see you either." I said, as snippy as I could manage in the moment without snapping.

"Pff, he will never get over me. Don't kid yourself that you mean anything."

Now my blood was really boiling. I started to say something and Victoria grabbed me and pulled me out of the bathroom. All I wanted to do was run back in there and stab her with my heel. She had me across the room to the guys before I could even get my shoe off.

"We need to go."

"What? Why?" Lucas asked.

"Just get her outside before things get bad," Victoria said. In the hand-off, I tried to make a dash back to the bathroom but Lucas swooped me up and took me outside. I slammed my purse on the ground and stormed off to the car, but Lucas grabbed my hand.

"Drea, wait. What happened?!"

"Go ask blondie!" I shouted. Why was I shouting at Lucas? I closed my eyes. Took a deep breath and bit my lower lip as hard as I could. "I'm sorry, I didn't mean to yell at you. Blonde bitch Brook was in the bathroom."

"Blonde bitch Brook, that's a good one. Can I use that?"

He always knows how to lighten the mood. Or maybe shrug it off.

"What did she say to piss you off so bad?"

"Please don't make me say it. Can you talk to Victoria, please? I need a moment."

Reluctantly, he went back into the theater to talk to Victoria and Tyler. The moment he went back in the door, I was sobbing. Deep down I knew she is lying, but there was still that stupid part of me that wondered if she was right. He did ask her to marry him. She ran out on him with no explanation. He never got closure. Maybe he hoped she would come back. I start hugging myself and rocking back and forth, trying to calm my erratic mind. When the door opened back up and Lucas saw my state, he was at my feet.

"Drea, why are you crying?" he asked, using both his thumbs to wipe the tears from under my eyes.

"Because I am having a moment. Remember?" I said between sniffles.

"Listen to me. Brook means nothing. She did for a long time and I was hung up on her for a long time until I met you. Everything changed when I met you. Yes, seeing her still isn't high on my priority list but that isn't because I am not over her. She is just the blonde bitch who broke my heart."

I looked up at him and could tell the moment our eyes met that he was being completely sincere. I wrapped my arms around his neck and sniffled into his shoulder. He picked me up off the bench so he could fully embrace me. As he set me back down, he wiped the remaining tears away and tenderly kissed my lips.

"Tyler and Victoria are saving us seats if you want to go back in. If not, we can go home."

As much as I wanted to go home, I couldn't leave Victoria alone on her first date. I took out my mirror, fixed up my face so I had no runny makeup, and told him I was ready to go back inside. As we walked in, Brook was sitting on the bench outside the bathroom with a blonde dude. All I could think about was kissing Lucas just to spite her, but just as I told myself I am better than that, Lucas picked me up into his arms and kissed me. A deep, passionate, "No one hurts my girl and gets away with it" kind of kiss. Without missing a beat, he placed me back on my feet and we walked into the theater. As we tried to find our way through the dark, I heard Victoria say my name and flail an arm. Sure enough, they had kept two seats open for us. I took my place next to Victoria, and Lucas sat beside me. Tyler was smirking. Another family trait. Victoria leaned over and whispered in my ear, "I was worried you weren't going to come back."

"Trust me, I thought about it, but I couldn't ditch you on your first date."

"You really are a good friend but I am glad you didn't. If he doesn't stop smirking I am going to strip him in this theater."

We giggled. "Welcome to my world."

"Shhhhh," teased Tyler.

We were good for the rest of the movie and remained silent. Lucas periodically took my hand and kissed my knuckles. That had become our thing, a sweet yet subtle gesture. One of the few that didn't send instant heat to my nether regions. At the end of the movie, the entire fiasco was long forgotten. We rode home and discussed what we liked and didn't like about the movie. Victoria had fully come out of her shell and was being her witty, dirty self. Tyler seemed to enjoy it. When we got back to Victoria's house, we all spent some time outside her house chatting. I know Lucas said Tyler was really hurting, but he certainly wasn't showing it tonight. Even if it didn't work out between them, I would say it was a successful date. Tyler asked to use Victoria's restroom. She directed him and he disappeared, leaving the three of us out front.

"Lucas, thank you for giving this a shot," Victoria gushed.

"I have to admit I was nervous, but it worked out well. You ready to go?" he asked, looking at me.

"What about Tyler?"

"Oh, he's not coming back." He winked at Victoria.

"He's not? How do you know?" I asked.

"He's my brother. I know his tricks. This isn't out first double date."

"Wait... seriously? That gorgeous man wants to stay here with me?" Victoria asked in shock.

"It doesn't take us that long to pee. He is waiting on you."

"I can't do this. I'm not ready," Victoria said as she starts to hyperventilate.

I put my hands on her shoulders and together we breathed slowly. I reminded her there is nothing in the handbook that said they have to sleep together, but she might as well enjoy his company and get to know him. He obviously wanted to stay, and that was a good sign. Still taking deep breaths, she nodded and went to the house. Lucas wrapped his arm around my shoulders and escorted me back to the truck. As we pulled up to the house, it was my turn to make a little joke.

"So, do you have to pee or are you off and running tonight?"

"I definitely have to pee. Hearing that his girl wanted to beat down his ex makes a guy really have to pee."

TWENTY-SEVEN

The next morning I couldn't wake up soon enough. I had to hear how the rest of Victoria's night went. Did he stay? What did they talk about? Were they having breakfast together? Apparently my tossing and turning waiting for the phone to ring did not please Lucas.

"What is going on over there? It's like being in bed with a wildcat."

"I'm waiting for Victoria to call!"

"Baby, it's 6:30 on a Saturday. She is probably sleeping. Like we should be."

"I can't!" I threw the covers off and went to the kitchen to make coffee. Lucas didn't even bother to follow me. Just put a pillow over his head and attempted to go back to sleep. I got out my computer and started looking for potential teaching jobs. Talking about it the night before made me realize I missed teaching. I could do it part time or even on a sub basis and still keep up my work at TLC. I had plenty of connections in the area who could help. I decided to take a chance and email the principal of the high school I used to work at. I figured the worst that could happen was he would say no.

Since I was thinking about work, I figured my resume could use a spruce-up. If the principal did say no, I would need a resume to send out to other potential jobs. Just as I was almost finished, my cell phone buzzed across the table. Sure enough, it was Victoria. She never disappoints. I answered, and she herself was buzzing. Apparently they stayed up all night talking. Sharing stories and drinks together. He even told her about the heartbreak that Lucas had hinted at. She said she had never felt so comfortable with someone on a first date ever. I shared her enthusiasm and asked if they would be going out again soon. She surprised me by saying they were tonight. And I thought Lucas and I moved quickly! I wondered what his thoughts would be on all this. Once she gave me the run-down, she said she had to get off the phone to shower and prep for tonight, even if it was only 11. As she hung up I felt an overpowering sense of joy to hear my friend so happy. I couldn't think of anyone who deserved it more. It also brought an interesting thought to my mind. If it worked out with them, AND it works out for me and Lucas, we wouldn't just be best friends. We would be sisters-in-law! Oh, their family would be in so over their heads.

Wait. It's 11 a.m. and Lucas is still in bed? I couldn't have worn him out that much. Smiling, I went to the bedroom and sure enough he was sprawled out, sound asleep. The question was, how do I wake him? With water? No, then the bed is all wet and I don't want to deal with that. Should I bite his neck? His weakness. No, that would probably just turn into him taking control of me. I remembered him smelling my hair and got an idea. I turned on the shower and let it run to get hot as I reached for my shampoo.

Taking it into the bed, I put a small dab on the pillow next to his nose and then rushed back to the shower. Turning on some music, I started to sing. If my smell didn't get him, my horrible singing would.

In no time at all I saw his shadow enter the bathroom. I turned away and let the hot water run down my face and hair. Just as I was getting ready to shampoo my hair, his hand found my lower back, and the other took the shampoo from my hand. I turned to face him as he put some shampoo in his hands and began to wash my hair. He was careful and gentle and I am pretty sure I was falling asleep on my feet as he eased me back into the water to rinse. The water ran down my closed eyes as he continued to gently rinse the shampoo out of my hair. As he worked, he planted a soft kiss on my lips. He repeated the process with the conditioner before moving on to my body. This wake-up plan had been even better than imagined. He started washing my feet and slowly worked his way up, cleaning every inch, and I was switching from being very relaxed and sleepy to extremely turned on. When he was done, he nonchalantly went to washing himself. *Oh no, Lucas. Two can play this game.*

Once we were thoroughly cleaned, Lucas stood in front of the fridge looking for something to eat as I went back to work on my resume.

"Did you put shampoo on my pillow?" he asked, eyes still on the fridge.

"Shampoo on your pillow? That's crazy. No."

He closed the fridge and said, "Why must you lie?"

"What makes you think I am lying?"

"There is no way your shampoo scent made it that far..." And before I could interject, he added, "Plus, there was a wet spot on my pillow that smelled exactly like your shampoo."

"Guilty."

"You are fucking cute, you know that?"

Good to know I was cute. I definitely didn't want him to think I was crazy. If I poured water on his head, that would be crazy. So glad I decided against that. I decided to fill him in on the Victoria and Tyler situation.

"Victoria and Tyler are going out again."

"Oh good."

"Tonight."

"No shit!" Lucas sat at the table with me eating a sandwich he had thrown together.

"No shit."

"This is huge."

"Oh, it gets better."

He gestured for me to go on as he demolished his sandwich.

"He told her about the girl who broke his heart that you brought up at dinner."

Lucas looked like he was about to choke, so I patted his back. I was wondering if this was out of character or not. Wasn't sure if this was a part of some elaborate "get the girl in bed" scheme.

"Wow, I guess it was a good setup. My brother doesn't talk to anyone aside from me, and he wouldn't even tell me about her."

"Victoria does have a sparkling personality."

Lucas hung out for a while before finally saying he had to go tend to things at the new house. Apparently there were things that needed to be "corrected" before he could be completely settled, and he wanted to be done with it. I asked if it could wait until Monday, and he insisted he couldn't but promised to be back tomorrow. I figured it was the perfect time to start a new book and find my way out to my hammock.

Later that evening, I got a text from Greg saying the crew was meeting up at his house for a few beers and some cornhole if I wanted to join. I figured why not. The bigger my support system, the better. I stopped by the liquor store to get a case of beer. I didn't want to show up empty-handed, and between everyone I knew it would never go to waste. When I showed up there were several new faces I recognized but didn't. Basically guys I knew I had met but whose name I didn't remember—which I hated. I guess grief will do that, though. I walked over to the group and handed Greg the case of beer.

"Good to see you again, Drea." He smiled, taking the beer from my arms.

"Thank you for inviting me."

"Hey Greg, who is the skirt?" one of the new faces asked. Apparently I am not the only one who doesn't exactly remember.

"Easy, Matt, this is Ryan's old lady."

"Oh shit," he said, walking over to me. "I'm sorry I didn't recognize you." He continued pulling me into a giant hug. I have to say these big, burly men give the best hugs. Strong and firm, but welcoming and warm. I wonder if they secretly teach that at boot camp.

"It's OK. I honestly didn't remember you either. I knew your face but couldn't tell you anything else."

"Grief's a bitch, huh?" he asked.

I nodded as I found a spot among them. They were all telling old battle stories. Moments they didn't think they would escape. Moments they didn't understand why the enemy even bothered and moments when they were thankful for overwatch. This sparked a memory and prompted my own question.

"Hey, can I ask you guys something?"

They all nodded and some said, "Shoot."

"While you were in battle did you ever... smell something that wasn't there?"

"Can you give us a little more to go on?" Matt asked.

"OK, just don't make fun of me... I had a dream of Ryan telling me he would have moments where he could smell me. Like the wind would change and he would get a whiff of my lotion and it was like a reminder of what he had waiting. Wow... OK... saying that out loud makes it sound really stupid. Just forget--"

"Absofuckinglutely that happens," Greg said, cutting me off before I could finish insulting myself.

"Really??"

"Yeah. I could be in the heat of battle, bullets flying over my head, and suddenly smell my wife's favorite Chapstick like she had just kissed me."

"Same, just not Chapstick. It was usually my girl's perfume."

One by one they all said they had experienced at one point or another the small assault. Usually more than once. Which prompted them to tell more stories of any time it happened to one of them. I was taking notes in my head to tell Lucas later. It did have me wondering if it was only a "military thing" or if it happened in any sort of separation or long-distance relationship. The thing that really got me thinking was I never remembered it happening to me. I don't even remember having a moment when I just smelled Ryan. Did I not need the reminder, or was it just because they were wondering if they were having their final moment and life sent them a sweet reminder? It made me want to go sit in front of my computer for hours trying to figure out this phenomenon. As I was half listening and half contemplating, my phone rang. Reaching into my pocket, I saw Victoria was calling. She should be on her date. I hoped everything was OK.

"Hey, sugar!" Well, she sounded happy, at least.

"Hey, everything OK?"

"Oh, yeah, it's great, just wanted to see if you and Lucas would want to join us at that dance club you pointed out the other day?" Did Victoria just ask me to go dancing? She didn't go dancing. What the hell was happening here?

"You want to go dancing?"

"Yeah, Tyler convinced me and we know you two love this stuff, so let's go!"

Too bad Lucas was busy, but I don't see why I couldn't go solo. Dancing is one thing I am never ashamed to do.

"Lucas is working on the house, but I'm down."

"You sure? Don't want you to feel like a third wheel."

"Yup. Totally sure. I can dance with or without someone."

"Great. See you there at 10."

I could never say no to a night of dancing. It truly was the one thing I didn't mind doing solo. I just hoped that creepy guy wasn't there again this time. I wouldn't have anyone to scare him away. I sat and chatted with the guys for a while longer before making my exit. I thanked Greg again for including me, and he said he was just happy I finally came around. Driving home I was tempted to call Lucas to see if I could steal him away from the house but figured it was better to let him just work and get it done with. Plus, then we could start hanging out at his house. I couldn't wait to have coffee on the deck and to see the mountain view during the day.

Once home, I grabbed a quick shower, not bothering to wash my hair. I was going to get sweaty anyway, and a messy bun with some loose pieces hanging down would do just fine. I added some lipstick to dress up the look before heading to my closet for something to wear. I debated my favorite dress for a few beats but decided to go the more comfortable route this time. I put on a black bodysuit with a lowcut back, a pair of skinny jeans, and some strappy black heels. Sexy but comfortable. I took a look in the mirror before leaving and decided I was missing one thing. My hoops. I have always loved hoop earrings. They get a lot of flak and people have certain "theories" about them, but I don't care. My look was now complete.

Driving over, I put on some Latin music to get me in the mood and car danced. I considered it warmup. Every time I stopped at a light, people either looked at me like I was crazy or started dancing too. Once parked, I went inside and got myself a drink. Sitting at a table, I looked out onto the dance floor and spotted Victoria and Tyler already getting their groove on. To my surprise Victoria was doing really well, and Tyler... well, this must be another of those things they learned together. Man, I would of loved to be in that dance class. Just like Lucas, he was a natural. I enjoyed my drink and watched the two of them learn from each other. Victoria was smiling ear to ear, following in Tyler's lead. Actually, she was beaming. I found myself praying to God this would work out. I finished my drink and decide to go crash their party. It was time to give Tyler the best friend talk.

"Can I cut in?" I asked.

"Oh, hey!" Victoria said, wrapping her arms around me. "Yes, you can. I could use a drink and a potty break." And she darted off for the bathroom. I stepped into the space Victoria had just vacated and fell into step with Tyler.

"Well good evening, Drea."

"Being quite formal, aren't we, Tyler?" I asked.

He laughed. "I have a feeling I know where this is going," he replied.

"That I'll kill you if you hurt her speech?"

"That's the one."

"Well. I am glad we at least understand each other then."

"I really like her."

"It's been two damn days!"

"I know, it makes no fucking sense but we just... we really... hit it off."

"I have no room to talk, really. Just... be good to her. Please."

He nodded.

I decided to continue probing him. "Can I ask you something?"

"Yeah, of course."

"What made you decide to give Victoria a try when your heart was just broken?"

He smirked. "Well, that is a loaded question. Honestly, Lucas convinced me. Said that if it didn't work I had nothing to lose, but if it did work and I didn't try I wouldn't even know what I let slip through my fingers."

"He can be really convincing, can't he?"

He nodded but now it was his turn to question me. "How did you do it? Get through to him?"

"I honestly don't know. I just kept trying to relate to him and we eventually just... connected."

"I'm glad you did. He needed you more than he would probably ever admit."

Now that he had me smiling like a goon, he twirled me around the dance floor. It felt odd to be dancing with someone other than Lucas. I had become so used to him, but I could tell they were brothers. As he spun me again I recognize a face in the crowd. It was blonde bitch Brook. *How can I not stay away from the woman? It's not like this town is tiny.* I guess I did see her here before, but this can't be the only place to dance. She walked over to a group and put her arms around someone I couldn't quiet see. At least she was here with someone this time. It would keep her occupied and away from me. Just as I was going to bring my focus back to Tyler, she and her mystery man turned to come toward the dance floor. What I saw knocked me completely on my ass. Lucas.

The bile started to crawl up my throat as I left Tyler confused in the middle of the floor. I wasn't sure if I should walk out and pretend I didn't see it or go to him. Tyler's hand was on my shoulder.

"Drea, what..." he trailed off as he spotted his brother in the crowd. With her. "Oh shit."

"Did you know about this?" I asked through gritted teeth.

"No. I had no fucking clue." I believed him. He seemed just as confused. They were headed right for us, and I couldn't seem to move my feet. Until he saw me. He stopped dead in his tracks, his arm falling from around her waist. We held eyes for a moment until I couldn't hold my composure anymore and went for the door. Tyler yelled something after me but I couldn't hear him. Pushing through the crowd, I heard both of them now. Their voices were similar, but I could tell they were arguing. Just as I got out the door, Lucas's hand grabbed mine and I was back face to face with him.

"Don't. Touch. Me."

"Drea, let me explain."

"Explain? There is nothing to explain, Lucas. This isn't your house, and you are here with..." I couldn't even speak her name. Tyler was standing in the background debating coming to my aide. I shook my head no and he didn't move. I had turned to go to my car when he spoke again.

"It's not what you think..."

I felt the anger roaring inside me.

"It's not what I think? What I think is you are supposed to be working on the house that you supposedly bought with ME in mind. What I think is this was all just some fucked up game to you. What I think is that Brook was right. You aren't over her. And you never will be."

"That's not true..."

"Ha."

"I can't do this..."

"Do what exactly?"

"I don't know... this..." he said, running his hands through his hair.

"Well good, because there is no this anymore."

TWENTY-EIGHT

To be continued.....

A MESSAGE FROM THE AUTHOR

If you have enjoyed this book, it would not only mean a lot to me, it would make a huge difference if you leave a review on Amazon and Goodreads. Being an independent author, reviews are our life blood. It is how our work gets out there and the few minutes you take out of your day could mean a world of difference to me. Please feel free to reach out to me, I love hearing from readers.

Thank You

ABOUT THE AUTHOR

Rietta is an author who writes romance books that can be racy but are always soulful and witty. Her writing doesn't stop there; she also blogs about her outdoor adventures, books she loves and life as a Marine spouse. She shares a podcast with her cousin Connie called How to Deal When the Shit Gets Real where their guests share inspiring stories and she is a mama to an amazing son. When she isn't busy creating she loves road trips with the windows down, animals and crazy outdoors adventures. If you would like to connect with Rietta or just know when the next book is coming visit her website riettaboksha.com. You can also connect with Rietta on Instagram.

Made in the USA
Coppell, TX
11 November 2022